DESERVING YOU

A MCCORD FAMILY NOVEL
BOOK 3

AMANDA SIEGRIST

Short Stories

Paint By Murder

Follow Me, Sweet Darling

Sleighville Novel

Dashing Through the Fear

Here Comes Chaos

The Last Noel

Standalone Novel

The Danger with Love

Conquering Fear Novel

Co-written with Jane Blythe

Drowning in You

Out of the Darkness

Closing In

SHE DOESN'T THINK SHE'S WORTHY OF HIS LOVE.

HE KNOWS SHE'S THE ONLY ONE FOR HIM.

BUT THE GHOSTS OF HER PAST COULD SHATTER ANY CHANCE THEY HAVE AT HAPPINESS.

1
———

THE SLOW, deep breath didn't help to diminish the anxiety rushing through her veins like a raging river crashing against the shoreline. She'd like to say it was just another day.

Today was anything but normal. Today would either fill her up with intense joy, or bring her down to the lowest pits of hell. Throwing her phone, lip gloss, and keys in her purse, she scanned her desk again as one more shaky breath escaped.

The present.

She couldn't forget that.

Opening the top drawer, she yanked out the small gift bag hidden in the back and tossed it into her purse as well.

She had no idea why she hid it. It wasn't as if Emmett went digging through her desk. He knew better. She'd likely bite his head off for doing such a thing.

So, why did she hide it?

Pretending today wasn't finally here, maybe.

She jumped as a roll of thunder echoed in the distance.

Today, of all days, it had to storm. It was a sign. A bad sign. Today wasn't going to be a happy, joyous day as she planned.

"Hey, Deja."

Jumping again, this time almost falling backwards, she shivered at Emmett's warm touch as he grabbed her arm, preventing her from falling.

"Are you okay? I didn't mean to scare you." He smiled. The sweet one she wished she didn't like.

"I'm fine. I'm running late, and I don't want to be late." She gently shrugged his hand off.

She couldn't stand it when he touched her. Not that he touched her often. But on rare occasions like this, when he did, his touch did things to her that were best not to think about. Those emotions needed to stay locked away. She didn't deserve a good man like Emmett. She didn't deserve to feel the aching need that rushed through her body.

"You work too much. I told you to take the entire day off. I have no idea why you came in today."

She rolled her eyes. "Because I didn't need the whole day off. Just the afternoon. Honestly, what would you do without me running the office? You'd be lost without me." She grinned as she threw the strap of her purse over her shoulder.

His eyes sparkled with what she swore was heated desire. "I *would* be lost without you." He cleared his throat as the desire melted away. Or maybe she just imagined it. "Where are you going?"

"I have an appointment." She averted her eyes, unwilling to share anything else.

He might think she was the best secretary he ever had to run his business as smoothly as possible, but if he *really* knew her, he wouldn't like her. Most likely, he'd fire her without blinking an eye.

"Gotta run, E-man. See you tomorrow." Walking around him as quickly as possible before he could say anything else, she prayed she wouldn't be late.

"Have a great day, Deja."

Her hand rested on the door handle. She turned around to look at him. He had that sweet smile back on his face. She wished he'd stop looking at her like that.

"You, too, E-man." She ran out of the building and ducked into her car before the rain decided to appear. Bursts of thunder still pounded in the distance. A nasty storm was headed their way.

How bad would the storm be when she arrived at her destination? Would he be happy to see her? Would he ignore her as he had the past ten years? Would he like the gift she bought him?

Well, she'd find out soon enough.

Turning out of the parking lot, more thunder rolled in the distance.

Yep, the storm was making its way with a vengeance. A very bad sign.

"He'll be happy to see me. He will." Or not.

No amount of pep talk would change the fact her brother didn't want to see her. He ignored her the past ten years while sitting behind bars.

Well, tough. He was her brother. He was finally free. She'd welcome him with open arms, whether he liked it or not.

Lightning flashed before her eyes, thunder crashing alongside it. She wished she could consider this the eye of the storm. It wasn't.

Seeing her brother again would be the eye. The real test of her strength. She loved him. No matter what.

He killed their parents. But she still loved him.

"You slept with Brad, didn't you? He said you did." Chelsea cackled as she rolled her eyes.

At least, it sounded like a cackle. An evil laugh that said she was about to decimate Deja into a tiny million pieces. Chelsea was such a snob. She couldn't stand her.

Deja grabbed her backpack from the floor and slung it onto her back. Chelsea stepped in front of her when she tried to walk away. Why did she think coming to the mall was a good idea? On a Friday night, she knew half the school would be here. Maybe she was a glutton for punishment.

"What, cat got your tongue? Who's next on your list? Gonna sleep with the entire class?" Chelsea laughed, glancing at the other three girls behind her, who laughed in unison.

Deja squared her shoulders, refusing to let these bitches get to her. "You're just jealous Brad wanted to go out with me and not you. Get over yourself, Chelsea."

Deja walked around Chelsea, ignoring the continued teasing they were dishing out. It didn't matter. None of what they said mattered. She didn't sleep with Brad the Ass. That's exactly what he was—an ass. No more Brad Bear, just a complete asshole.

She wasn't ready for sex. When she told him that, he dumped her and immediately started to spread she slept with him—and wasn't very good either. It was one thing to brag she had sex with him, but the asshole had to say she wasn't good.

Wiping a tear from her cheek, she steeled her shoulders. She wouldn't cry. None of them mattered.

Brad better watch out. One little word to her brother, Dare, and he'd be a dead man. Dare didn't tolerate anyone messing with her. It'd serve him right if she did.

Deja took her time walking home, grateful the mall was less than a mile away. Enough time for her to get her emotions in check, but short enough that she wouldn't be exhausted by the time she got home.

Why did she go to the dumb mall?

Maybe she had hoped they wouldn't tease her. That they'd know Brad was a liar. Of course, she shouldn't be surprised. She never got along with Chelsea, especially after she started to date Brad. With Chelsea fueling the rumor she slept with him, everyone now believed it.

One more year.

One more year, then she'd be sixteen and she could get her license and disappear. Drive far, far away from all these stupid people. She hated them all.

Swiping another lone tear away, she sucked in a deep breath as she climbed the porch steps. The house was dark.

Strange.

Her parents never mentioned going out tonight. Her brother liked to party on Friday nights, but he normally didn't leave until later. Where was everybody?

She turned on the living room lights, then tossed on each light as she walked to the kitchen. For some reason, the dark was giving her the heebie-jeebies.

A roll of thunder echoed in the distance.

Well, at least the night was kind in that regard. She didn't have to walk in the rain. After dealing with Chelsea's cruelness, that would've been too much. The ground had been wet, telling her it rained before she left the mall. She could only thank her lucky stars it stopped when she decided to leave. Apparently, it was gearing up for another round.

She looked at the clock on the microwave.

8:10 P.M.

Where were her parents and brother?

She opened the fridge and grabbed a pop, gulping half of it before heading to the pantry for a snack. She'd eat her misery *away. At least for a little while. Then she'd scour her closet for the best damn outfit she owned and show Chelsea, Brad, and all the other jerks who liked to tease her exactly who they were messing with.*

They could call her a slut. They could tease her up and down until they turned blue. But no one would make her feel useless and pitiful. She was stronger than that. She'd put on her armor and show everyone she wasn't fazed by their words. They couldn't hurt her.

A knock sounded on the door.

She tossed the bag of chips she'd grabbed from the pantry onto the counter. Opening the door, her heart nearly fell out of her chest.

Two officers stood on her porch step wearing solemn expressions that didn't bode well for her.

"Deja Wilson?" the officer with pitch-black hair asked, a frown molded permanently on his face.

Nodding, unable to form words, she almost slammed the door in their faces. She didn't want to hear what they had to say.

"Is anyone else here with you?" the other officer with bright blonde hair, making her think he bleached it recently, asked. His softer expression displayed too much sympathy.

Why did they both look at her so forlorn?

"No. My parents aren't home. Neither is my brother. I don't know where they went. What's going on?"

The officer with the blonde hair twisted his hands, then suddenly dropped them to his sides. "We have some terrible news."

"OH, SHIT!" Deja swerved her car to the right. Her heart pounded as her body jerked roughly against the seatbelt, then her head snapped painfully as the car lurched into the ditch.

The deer came out of nowhere, but she couldn't blame the dumb animal. Her mind had wandered, thinking about the day her life changed forever. Changed to loneliness and despair for the longest time.

Until she met Sophie.

"Oh, Soph, shit! I'm so sorry." Deja rested her head on the steering wheel as she thought about how she'd tell Sophie she just crashed her car.

Saving money was a daily struggle. Since Emmett hired her, she had been making decent money, but it still took time to save up. It had been only nine months since she met Sophie. The first person in her life to ever look the other way and help her instead of blaming her. Berating her. Teasing her. Mocking her. Using her.

She refused to be treated like a charity case. She almost had enough money to buy her own vehicle. Now, she'd have to use all her savings to fix Sophie's car.

Normally, she walked to work, considering the office was only two miles away from the house. It was a long walk, but she enjoyed the fresh air and the energy boost the jaunt gave her. On occasion, she got a ride from Sophie. Rarely did she borrow her car. Today was important. Sophie never asked why she needed to borrow her car. She just handed the keys over with a friendly smile. She never asked questions about Deja's background. Just as Deja respected her privacy.

Two wounded souls.

That's what Sophie called them when they first met. She had been trying to break into Sophie's shed, hoping to find something good she could sell for money. Hunger did things to people. She still felt sick and shameful about her actions. The lowest of the lowest she ever acted.

Instead of calling the cops, something that should've happened, Sophie offered refuge. Help. A bit of friendliness that no other person on the planet ever offered her.

She hadn't been worthy of Sophie's kindness. Especially when a few days before she tried to break into the shed, she had broken into her neighbor's house and stolen two hundred bucks.

The house of Austin McCord, Emmett's cousin.

She still couldn't believe how that family could accept her with open arms and forgive her. Austin didn't turn her into the cops. He let her pay him back every cent she took and the amount it cost to fix the window she broke.

All because of Sophie. Her savior.

Now she just ruined her car. She was a horrible friend.

Turning to reach for her purse, she cried out in pain. Her head hurt. A massive headache was already forming. She had insurance, grateful, yet again, to Emmett's kindness and offering her a job when he did. But she didn't have time to go to the hospital. She needed to pick up her brother.

Ignoring the ache, she grabbed the phone from her purse and started to search for a cab. Not exactly how she wanted to greet her brother, but it'd have to do.

As soon as she got her brother settled, she'd call a tow company and take care of Sophie's car. Nothing she could do about it now.

A tap on her window had her dropping the phone in her lap.

Shit! The police.

"Ma'am, are you all right?" the officer asked, as he motioned for her to roll down the window.

She didn't even try turning the car back on. Would it even start? How bad did she ruin the car? Would Sophie be upset? Probably not. Sophie was an angel. Austin even called her his *pixie angel*.

Austin and Sophie's wedding was only two months away. Sophie asked her to be her maid of honor. She wasn't worthy of such an honor.

"Ma'am? Do you need medical attention?"

What she needed was a magic wand to erase all the bad from her life. Or to disappear. Running away from everything sounded like a lovely idea.

Instead, she shook her head, ignoring the ache, and opened her door. She didn't even try to start the car. She knew deep in the pit of her stomach it wouldn't start. If it wouldn't start, she couldn't roll down the window. Here's to hoping the officer understood that predicament as she stepped out of the vehicle. "I'm fine, officer. A deer jumped in front of me. I tried not to hit it."

The officer glanced around the road, then nodded. "Doesn't look like you did. Hit the ditch hard, though. Gonna need a tow truck. Are you sure you're okay? The front end is pretty banged up. Doesn't look like your airbag went off."

Deja smiled, hoping to give off reassurance. "I'm fine."

"Well, let me help you call a tow truck. Can I see your license, registration, and insurance card?" He smiled back. A friendly smile. Not one that indicated trouble.

She still felt like she was in so much trouble. Dealing with cops never put her at ease. They never had. Not since the day two cops turned her world upside down.

This officer wasn't so bad. In fact, he was downright amazing. Regardless, she went through the motions with him, barely containing her edginess. She would be late. No doubt about it now.

Thirty minutes later, the officer had written a report for

her accident, called a tow truck, and waited until her cab arrived. He shyly smiled at her before she hopped into the cab. That made her jump in even quicker. She knew what that smile meant. Only when a man wanted to ask her out did they exhibit that kind of smile.

She didn't need a man in her life right now.

He was the wrong one, anyway.

Only one man had a chance...

Nope. She wouldn't even think about it.

She was late. That's what mattered. The last thing she wanted to do today was be late. Would her brother still be there?

Only one way to find out. She rattled off the address to the St. Cloud Prison to the cab driver, and twenty minutes later, they arrived.

The parking lot wasn't full of cars or people. It helped her to see everything so clearly.

"Wait here, please." Deja hopped out of the cab and started to run. "Dare, stop."

Walking toward the road, head hanging down, was her brother. He turned around, eyed her warily, and dismissed her with one simple glance.

Deja ran faster. Grabbing a hold of his arm, she turned him around. "Where are you going? I'm sorry I was late."

Dare's face was impassive. No expression whatsoever. "Go home, Deja."

"My home is your home. I came here to pick you up."

"Just forget about me." Dare shrugged her hand off and continued to walk.

Oh, hell, no. He wasn't about to walk away from her.

Deja caught up to him again and quickly stepped in front of him. "You can't just walk away from me. What's wrong with you? You've shut me out for the past ten years. I thought it was because you didn't want me to see you behind bars. Why can't I get a hug? Or a simple hello? Why are you treating me like I don't matter?"

He frowned, a flicker of emotion, maybe regret, shimmered within his eyes. "I didn't want to see you then, and I don't want to see you now. Go home."

"Tough. You're my brother and I'm here for you. Quit pushing me away."

His face became hard as stone as he leaned closer. "Don't make me hurt you, Deja. You know what I'm capable of. Leave me the hell alone."

Deja stood frozen at those words as he walked around her. Shell-shocked, she let him. He couldn't possibly mean that. He was the only family she had left.

"Dare...it was an accident."

"Goddamnit, Deja!" He whipped around. "The hell it was. You know what it was. I killed our parents. Murdered them. That's what I am. A murderer."

She stood in silence as he walked away, yet again. Tears rolled down as the first raindrop finally fell.

The storm had arrived. Worse than she imagined.

The anguish. The hurt. Her brother needed her. She needed him. Why couldn't he see that?

A murderer? She could never see her brother as a murderer.

EMMETT LOCKED the door for the evening, his chest heaving with a slight pain he wasn't familiar with. He knew *why* the pain was there. It just normally never happened. If he didn't know why, he'd think he was having a heart attack. But no. The answer was pretty simple.

Deja.

She always locked the office at night. He never had a need to come to the office after working hard during the day. He did anyway. To see her. Like a pathetic, lovesick boy.

He was her boss. That's it. She'd never see him as more. Well, that's not true. She probably saw him as a friend as well. She was best friends with Sophie, his cousin Austin's fiancée. He tended to hang out with Austin. A lot. He was pretty sure Austin knew the reason why. He wanted to see more of Deja.

She was too good for him. Too beautiful. Too amazing.

Yet, she never saw him as anything other than her boss. A simple friend.

Since the beginning, shortly after they met, she had dubbed him with the ridiculous nickname E-man. It popped out of her mouth and she had yet to change back and call him Emmett.

Did she want to distance herself from him? Was it a good sign? Like a pet name? He couldn't decide. What he did want was for her to call him Emmett. He enjoyed the way his name rolled off her tongue. The rare times she actually used it, that is.

Probably best she didn't call him that. He needed to keep it professional with her. Right before he offered her a job, her manager at her last job had grabbed her ass without permission. He fired her after she slapped him. Of course, once Ava, his cousin Zane's wife, found out, she had Deja's manager arrested for sexual assault.

She didn't want to work there anymore, even after the owner of the diner said she could.

She had stolen from Austin. Broke into his home. But she proved to him and the rest of the family she was remorseful for her actions. He wanted to help her. He also needed a damn good secretary to help him run his business. Offering her a job had seemed like the easiest solution.

At first, she declined. He couldn't understand it.

Maybe it had been the way he offered the job, scrambling his words up and sounding like an idiot. *I need a secretary. I won't grab your ass without permission.*

Yeah, what a great way to ease a woman's worry about working for a man.

Eventually, she accepted. He couldn't have been happier. One, because he couldn't get enough of seeing her gorgeous face. Two, because she was the best damn secretary on the planet.

He owned a landscaping company. He loved working with his hands. Hell, even digging in the dirt, taking a bit of ugliness and turning it into something beautiful always made him feel great.

Which made his business sense slack. A lot. He forgot the simplest things, like where he jotted down a client's number. He never filed anything, and his inventory wasn't always kept up-to-date, needing to scramble at the last minute to order something for a client.

Then Deja stepped in.

She had taken one look at his office, cringed with disgust, and looked at him. "E-man, once I clean this sty up, I'll bash you over the head with my tire iron if you don't keep this shit clean."

And he had. He didn't doubt her for one second. While he knew she was just saying it to get her point across, knowing she'd never hurt him, she had a hardness about her that he didn't doubt she could get lethal.

She also had a lingering pain. Not that she displayed it too often. Today was an exception. Her eyes bled with suffering. He wanted to know why. Burned with agony to know.

She dodged him like she always did when he tried to get a little personal. She rarely shared much about herself. He wanted to know it all.

Emmett parked his car in front of Austin's house and got out before he changed his mind. He had no reason to stop by for a visit. Hopefully, a good excuse would come to him by the time he knocked on the door. Would talking about the weather and the nasty storm they had earlier be a dumb reason? Probably.

The lights were on in the house next to Austin's—Sophie's house. About two months ago, Sophie finally caved in and moved in with Austin. She enjoyed her freedom. Her space. Austin basically lived with Sophie in her house, sleeping over almost every night. It didn't seem practical to live out of both houses. The most logical reason of all, they were getting married. They had a choice to make. Whose house did they live in?

Austin had a mortgage. Sophie's house was paid off. Her father left it to her when he died. The wonderful friend that Sophie was, she told Deja she could keep living there. Deja insisted on paying her rent. Emmett respected her for that. He knew Sophie didn't want her money. But Deja wanted to know she could make it on her own. Paying rent said she could.

Damn, he wanted to know her every little secret. Would she ever share with him?

He knocked on the door. A few seconds later, it opened to the sweetest smile he always loved seeing. "My favorite girl. I missed you. How are you?" He stepped inside and pulled Sophie into a hug.

She chuckled as she squeezed him tightly. "You saw me

yesterday. How could you miss me that much?"

He laughed when he caught Austin's glare. "Not flirting. I swear."

"Better not be. I'd kick your ass." Austin stood up from the couch and grinned at Sophie. "Sorry, my pixie angel, I didn't mean to swear."

"Of course you didn't." Sophie closed the door. "Did you eat yet, Emmett? I can heat you up some dinner."

Emmett shook his head. "I'm good. I'm not too hungry, unless you have pie."

"Actually, I do." She smiled a bit deviously. "It's for Deja, though. It's cooling down. Could you be a doll and bring it to her?"

"Uh..." Emmett watched as Sophie walked away before he could properly answer. He turned to Austin. "Am I that obvious?"

Austin walked around the couch, laughing like a jackal. "That you like Deja like there's no tomorrow? Hell, yes."

Emmett groaned. "Do you think Deja knows? I'm trying to keep it professional. I'm her boss. Not to mention, she never looks at me like I want her to. She's a woman that is very unattainable."

"You're an idiot, Emmett. She's not unattainable. She just has secrets that are holding her back. Did she call you?"

"No. Why?" Emmett didn't like the frown that crossed over Austin's face. "Did something happen?"

Austin nodded. "She almost hit a deer. Sophie's car might be totaled. She hit the ditch pretty hard and the front is banged up. We'll know more tomorrow."

Emmett's heart plummeted to the floor. He forced himself to slow his breathing down and not rush across the yard to Deja's house. "Is she okay? Did she get hurt?"

"She said she's fine and—"

"It sounds like you don't know for sure. Does she need to go to the hospital? What happe—"

Emmett turned as a soft hand touched his shoulder. Sophie smiled warmly. "She's okay, Emmett. Calm down." She held out a pie. "Go see for yourself. You know how tough Deja acts. If she says she's fine, she is. It doesn't mean she couldn't use a friend to keep her company."

He nodded and took the pie from her. "Apple pie. It smells delicious, Soph." He started for the front door. A soft chuckle rumbled behind him. He glanced at Austin. "Something funny?"

Austin joined Sophie and wrapped his arm around her. "Just curious about the reason for your visit. Did you have one?"

"I can't say hi to my cousin and his beautiful fiancée? Is that a crime?" Emmett refused to let the embarrassment show that he was so transparent when it came to Deja. Yet, he could feel the heat rising from his neck to his cheeks. Blushing, over a damn woman. Well, there was a first time for everything. Never in his life had he blushed over a woman. Until now.

Austin laughed. "If you say so, buddy."

Ignoring Austin and his aggravating laugh, he walked out of the house. He hadn't been teased about a woman since the ninth grade when he wanted to ask Julie Callohoun to the homecoming dance. She had been a senior, way out of his league, but so damn beautiful and popular he couldn't help but want to take her to the dance. He lost his chance when he took too long to ask her. Brett Johnson, the star quarterback, also a senior, beat him to it. He probably wouldn't have had a chance in the world if he would've asked her out.

He probably didn't have a chance in the world if he asked out Deja. Way too unattainable.

"Keep your cool. Don't freak out. Austin and Sophie said she's fine." Emmett blew out a deep breath and knocked once on the door.

A few seconds later, Deja opened it. Her beauty, as always, nearly knocked him on his ass. Her blonde hair lay beautifully in soft waves, yet almost appeared bedraggled. Not nearly as perfect as when he saw her earlier. She looked okay. On the outside.

But her eyes.

Her gorgeous blue eyes that always sparkled like the deep blue sea shined with agony. It's as if she wasn't even trying to hide it from him.

"Hi, E-man. Why do you have pie?"

He lifted it with a smile. "Sophie asked me to deliver it to you. I'm hoping I get a piece."

She laughed and rolled her eyes, the sound lifting his spirits. "Of course you do. Come in."

Holding the door open a little wider, he stepped inside and turned around as she closed the door. "You're not going to make me beg for a piece?"

"I should." She tried to smile, but it didn't reach her eyes. "You're a great boss, though. You can have a small piece. Small. Sophie did make the pie for me." She pointed at him, as if she was trying to exert her meanness. All he could see was her pain.

Who caused it? What happened today besides the accident?

He followed her to the kitchen and set the pie on the counter. Deja grabbed two plates from the cupboard and snatched two forks and a knife from the drawer near the refrigerator.

She started to cut two pieces of pie. One slice was large, while the other, tiny. As much as he loved Sophie's pie, he wasn't in the mood for even a tiny piece. He didn't care what piece Deja was planning to give him. That said enough. The worry was swimming through his veins.

"Are you okay?"

She glanced at him. The knife froze in her hand. "Of course. Why wouldn't I be?"

"Austin said you almost hit a deer. Are you sure you're not hurt? The car hit the ditch." Emmett wanted to wrap her in his arms. Her facial expression didn't bode well that she'd be receptive to that kind of gesture. So he didn't move a muscle.

"I'm fine. Not a scratch on me." She handed him a plate, the large piece of pie on it.

He followed her to the table and took a seat across from her. "Doesn't mean you didn't get hurt."

Her knuckles turned white, as if she were exerting too much pressure holding the fork. "I said I was fine, E-man."

"How did your appointment go? Did you hit the deer before or after? I hope you weren't late."

His hand paused, the fork dangling in front of his mouth as her face became ashy-white. Tears started to form in the corner of her eyes. He had never seen her look so vulnerable. "Deja...what did I say? What—"

"I didn't hit the deer." Her face became hard as the water in her eyes disappeared.

"You're avoiding my original question. Does that mean your appointment didn't go well? Where did you go?"

She stood up so fast from the table she knocked her chair over. "I think it's time you leave, E-man. I don't want to talk about it. I won't be put on an interrogation." She grabbed her plate, her pie barely touched, and tossed it into the sink.

Standing up, not one bite of his pie consumed, he couldn't make his feet work. He didn't want to leave. He wanted to pull her into his arms and soothe her torment away. Why did she almost cry? Never, not once, had he ever seen tears in her eyes.

"It's okay to talk sometimes. It's okay to let someone else in. You don't have to be strong and tough all the time, Deja. We're friends. I'm here for you. For anything. I wasn't interrogating you. I was trying to be your friend. You have no idea how much I want to pull you into my arms and hug you. You look like you need a hug so badly." He sighed, knowing that was probably the dumbest thing he ever said to her. "I know you're not going to budge, though, and more than likely, find that trusty tire iron of yours. So I'll leave. See you tomorrow."

He walked out of the kitchen before he went against his word and yanked her into his arms anyway. He had talked to her back the entire time. She was effectively shielding herself from him, not even letting him read her eyes. Did she know how well he could read her? How well he could see the pain she tried so hard to conceal?

He grabbed the door handle.

"Emmett..."

His body froze as his name rolled off her tongue with such delicate softness. She hadn't uttered his real name in months. He wanted to hear it again.

"I could really use that hug."

2

So DAMN WEAK. She couldn't believe she followed him out of the kitchen and stopped him from leaving. Actually said that she could use a hug. The way he said it, she knew she had to take it from him. Could he make the hurt disappear... just for a moment?

Emmett glanced over his shoulder, dropped his hand from the doorknob, and took three long strides before he reached her. He didn't hesitate. She didn't push him away.

His warmth wrapped around her, cocooning her. A sense of safety overwhelmed her. How long had it been since she felt safe? How long had it been since she felt like someone cared?

She knew Sophie cared. As a friend. This hug. This moment in his arms. This felt like more than friendship.

Her arms snaked around his waist and her hands slid up his back. He shivered. Did she get to him as much as he got to her?

She could wipe her pain away easily. It would all fade away if she let Emmett consume her, take her to the height of pleasure. But at what cost?

Her head rested against his chest, the steady beat of his heart soothing. Neither of them spoke. She didn't know what to say. Perhaps he didn't either. Was he as shocked as her that she asked for the hug he offered? A hug that felt like so much more. Or did her wild imagination want it to be something more? Wanting Emmett was bad. She knew this. Hiding her emotions toward him was crucial. But his warm arms around her made her forget why she needed to avoid him.

Her hands moved higher on their own accord, running her fingertips through his hair. He shivered again at her touch. Lifting her head, she pressed her lips to his before she could think about what she was doing.

He jerked, then opened his mouth to her insistence. Their tongues swirled together, her body molding closer to his. She could feel his hard arousal against her. He wanted her. How could he want someone like her?

He only offered a hug. Here she was, taking more, demanding more than he offered.

She didn't care. Increasing the kiss, she tried to press into him some more. The movement made him stumble back a few steps. She kept in tune with his steps until she had him pressed against the wall. The kiss turned hotter.

Emmett grabbed her face gently and pushed her lips away. "What is this, Deja? Because this doesn't feel like a simple hug anymore."

"Don't you want me? Because you're feeling mighty nice to me right now." She rubbed against him, even as she did, hating herself for it. She was using him. Burying the hurt in mindless sex would erase the memories from earlier. At least for a while.

"What happened today?"

He obviously read her like a book. Just like that, the

memories assaulted her. She shoved away and turned her back to him. What did she do?

A large hand touched her shoulder. Touched her heart. "As much as I enjoyed that kiss, I want you to talk to me. You're hurting. I want to help."

Turning around, his hand dropped. She slid her hands up his chest, relishing in the way he shivered, yet again, at her light touch. "You can help me."

He grabbed her hands and clutched them tightly, but didn't remove them from his chest. "Not like this. Don't make this into something cheap. I won't let you do that. Talk to me first, then I'll make you feel good."

His words lit her body on fire. She didn't want to talk. She wanted his hands roaming her body until she forgot every little thing that happened today.

"Emmett…" She purred his name, knowing as she did, she would regret her actions tomorrow. "How long have you wanted me? I never knew."

His eyes narrowed. "Call me E-man if you're going to talk to me like that. You can't hide behind sex, Deja. What happened today?"

She laughed. Almost an evil sounding laugh. "I could make you feel good, E-man."

His lips thinned into a hard line. He didn't speak for several seconds. It felt like hours. Then, to her surprise, he squeezed her hands hard and dropped his lips to hers. The kiss scorched her to the bone. Nothing in the kiss said soft and tender. It felt like a raging inferno, a volcano that just erupted. As if all his pent-up emotions, all he hid from her, poured into the kiss. Did that mean he had wanted her for a long time? She had been joking. Maybe there was actual truth to what she said. What was she doing to this man? What kind of bridge did she just create between them?

Because no matter how deeply involved this kiss was, he would hate her in the morning. She would hate herself.

He broke away from her, his chest heaving, his breaths heavy. "That's all you get from me until you talk. I won't let you belittle yourself. Demean yourself. You're not acting like yourself. Stop it."

"This is who I am. I'm a slut. I sleep with any man, for any reason."

HE STARED at her in disbelief. Did she actually believe what she was saying? Because he didn't believe it for a second. None of it.

This was the sorrow talking. Why wouldn't she just tell him what happened today?

He wanted her so badly, his resistance was slowly withering to pieces.

But no. Not like this. He couldn't. He wanted her to want him for him. No other reason.

Emmett rubbed his thumbs over her hands, trying to soothe, to erase the pain in increments. This could take him a long time to ease whatever was torturing her. Because he could see the truth reflected in her crystal-blue eyes. She believed every word she said.

"I don't believe you. I've known you for almost a year. I've never even seen you date. Not once."

She tried to remove her hands from his, but he held on tight. He wouldn't let her pull away. They needed to sort this out. Now that he tasted her, he wanted more, but only after she squashed her demons. He'd never take her this way.

"I don't date. I just screw 'em and leave 'em," Deja said with a nasty smirk.

Moving closer, his lips brushed her ear as he whispered, "You're lying." He rubbed his thumbs across her hands some more as she trembled in his arms. "Talk to me, Deja. Really talk. Just tell me what happened today."

He kissed her neck below her ear and pulled away. Her eyes would tell him everything he needed to know. And they did. Desire reflected in the depths, as did the awe. He had the distinct feeling she never felt true passion before. He'd be more than happy to show her—after she told him what happened.

Just as swiftly, the desire disappeared. "Don't, Emmett. Just don't." Her features turned hard as she stared him down with the evil eye he knew so well.

Deflection. That's what that look was. He had learned the ins and outs of her so well. The last nine months had given him plenty of time to learn her quirks. She was truly a soft-hearted person inside. Her hard persona was an act. So much anguish she held inside.

"Don't what, Deja? Don't try to be a friend? Don't hold you like you matter to me? Don't let you see how much I care about you? Don't make you talk? I don't listen very well sometimes. Get used to it."

"Excuse me?" One brow rose as she pursed her lips.

He leaned closer, brushing his lips against hers. She trembled at the touch. He didn't mind giving her little tastes of how good they could be together. She'd give in eventually. She'd talk and then he would show her how much he cared about her.

"I said get used to it." His lips made one more light sweep across her delectable mouth. "I can see you're hurting. Something bad happened today—besides the car accident—and I want to help. I'll show you real desire as soon as you talk to me. I've wanted you for a long time. It's nice to know you want me, too. So, get used to it. Get used to me. I'm not going anywhere."

"I don't want you. I just want sex," she scoffed, as if she were trying to make it sound believable. He knew better.

"You're so cute when you lie."

"I'm not lying."

"Did I ever tell you that you have such gorgeous eyes? They sparkle like the deep blue ocean." He smiled. "When you lie, they flash a shade of purple. It's the strangest thing I've ever seen. It's so damn beautiful."

"Let me go, Emmett."

He didn't release his hold. If anything, he held her hands tighter. "Did I ever tell you that I love how you say my name? The nickname you gave me just doesn't have the same ring to it."

"Stop it."

"Did I ever tell you that you look so adorable when you're trying to look hard and tough? But you know what? You're a softie. So sweet and delicate."

"Knock it off."

"Did I ever tell you—"

"Shut up, Emmett!"

"Did I ever tell you—"

She let out a mangled cry that cut his words right off. Burying her head into his chest, her tears soaked right through him. They were fast and rough. So much pain it broke his heart.

He let go of her hands and wrapped her as tightly as he possibly could. "You don't have to do things alone anymore, Deja. You have so many people who care about you. It's okay to let us help once in a while."

"Sophie cares. I know this. She's the best friend I never

had. But the rest of you...it's probably just for her sake," she said between muffled tears.

"Shit, Deja. Do you honestly believe that?"

Silence met his question. She *did* believe that. How could she think they didn't care about her? That he didn't care? He cared too much. Did he hide his feelings too well from her? He never meant to make her feel like that.

He doubted that was the case. She had too much pain inside, too much hidden. She believed that for another reason. A reason he needed to know.

"Believe it or not, I care. Austin cares. Ava and Zane care. Ethan and Gabe care. It's not just Sophie. You're part of our family. Why would you think we don't care?"

Her tears became quieter, as if she had stopped crying, but she refused to answer his question or lift her head. He couldn't believe she was crying. She never showed this sort of weakness. Not that he saw it as weakness, but he knew damn well she thought that. Whatever she was hiding was bad. He wasn't leaving until she told him. He'd sleep on the couch if he had to. Hell, the porch if she kicked him out of the house.

"I'm not leaving. You'll have to grab your tire iron and forcibly remove me before I leave. Talk to me." He'd let her hit him repeatedly with her tire iron if it made her feel better. But he refused to leave.

That's all she had to her name when she met Sophie. He could still remember what Sophie told him that Deja said. *All I have is my tire iron and my wits.* What sort of hard life did she have before she waltzed into their lives? He wanted to know so badly.

"I should beat you with my tire iron." She said it so softly, yet laced with humor, it made him chuckle.

"If it'll make you feel better. Deja, please, talk to me."

She lifted her head, her eyes red-rimmed and so sad looking it tore his heart into pieces. He'd do anything for her. Anything to put a little happiness in her eyes. "You'll hate me, Emmett. You all will."

"I could never hate you. It can't be that bad." He brushed a hand across her cheek, wiping a few stray tears away.

"I'm not worthy of your kindness. Just stop it."

"I've never seen you put yourself down like this before. Who made you feel this way? It's not true."

Her eyes were hard as steel, blazing like a fire—an icy fire. "Everyone. My whole life I've been unworthy."

"Your parents—"

"Are dead." She said it with such heartache he wanted to cloak her with love. Drown out all her sorrows with love.

She tensed. The ringing in the kitchen should've broken the stress developing between them. Instead, it increased.

"I should get that. Can you let me go now, Emmett?"

He nodded. "Sure. But I'm not leaving."

She rolled her eyes as she stepped out of his arms and beelined it for the kitchen. Did she think running away from him would work? He wouldn't be that easily swayed. He'd wanted her for so long. Her body. Her thoughts. Her sweet smiles directed his way. Just her. The complete package. He was ready to stop hiding his feelings.

Emmett leaned against the wall near the opening of the kitchen as she said hello to Ava. Maybe she thought he'd leave. Not gonna happen.

"Shit. You're kidding me. What did he do?" She paused as all the blood drained from her face. Then her voice dropped to a whisper. "Did he ask you to call me?"

Emmett stood up, his body taut with tension. Who was *he*? Was she dating someone? Did he just make a complete fool of himself? Would Deja try to sleep with him knowing she was with someone else? What the hell was going on?

"I'll be right there. Thanks for calling, Ava. I appreciate it."

She ended the call and clutched the phone, refusing to meet his gaze.

"What happened? What did Ava call about?" Emmett waited a few moments, the silence starting to get on his damn nerves. "Damn it, Deja, just talk to me."

She lifted her eyes, the life in them gone. "You want to hear it all? Fine, Emmett. You asked for it. Don't tell me I didn't warn you." She smirked suddenly. "You sure you don't want some hot, sweaty sex before I do? You won't want me after this."

"Your attempt at jokes isn't funny. You also didn't listen to a damn word I said earlier." He pressed his lips together firmly before he said something he'd regret. She was starting to truly piss him off. He hated how she put herself down.

"Screw you, Emmett." She snatched her purse from the counter and shuffled past him with quick footsteps.

"I thought you were going to tell me. Now you're walking away. Running again. How many times have you ran?"

"I have somewhere to be." She grabbed her coat from the hallway closet and slammed the closet door shut.

"How are you going to get there? You don't have a car. I'll drive you. Where do you need to go?"

Shoving her coat on, she looked at him. Her blue eyes scorched him to the bone. "The precinct. My brother was arrested."

Not what he was expecting. He had no idea she had a brother. Why would he? She never talked about herself. Never revealed anything remotely personal.

"I'll drive you. We'll take care of this. Hopefully, we can get him out tonight. I know I wouldn't want my brothers spending a night in jail. I imagine, neither do you."

Deja laughed, although, there was no humor laced within it. "This is nothing new. He couldn't even survive an entire day without going back. He's not getting out tonight."

"What?"

She pulled open the door. The cold night air seeped in. That wasn't the only thing chilling him to the core. "That's where I went today, Emmett. To pick my brother up from prison. They finally released him, and just like that, he's back behind bars. Our reunion didn't go as well as I had hoped. He probably doesn't want to see me tonight, just as he didn't want to see me this afternoon. Well, screw him. I'm going. And screw you."

"You keep saying that to me, but it just doesn't sound believable. What was he in prison for?"

"Murder."

3

WHY DID she act that way?

Throwing herself at Emmett like a two-cent whore. Of course he didn't want her. All those times she swore she saw desire in his eyes had been a delusion on her part. He didn't want her.

Well, good. She wasn't a slut. No matter how many times people called her that. She wasn't a whore. There had been a few times in her life where things got to be so low she had no choice but to resort to things she wished she didn't have to do. Breaking and entering was a fine example. But no matter how hard life had gotten, she had never sold her body to a soul. Never. Still wouldn't. God, Emmett would laugh at her if he knew the truth about her.

Stripping. Now that was different. She had been a stripper for two months. Worst two months of her life. Just another low she suffered. She decided breaking and entering to find cash for food was so much better than letting disgusting men ogle her. She felt dirty just thinking about it.

Why did she open her mouth? Why didn't she fight him a little?

The silence in Emmett's truck skewered her to the bone.

Murder.

One word. That shut Emmett's mouth up pretty quickly. His face turned expressionless and almost cold-like. The kindness in his eyes had vanished. Just the reaction she expected. Did she still have a job? Who would want to employ a woman whose brother killed two people?

Walking out of the house without another word, intending on getting far enough away from him before calling a cab, she barely made it two feet before he gently grabbed her arm, his warm touch soothing, yet his eyes still cold, and said three simple words. "I'll drive you."

The drive was silent. All that talk from him about wanting to hear her problems, wanting to comfort her, wanting to be her friend—lies. Nothing but lies. Another typical man saying things just to shove it all in her face.

She honestly thought Emmett was a better man than that. She should've told him to go screw himself—again. He didn't listen the first few times she said it. He probably wouldn't have listened again and forcibly put her in his truck.

A sigh released when the precinct came into view. She needed air. Lots of it. Emmett pulled into the parking lot and shut the truck off.

"Thanks, E-man." She scrambled out of the vehicle before he could utter one word. Not that he had anything left to say. His silence the entire ride said enough.

Her hand trembled as she grabbed for the door to the precinct. "Get your shit together, Deja. You can do this." The shaking stopped. She wouldn't—couldn't—be afraid.

It wasn't that she was afraid of her brother in a physical

sense. She just didn't know how much more she could take of him pushing her away. More tears wanted to fall thinking about it.

No more crying. She refused to shed another tear, especially after how dumb she looked crying on Emmett's chest. Talk about looking pathetic. She hadn't cried this much since her parents died and the police hauled Dare away.

Yanking open the door, she shuffled all of that away. That stuff didn't matter. Trying to get Dare out of this horrible situation mattered.

She approached the front counter where a stern looking man with gray hair sat. She knew Ava well only because of Sophie. Besides that, she avoided anyone in law enforcement. That task could be difficult, especially since Ava worked in the crime lab, and whenever she had a party, she liked to invite people from her work. Deja rarely attended those parties. She wasn't a fan of cops. Never had been. Not since the day two cops tore her world to pieces.

"Can I help you?" the officer asked with a slight annoyance in his tone.

Another good reason she didn't like cops. Did he have to speak to her like that? Was it the way she looked? She was dressed decently, like a respectable citizen. That wasn't always the case in her life.

Clenching her fists, a smart retort was on the tip of her tongue when a rough hand smoothed one of her fists out and laced his fingers with hers. She looked up into Emmett's eyes. He still showed no expression. Why was he holding her hand?

"Hey, Greg, how's your wife? She's due any day now, isn't she?" Emmett flashed a bright smile, to her surprise.

Of course, Emmett knew who he was. The entire

McCord family knew every single cop in town. Hell, the chief of police was like their honorary uncle.

"She's hanging in there. Stopped working about a week ago and pretty much keeps her feet up. Her back hurts a lot and it's difficult to walk at times. I don't know how Ava worked until she had the baby. I'm worried about Jan, and she's not even working now. I can't imagine how Zane felt." He laughed, yet the smile didn't reach his eyes.

Deja studied him harder, finally noticing the tired wrinkles around his eyes, the worry lines creasing his forehead. Was that why he was so short with her? Because his mind was preoccupied with concern for his wife? It didn't excuse his behavior, but it did make him a little more likable in her eyes. As long as his abruptness wasn't because of her.

"What can I do for you?" Greg looked back and forth between the two.

"Ava called me. My brother...was arrested." Deja couldn't believe she hesitated. Where was her toughness? How come she didn't sound brave? She didn't need Emmett to see any more weakness from her.

He squeezed her hand. She refused to look at him. Was he honestly trying to comfort her? Why didn't he do that in the truck?

Fake. His behavior was all fake. He was only offering her comfort now because they had an audience.

Trying not to make a scene, she yanked her hand out of his unobtrusively. She didn't want his fake sympathy.

"She's in the back. Let me give her a ring." Greg suddenly eyed her warily, the distrust forming in his eyes.

There we go. That look appeared much more normal. Now he was back to judging her.

Less than a minute later, Ava rounded the corner, not even looking like she had a baby two months ago. Although, when it came to Ava, she didn't slow down for anything. Deja learned that early on.

"Emmett, I didn't expect to see you," Ava said as a sly smile emerged. What was with the smile?

"I was having pie with Deja when you called. I offered to drive her."

Deja wanted to snort. Offered? More like, gave her no choice when he grabbed her arm. His touch had been soft and gentle. She could've pulled away at any point. Just like she did here when he was holding her hand. So why didn't she? Why did she let him drive?

"Thanks for the ride, E-man. You can go now." She didn't need—want—him here. She stepped around him and walked closer to Ava. "Where is he?"

Ava glanced behind her shoulder to the obstinate man, who obviously wasn't going to leave, then looked at her. "No paperwork has been filed yet."

Deja frowned. "What do you mean?"

"Come on." Ava waved her hand for her to follow.

Deja listened obediently, large footsteps trailing behind her. Damn him! Why couldn't he just leave? Ava stopped in the middle of the hallway. Emmett stood right next to her. Too close for her comfort. What was he trying to prove? He didn't care in the car. Why was he acting like he cared now?

"I've always respected you, Deja." Ava stopped talking when Deja started to laugh. "What?"

Deja rolled her eyes. "You hated my guts and wanted to arrest me when you first met me. I wouldn't call that always respecting me."

Ava smirked. "Okay. I concede that point. Once I got to know you and your determination to right a wrong, I respected you. I respect your privacy."

Deja shivered as Emmett's arm brushed her shoulder.

Why couldn't the man leave? How many times did she have to say it? "What's your point? What does this have to do with my brother?"

"I was wrapping a few things up, eager to get home to Jimmy and Zane, when Officer Dorscher brought in an arrest. He was silent, brooding, and his eyes...they looked so familiar. You and your brother have the same eyes." Ava smiled. A friendly one. "I asked Officer Dorscher if I could have a word and inquired about the arrest. I knew he was your brother as soon as I saw the last name. I politely asked him to hold off filling out any paperwork until I could talk to you."

Deja steeled her features. She wouldn't cry. "Why? What did he do?"

"I heard you got into an accident on the way to an appointment," Ava said slowly. "Was that appointment to pick up your brother?"

"What's your point, Ava? He's on parole. This arrest is gonna have his ass back behind bars. Fine." Deja shrugged like she didn't care. Problem was she cared too much.

She didn't want to talk about this. She certainly didn't want to talk about it in front of Emmett. She already lost his respect.

"I'm sorry about your parents. That must've been hard on both of you. It was an accident." Ava touched her shoulder, offering her comfort, the one thing nobody ever did. Not those two cops who came to her door. Nobody during the trial. Not even her brother.

"An accident? You said he was in prison for murder," Emmett said quietly, a hint of suspicion in his tone.

Ava scoffed. "Is that what you believe, Deja?"

"That's what Dare believes." Deja shrugged again.

Ava brushed her hair away from her face and sighed.

"Here I am again, meddling in other people's business. I can't help myself. Especially when it involves people I care about. I care about you."

"Why?" Deja honestly couldn't understand. She didn't understand in the beginning, and she still didn't.

"A conversation for another time." Ava nodded down the hallway. "He's sitting at the desk, probably sweating bullets. Or not. He looks at peace, almost as if he purposely tried to get arrested. Did you see him today?"

Deja nodded. "It wasn't a happy family reunion. He wants nothing to do with me."

Ava slowly smiled. "And yet, here you are."

"I don't turn my back on my family. He's all the family I have." Deja clenched her fists.

"He was arrested for disorderly conduct. He got into it with a few other patrons and the bartender asked him to leave. According to the bartender, he refused, so he called the cops. Officer Dorscher ran his record and slapped the cuffs on him. I could probably talk him out of filing the report and giving him another chance. Everyone deserves a second chance." Ava reached out and touched her shoulder. "Don't they?"

"His second chance was when they released him today. The first thing he does is have a drink." Deja shook her head as the memories assaulted her. Memories she hadn't let prick her mind in a long time. "Why'd you call me?"

"Because I thought you'd want to know. Because I thought seeing you might change his mind and clean up his act a little better." Ava shrugged. "Me meddling. Can't help it."

Deja refused to cry, yet she could feel tears forming. "Can I talk to him?"

"Sure." Ava waved for her to follow her once again.

Deja turned to Emmett. "Just leave already. I don't want you here." She walked away before he could argue with her or she could attempt to change his expression. It was still oddly blank.

They turned another corner that led into a big room filled with desks. A few officers sat in front of their computers tapping away or working on some paperwork. The only desk that mattered to her was the one occupied by her brother. His head was down, eyes in his lap. It gave her time to study him, unlike this afternoon.

His blonde hair was long, almost to his shoulders. She could still remember the short buzz cuts he always wore. He never let it grow longer than an inch. Now, it was borderline girlish. She had no idea where he got any clothes. He certainly wasn't wearing the clothes he walked into the prison with ten years ago. He had on a black T-shirt with a pair of faded jeans that looked a size too big for him.

He'd lost too much weight. Not that he was fat ten years ago, but now he was lean and firm. She could tell he had to have been working out with the way his biceps bulged out. He looked almost ripped, yet his face looked slim with sharp angles. Hardened and fierce. Like someone who spent the last ten years behind bars.

Ava stopped and gestured for her to keep going. "I'll just hang back here. Take your time."

Deja nodded and took a few long strides before she was standing less than a foot away from her brother. "Dare?"

His head shot up so fast she was afraid he developed whiplash. Surprise, disgust, and maybe even a little hope flashed in his eyes before they turned black, devoid of any emotion.

"What the hell are you doing here? Go away, Deja." He looked away.

"I have a spare room. I have a few clothes I found at garage sales, but I figured we could go shopping tomorrow." She waited for him to look her way. "I can help you find a job."

He lifted his hands, jangling the cuffs that were wrapped around his wrists. "See anything interesting? The only thing I'm doing is going back to prison."

"Is that what you want?"

He stared at her for the longest time. "What do you want from me? Just go home. I don't want to see you."

Deja didn't know what to say. How many times could she offer her love, her support? How many times could she ask for her brother's love? Why did he keep pushing her away? She didn't blame him. It was an accident. Just like Ava said, which surprised the hell out of her.

"Dare, it was an accid—"

"Shut the hell up, Deja. Don't you dare say that. Leave me the hell alone." His lips were tight, his face red with anger, his fists clenched in his lap.

"Listen up, asshole. Nobody speaks to her that way. Not even her brother. Show a little respect." Emmett stood in front of her brother, the anger plastered on his face. "She's the only reason your ass isn't sitting in a cell waiting to be escorted back to prison. This is your only chance to start doing things the correct way. You're not going to get another pass, that's for sure."

Where did Emmet come from? She could tell Dare wanted to stand up and get in Emmett's face. Instead, he sat there, his jaw clenched, the tiny muscles in his cheek twitching. "Who the hell are you?"

Emmett glanced at her, the fire blazing in his eyes. Anger. Rage. Desire?

Why didn't he leave yet? Why was he standing up to her brother defending her?

He turned away and looked at Dare. "I'm her boss...and her friend."

I WANT to be so much more.

Emmett couldn't say that. Maybe he should. Maybe that would wipe away the anger and sorrow from her face. He couldn't blame it all on her brother. He put some of it there. Like an idiot, he got tongue-tied when she uttered the word murder. Or, more like, silent.

What do you say to that? *Wow. Okay. That's nice. Crazy.* Nothing seemed appropriate.

"Emmett?"

He turned to Deja, noting the anger still present. Her eyes sparkled bright blue. Brighter than ever before. Her lips were tight, her stance stiff. She could be pissed at him. He wasn't about to let anyone, including her brother, talk to her that way. It was uncalled for.

"I won't apologize, Deja. You deserve better. You're trying to help, and he's acting like an asshole. I won't stand here and let that happen. Be pissed all you want."

Her eyes glittered. With what, he couldn't tell. "You didn't care on the ride here."

"I care. Some days I care too damn much." Emmett averted his eyes and glared at Dare, who gave him a funny look. "Are you going to let her help you, or continue to act like a jackass?"

Dare stared him down for a few beats before speaking. "Do you even know what I did?"

"Not really. At this point, I don't care. You're hurting your sister by pushing her away. She's all the family you have. Why push her away?" Emmett raised his brows as he waited for an honest answer.

Dare loosened his fists and shrugged. "Fine. Get me the hell out of here."

"Really, Dare?" Hope sprang into Deja's eyes.

Emmett shook his head. No way in hell anything was happening unless he felt satisfied. Deja would just have to deal with it. He couldn't see her hurting as he did back at the house. Now he knew why. Her brother put the pain in her eyes.

"Apologize first."

Dare cocked a brow and smirked. "Make me, asshole. It's none of your business the shit between my sister and me."

Emmett leaned closer, getting right into his face. "I'm making it my business. You're not leaving until you apologize for talking to her like that."

"Emmett, stop. He doesn't have to apologize."

He backed away from Dare and threw a hand in his direction. "So, you're okay with him speaking to you that way? You're okay with him constantly hurting your feelings? I've never seen you let anyone hurt you like that. Why would you allow your brother to?"

Her face became hard, just like the many times since he met her. A wall was creeping up between them. He drove that wall down, brick by brick, and now it was springing back to life. Because he suddenly couldn't keep his emotions in check.

"Like my brother said, it's none of your damn business what's going on between us. I'm pretty sure I asked you to leave several times. Please do so."

He clamped his mouth shut before he said something he would regret. He shouldn't walk away. He should grab her brother by the shirt and make him apologize, but if Deja didn't want him here, then fine. He wouldn't stay where he wasn't welcome.

Emmett stepped in front of Deja, shielding her from Dare. With a light brush, he caressed her cheek before letting his hand fall to his side. "You don't deserve to be treated that way. By anyone. I don't care what he did. He doesn't scare me. You can keep pushing me away all you want, but I'll always be here for you. Just remember that. One phone call and I'm there. Don't hesitate."

He walked away. She wanted to handle her problems by herself, so be it.

For now.

He'd be back later to try to help her. To convince her to talk.

Emmett tried to walk past Ava without her stopping him, but it was impossible.

"Didn't go like you wanted, huh?" Ava asked with a tender smile.

"I don't like that guy. It doesn't seem like he should get a free pass right now."

"They've been through a lot. He's probably dealing with a lot of guilt right now. It's always easier to push people away rather than let them in."

Emmett ran a hand through his thick, black hair. "What happened?"

Ava glanced behind her to look at Deja and Dare. His eyes followed. Deja was saying something to her brother, and by the looks of it, he didn't care what she was saying. Clenching his fists, he forced away the temptation to walk back over there.

"I've already meddled enough. If Deja wants you to know, she'll tell you. I'm sorry, Emmett."

He nodded. Surprisingly, he preferred that, too. He wanted Deja to trust him enough to tell him the story. "Make sure he's not a complete dick before they leave. I don't trust him."

"Don't worry about a thing."

Emmett walked away, knowing he would worry about too much. Things he had no right to worry about. Things he shouldn't even think about.

Going home to an empty house sounded lonely. Normally, it didn't bother him. Tonight, it bugged the shit out of him. Before he knew it, he was pulling into his brother Ethan's driveway. One quick knock and he heard a voice holler, "Yo, it's open."

Ethan wouldn't say that to any knock. He just knew it was one of his brothers—either him or Gabe. He never did anything special either, just one quick tap. Maybe that's what made it so distinct.

Emmett swung the door open and slammed it shut. Not intentionally. At least, he didn't think so.

"Who cranked your engine? Go get a beer. Grab me one while you're at it. Mine's empty." Ethan held out an empty beer bottle with a sly smirk.

"Lazy much?" Emmett swiped the bottle from his hands and grabbed two from the fridge before taking a seat on the couch not far from Ethan, handing him one of the beers.

"So?"

Emmett took a swig of beer. "What?"

Ethan cocked a brow. "You normally don't slam the door like that. What's up? I heard Deja wrecked Soph's car. Is she hurt? I thought she didn't get a scratch. Is that what's got a bug up your ass?"

"She's fine. We got into a spat."

Ethan chuckled. "When do you two not get into a spat?"

"We don't fight all the time."

"You two squabble back and forth all the time, man. I call it sexual tension. Just announce your intentions toward her already and release that tension."

Emmett laughed, the sound not ringing true at all. "Trust me, it's all one-sided. I thought I hid my feelings better."

"Dude, you're so transparent when it comes to her. Since she popped into our lives."

"She sure told me where I could shove it. Told me *screw you* several times." Emmett smirked at Ethan before he could retort in a dirty way. "And not the good kind of screwing."

"That's too bad." Ethan's eyes sparkled with mischief, then turned somber. "So, what happened? Doesn't sound like normal fighting here."

"Her brother just got released from prison, and not a few hours later, he was arrested. Ava, being the nosy busybody she is, called Deja. She's willing to talk the officer out of making it an official arrest for Deja's sake. There's a whole lotta drama in that family."

Ethan sat up, twisting the beer bottle in his hands. "What was he in prison for?"

Emmett shrugged. "Don't know. Deja said..." Saying it out loud made it real, even though Ava made it sound like it wasn't true.

"Deja said what? The suspense, Emmett. Knock it off. It's Gabe who holds everything inside. Don't act like that." Ethan laughed, obviously trying to cut the tension in the room.

"Murder." Emmett sat up, mimicking his brother by twisting the bottle. He didn't need to look at Ethan to know he was speechless. Sort of the same reaction he had earlier.

"Ava made it sound like it wasn't quite like that, but she didn't tell me anything. I don't really care either. I want Deja to tell me. After tonight, I don't think she's going to keep working for me, let alone talk to me."

It sat on the tip of his tongue to tell Ethan what happened at her house. How good she felt in his arms. How sweet she tasted. Except he couldn't. Because then he'd have to tell him how fake everything was. A way for her to remove the hurt. Hide it for a while. She didn't want him for him. She just wanted to use him.

"Deja won't quit on you. She's one tough cookie. You two have gone head-to-head quite often about things and not once has she ever walked away."

Emmett chugged half his beer to keep from spilling about the kiss. "I might've gotten into her brother's face for the way he was treating her. She didn't appreciate it."

Ethan laughed. "No shit. When has Deja ever appreciated someone trying to help her? That woman likes her independence. Doesn't like to rely on anyone. The only one she doesn't argue with much is Soph. You know that."

"Yeah, well, I wasn't about to stand there and let him talk to her that way. Whether she wanted my help or not."

"Good for you." Ethan chuckled. "It's about damn time you start showing her what she means to you. I thought Gabe was slow with the ladies."

Emmett wanted to knock that stupid grin off his face. "Quit laughing. There is absolutely nothing funny about what happened tonight."

Ethan leaned back, pressing the bottle to his lips, a smile hiding behind it. "It's a little funny. Let me know when you finally kiss her."

"Why?"

"Because Gabe and I have a bet going on when you'll finally give in and kiss her. I don't wanna lose that bet."

Emmett remained silent. Sometimes being the oldest sucked. He had to deal with his younger brothers acting like a bunch of juveniles. He finished his beer. No way would he admit he kissed her tonight. Well, correction, she kissed him. He just happened to kiss her back. When he truly initiated the kiss, then he'd spill the beans and make whoever won the bet split it with him. Because, yeah, sometimes being the oldest had its perks. He always got his way.

If he even had the chance to kiss her again. Or the nerve.

More than likely, she wouldn't talk to him.

"I need another beer. Want one?" Emmett stood up.

"Drowning your sorrows isn't going to help." Ethan laughed.

"Just for that, you can get your own damn beer."

Ethan's laughter followed him all the way to the kitchen. Despite how much it annoyed him that his brother found this all funny, it lifted his spirits. This was why he came here. He knew Ethan would make everything seem not so bad. He found the humor in almost anything.

Emmett didn't. Not when he screwed it up with Deja.

4

DARE STEPPED INSIDE THE HOUSE, sighing silently. This house, besides the crappy look of peeling paint outside, looked like a real home. Cozy. Lived-in. Cheery.

He stood in the foyer, glancing down the hallway that led to the kitchen, the stairs leading to the second level, and the living room off to his left.

Pink curtains covered the living room windows, little frilly stuff hanging off the walls. A chair made out of pallets with intricate designs painted on it sat in the corner. And the smell. A lavender type aroma that made his nose itch.

This house didn't reflect his sister at all. But shit, what did he know? He hadn't spoken to his sister in the past ten years. It was for the best. Staying with her wouldn't make everything okay in the world. Nothing would.

"Are you hungry?"

Dare eyed his sister and shrugged. He suffered from plenty at the moment. Hunger wasn't one of them.

"Don't do this. Don't shut me out like this."

"I shouldn't be here."

"Fine. Get out." She threw her hand toward the door. "Go get drunk and arrested again."

Now, this. This was the sister he knew. The tough one. The one who didn't take shit from anybody. Not this girly shit decorating the house.

"I didn't drink tonight."

Deja propped her hands to her hips. "You smell like a damn brewery."

Dare narrowed his eyes. "That's because the asshole who got in my face threw his beer at me."

"Why did you go there?"

He turned away from her penetrating eyes. "Do you own this place?"

"I hate it when you ignore me like that."

He grinned, glancing at her. "Just acting like your brother. Just like you wanted me to. That's what I do."

"Fine. We'll ignore the elephant in the room. This is my friend Sophie's house. She's getting married soon and decided to move in with her fiancé next door. They were neighbors when they met. She said I could still stay here."

"Free of charge?"

"God, no. I'd never let her do that. I pay rent." She sighed. "Not as much as I would like because she's stubborn."

"How much?"

"Why?"

He cocked an eyebrow. "I'm having a conversation with my sister. I thought you'd appreciate that."

"You're such a jerk." She turned toward the kitchen and walked away. "Three hundred."

Nobody was *that* nice. Not in their world. "That's pretty damn low. What's the catch?" He followed her into the kitchen.

"There is none. Sophie's the best friend I never had growing up. She gets me. I get her." Deja stood at the counter, her eyes glued to a pie. "She gave me a new beginning when I didn't deserve one."

"Don't say shit like that. I'm the only bad seed in the family."

"Her fiancé—Austin—I broke into his house and stole money from him. A few days later, I tried to steal from her."

Never. His sister would never do something like that. She was the only bright light in their family. "I don't believe that for a minute."

She turned around and rested against the counter. "Believe it. If not for Sophie, I would've been arrested. Because of her, Austin let me pay him back the money I stole and the cost to fix his window I broke." She looked down at the floor. "When you left, life wasn't easy. I had to do things I'm not proud of. I was all alone. I still feel alone."

"Deja…" Shit. What should he say to that? Didn't she see how bad it would be if he stuck around? "That's why I should go."

Her head snapped up. "So I remain alone? It was an—"

"Shut up." He pressed his lips together to stop himself from spewing more hateful things. That asshole from the precinct was right. He needed to treat his sister better. He knew this, yet he couldn't stop himself. He didn't want to keep hearing her say it was an accident. The hell it was. He killed their parents. That was no accident.

"Life wasn't all rainbows and unicorns for us, Dare. I'm not saying I wanted them to die, but I don't miss them as much as I miss you. We were a team. You can't have a one-man team. I need you."

Brows puckered, fists clenched, her stance was like beams of steel. He still saw the pain, the anguish, the strength it took to say that. Those words made it feel like he was worthy of them. He was far from that. He didn't want to hear them.

"Don't say that. You don't know what you're saying. I'm bad."

"You're not."

"Deja, I was high as a kite that night. I should've never —" He eyed the pie behind her, anything to look at but her trusting face.

"We'll get you some clothes tomorrow and look for a job. Both of us."

Why did she insist on helping him? He should've kept those handcuffs on and let them toss him back into prison. He fit in there. Here, in her world, he felt like an interloper.

"You have a job."

He wanted to smile. At least someone was trying to take care of his sister. Something he should've been doing all along. Not sitting in prison the last ten years. Didn't mean the guy wasn't an asshole talking to him that way. Nobody talked to him that way.

Dare didn't think her face could get any more forlorn. It did. Without even trying, he was hurting his sister as each minute passed.

"After what happened today, I'm sure Emmett doesn't want me coming back to work."

"Did he say that? He whispered to you before he walked away. What the hell did he say?" He'd track him down and beat the shit out of him if he fired his sister for no damn reason.

"No. He didn't say that. But still..."

So she wouldn't tell him what he said. He could only imagine. He saw the look in his eyes. "He likes you."

Deja laughed with hardly any humor behind it. "Not likely."

He grinned, cocking a brow, probably looking like the devil himself. "I might've been behind bars the last ten years, sis, but I know when a man looks at a woman he likes. I'll kill him if he hurts you."

Her eyes went round with shock, her skin turning ashy-white in an instant. "Don't say things like that, Dare. You're not a killer."

"That's funny. That's why I was in prison."

He wanted to laugh. His sister liked this Emmett guy. Not that she'd admit it. His sister rarely admitted things like that to him. Because she knew he'd take care of any asshole who treated her wrong. Even the tiniest amount of disrespect warranted a punch in the face.

"We need to talk about it."

"Nope."

He glanced around the kitchen, noting more frivolous knickknacks hanging around. Perhaps her friend Sophie didn't take all her crap with her when she moved. His sister's bedroom, from what he could remember, was always clean, but sparse. She didn't hang posters on her walls or collect anything. She didn't buy things just to decorate a room and make it more colorful. Neither did he. They never had the money to do it. Still. This house didn't reflect the sister he remembered.

"Dare, please, I think—"

"They say you don't dream in cryosleep."

"What?"

"They say you don't—"

"I heard you the first time, idiot."

Smirking, he propped himself against the kitchen table

and crossed his arms and legs. "Then why'd you ask what for?"

"Could you try not to be a smartass all the time?"

"Just one of the many reasons you love me."

"I do. I love you, Dare."

He glanced down at his feet. He hated when she talked like that. Her love was precious and what he did... "I hate dreaming. You could call it nightmares." Looking at Deja, he saw the understanding in her eyes. "I'm not ready to talk. I might never be ready."

She smiled. The first real smile of the day. He missed that. He didn't realize it was something he needed in his life. "I'll wait. Forever if I have to. I'm not going to let you shove me out of your life. We're a team again. Whether you like it or not."

"Well, partner, just know I'll hurt anyone who hurts you, including that asshole Emmett."

"You have nothing to worry about. Emmett doesn't like me like that."

"Yeah, right. You're delusional as shit, D."

She smiled again. His sister was so beautiful when she smiled. Since this afternoon, all he did was made her frown. It was good to see her happy again. All he had to do was call her by her nickname.

"You need to watch your language. Sophie won't put up with that."

Dare laughed. A real laugh. "Whatever."

"You'll see. One look from her and you'll be watching what you say."

"I haven't seen you watch your mouth."

"Hmm...you bring it out of me so easily." She grinned, the mischievous smile he missed seeing.

They could never go back to the close relationship they once had, but he could try a little harder to be nice.

"That pie any good? Maybe I am a little hungry." He nodded to the pie sitting close by her.

"It's the best. I'll grab you a slice." Deja turned around to grab a plate from the cupboard.

Dare took a seat at the table. A piece of pie sat on a plate, the fork dangling on the edge. It looked like someone left in a hurry.

Because of him.

This would never work. He couldn't stay with his sister for long. He didn't want her to get too attached.

Hell, he didn't want to get too attached. Leaving would be better. For everyone.

"DARRIAN! DARRIAN! OH MY GOD."

Dare rolled his eyes as he turned up the volume on his music. His mother was in another mood for hysterics. When wasn't she? Her emotions were like a damn ping-pong ball, hopping all over the place.

The door swung open, slamming into the wall.

"Shit, Mom, what the hell?" Dare sat up on the bed.

"Your father, Darrian. Oh, dear." Her eyes were round with shock, tears streaming down her face.

He frowned. His mom was known for hysterics of all kinds, but rarely did tears appear. "What about him? He was hitting the bottle last I saw."

"He's having chest pains and looking red in the face. I think he needs to go to the hospital. I can't lose him, Darrian. He's all I have."

Standing up, he grabbed a shirt from the floor without both-

ering to sniff it. If his dad was having a heart attack, did it matter if he grabbed a dirty shirt? Dirty and clean were mixed all over the floor. Not that his parents cared. Clearly, his mother didn't even care about him as a person. Dad was all she had? What a crock of shit. Where was Deja when he needed her?

"Did you call for an ambulance? If he's having a heart attack, that's what you should be doing, Mom." Half the time he felt like the damn parent around here.

"The phone..." She trailed off as she ran out of the room.

Great. That translated into they didn't pay the phone bill again. Sometimes, he felt like the only damn adult in the house. Working his ass off at nineteen to keep the house from falling apart was bullshit. But he did it. For one reason only—Deja. He'd do anything for his younger sister. Including staying around this hellhole. The minute she turned eighteen, they were out of here.

Grabbing a blunt lying on his desk, he lit it up and took a large puff. Swiping his keys as well, he walked out to the living room where his father sat in the faded-brown recliner. He did look like shit. His dad might be the biggest loser, the biggest drunk he'd ever seen, but he'd get his ass to the hospital as fast as he could.

"Come on. I'll drive."

"Oh, Darrian!" The tears kept coming down in a steady stream on his mother's face.

"Mom, calm down. I'll drive to the hospital." Shoving the blunt between his lips, he stooped down and looped an arm around his dad's waist. "Come on, Dad. Let's go."

"Take care of your momma if I go. She needs someone to take care of her." His dad stumbled.

Dare tightened his hold and headed for the front door. He refused to answer that comment. Because he really wanted to ask, "What about Deja?" It's as if neither of them mattered to his parents. He knew this. He was used to it. Didn't make it hurt any less anytime they displayed it so blatantly.

Dare got his dad situated in the front seat as quickly as possible, buckling him in when his dad's hands kept fumbling with the clasp. Having a possible heart attack and drunk to boot. Figured.

His mother climbed into the backseat and crowded between them, sticking her head close to his dad's head. "It's all right, Barry baby. Darrian will get us there."

Dare backed out of the driveway, squealing tires as he headed for the hospital. Thunder rolled in the distance, dark clouds swarming the sky, haloing the drive in a gloomy way. He took another puff of the blunt, rolled down the window, and flicked the rest outside. The last thing he needed was to get pulled over for speeding with marijuana in his possession.

"Quit smoking that nasty stuff, Darrian. It's disgusting," his mother scoffed, clucking her tongue in disapproval.

"Mom, buckle up. Shit. What if we get in a damn accident?"

"I'm your mother. You don't tell me what to do. I tell you what to do." She leaned in farther toward the front, grabbing for his dad's hand.

"Whatever." Dare rolled his eyes, wishing he hadn't tossed the blunt so soon.

He was feeling pretty mellow, though. He took a few pills before his mom came bursting into his room. So much for partying with Rick tonight. Maybe he could drop them off at the hospital door and then hit up Rick. Dealing with his parents this long, he needed to get even higher. He could only stand his parents in low doses. They normally left him alone. Deja was another story. His mom was always on Deja's case for one thing or another.

The rain started to come down heavily out of nowhere. Dare hit the windshield wipers, slowing down a little.

"Darrian! Don't slow down. You can't slow down." His mother grabbed his shoulder, almost shaking him in the process.

He shoved her hand off and threw a nasty glare in her direction. "Shit, Mom. Shut up and buckle up. I can barely see with the rain. What the hell do you expect?"

"Don't take that tone with me, young man. I'll have—"

"Donna, baby doll, sit back and leave Darrian alone. It's raining hard."

His mother huffed but finally sat back. For once, his dad wasn't a useless deadbeat asshole. Drunk as a skunk and he still recognized how bad the weather had turned. Feeling ill must be sobering him up some.

"If your father doesn't make it to the hospital, I'll hold you responsible."

Dare wanted to laugh. His dad was too stubborn to kick the bucket so soon, that's for damn sure.

Halfway there. Thank God! It put him closer to partying it up with Rick. He couldn't wait to throw a case of beer back.

Shit. Deja.

He'd have to go home first and wait for Deja to get back. He'd have to give her hell for not telling him where she went. He always liked to know where she wandered off. Somebody needed to worry about her. Their parents didn't give two shits about either of them. Regardless, he had to tell Deja he was dropping Dad off at the hospital.

"Shit." Jerking the wheel and hitting the brakes hard, the car started to hydroplane as he attempted to avoid hitting the damn dog in the road.

The last thing he remembered before smacking into a tree head-on was the high-pitched scream as his mother flew through the windshield.

5

EMMETT TOOK a deep breath and pulled open the door. Deja's head snapped up and a tentative smile appeared. She came in. He hadn't been sure if she would show up. He took it as a good sign she didn't hate him too much.

"Morning."

She nodded and held out a piece of paper. "Good morning. Taylor didn't fill out his supply form. I don't make these forms for the hell of it. He needs to fill it out."

He grabbed the form. "Sure, I'll talk to him."

"Don't you have an appointment this morning?"

Did he go with honesty? Or pretend ignorance?

"I was worried. I didn't know if I'd see you behind this desk or not." Honesty it was. Deja always appreciated it straight. Why would he do any different?

She bit her bottom lip, then licked that same lip. "I wasn't sure if you'd want me behind this desk anymore. I'm sorry about how I acted last night."

Emmett knew she was saying something important, but all he processed was the delicious lip licking she just did. He wanted to kiss her again. Would she let him kiss her? Hold her in his arms again? What would she say if he pulled her into his arms right now? Would she slap him? Kiss him back?

"Emmett? Do you want me here?"

She was frowning. Her hand was shaking. He could tell by the slight movement of the pen she held; otherwise, he would've never been able to tell how nervous she was at the thought he wanted to fire her. He wanted her all right. In every possible way.

"Of course. We're good. No need to apologize. I should apologize. I'm sorry. I'll try to mind my own business." He smiled, trying to pull out any kind of smile from her. Even a fake one would do. "How's your brother settling in?"

"Fine." She turned her gaze away without posing any kind of smile and started to tap away at the keyboard.

Conversation over. He knew when to take a hint. After last night, she probably didn't want to talk to him about anything concerning her brother.

"I'll swing by the place Taylor's at and make sure he fills this out." He smiled again, hoping against hope she'd flash him one small smile.

"Thank you."

Nothing. Barely even looked at him. This sucked.

"I guess I'll go then."

"Bye, E-man."

That time she didn't even glance at him. Well, she didn't quit. He'd take the small victory.

Emmett left before he said something idiotic, or worse, did something idiotic, like pull her into his arms, regardless of what her body language was telling him. Cool indifference. He was nothing more than her boss. She probably didn't even consider him a friend anymore.

He swung by the house where Taylor was working. Late

April, and Taylor was hard at work cleaning up the mess from the winter. Mowing, trimming, fertilizing. One of the many reasons Deja wanted everyone's supply lists filled out monthly. He was never good at remembering to order things in a timely manner. Deja made sure everything was stocked —when they all remembered to tell her what they were low on, that is.

Emmett gave Taylor a quick, firm talk about remembering to fill out the form, with a smirk from Taylor, because yeah, Emmett was just as bad as him. The difference was he enjoyed the verbal squabbles they engaged in. She could get so lively, her eyes sparkling intensely, her hands on her hips. Even the hard look on her face was adorable. There wasn't much about her that he didn't think was adorable.

The day went fast, working his ass off, as usual. April was always a busy month when people were ready for their yards to transform from a wintry mess to a beautiful spring picture. He was hungry. Ravenous, in fact, for pie. Or whatever excuse he could think of to stop at Austin's house. He didn't have the guts to go over to Deja's house again, but if he saw her, then his night would end on a high note.

He swung his long legs out of the vehicle and tried to think of a good enough excuse for stopping by. When Austin opened the door, he knew no excuse would convince Austin about his intentions.

"I heard you and Deja got into it last night at the precinct." Austin closed the door behind him. "Want a beer?"

"Sure. And pie." Emmett grinned, hoping Sophie made another pie already.

"Didn't you have pie yesterday?"

"No."

Austin laughed, clapping him on the back. "Why is that? Did you finally make a move on her?"

He shrugged Austin off and headed for the kitchen where he could hear Sophie bustling around. "Of course not. Ava called and I never got the chance to eat any of it." Totally untrue, of course. Deja told him to get the hell out before he could eat his pie, then Ava called.

"Emmett, I'm so glad you stopped by," Sophie said with a sweet smile.

Emmett gave Axel, Sophie and Austin's dog, a pat on the head as he jumped on his leg in greeting. He loved it when she smiled. Sometimes, especially when she didn't smile, he could remember the terror written on her face when she thought her ex-boyfriend was going to come and hurt her. Nobody in the family would've let it happen. Of course, it still kind of happened. If Austin hadn't stepped in and saved her, who knew how bad it would've gotten. So yeah, he loved when she smiled. It was nice to see her so happy and carefree.

He grabbed a chair and sat down, letting Axel jump on his leg for more rubs behind the ear. "Why's that? Did you miss me?"

Sophie chuckled while Austin glared at him. "Why do you always flirt with my pixie angel? Go flirt with Deja."

"Soph knows I'm not flirting, just being friendly. Although, I am the more dashing gentleman in this room."

"Yeah, right." Austin crossed his arms, his features softening when Sophie kissed him on the lips.

"You're staying for supper, right, Emmett?" Sophie turned her sweet face in his direction.

"Sure. So, why are you glad I stopped by? You have a project you need help with?" Emmett wasn't a huge fan of stringing beads or gluing shit together, but for Sophie, he'd do it. She always smiled the brightest when he helped.

"Nope." She beamed at him with happiness and turned back to the stove. A knock sounded on the door. She turned to Austin, her eyes twinkling with delight. "Can you get that?"

"Of course." Austin kissed her cheek, smirked at him, and walked out of the room.

"What am I missing here?" He suddenly didn't like how mischievous they were both acting.

"I know you get nervous sometimes, but just relax and be yourself, Emmett. She'll come around. I know she will."

"What are you talking—" Emmett froze as he heard voices filter from the living room into the kitchen. "Is that Deja I hear?"

Sophie smiled so brightly at him, he thought she looked like a star from the sky. "I invited her over for supper. I'm so glad you stopped by as well."

Emmett tried not to tense up. Wasn't this the reason he stopped here with no handy excuse? He wanted to see Deja in any possible way. Now that it was happening, he wasn't ready.

He jerked up from the table. His lips started to curl into a grin, abruptly stopping when he saw who was trailing behind her. Dare. Her brother didn't look happy to see him. Axel sat down by his feet, unfazed by the newcomers. He wished he could feel the same way.

Austin took position by Sophie and wrapped his arms around her. "Dare, this is my wife, Sophie." He laughed when she raised a brow at him. "My beautiful pixie angel, this is Dare, Deja's brother."

Sophie stepped out of his embrace and walked over to Deja and Dare. Emmett did nothing but stand there looking lost and confused and ten times the idiot he felt like.

She held out her hand, barely a trace of her nervousness present, she hid it so well. She wasn't a fan of men. They made her nervous. "Nice to meet you, Dare."

Dare didn't even crack a small grin as he shook her hand. "You, too. You and your husband have a nice house."

Deja laughed, the beautiful sound music to Emmett's ears. "They aren't quite married yet."

"I'd elope tonight if she'd let me." Austin walked to the fridge and pulled it open. "Beer?" He looked at Deja and Dare.

Dare's face became rigid, his jaw clenching. Deja slightly stiffened next to him. She spoke first. "No, thanks, Austin. We'll have some iced tea."

Obviously getting the picture, Austin didn't argue, and pulled out the pitcher of tea.

Sophie tossed her hands out in a shooing motion. "Go. Take a seat in the dining room and I'll bring out the meal. We're having lasagna tonight."

"Sounds da...nuzeling good." Emmett coughed, trying to cover up the fact he almost swore. Sophie hated swearing, and he tried his hardest not to do it in front of her. He normally never failed. Damn nerves. Having Deja and Dare here wasn't helping him.

Dare looked at him strangely. Austin clapped him on the back and led the way to the dining room that connected with the living room. They all took a seat at the table. Austin sat on one side, leaving the seat next to him free for Sophie. Emmett sat across from Austin, curious and anxious to see who would sit by him.

Dare clearly didn't want Deja next to him, because he grabbed the chair by Emmett and sat down, giving him a side glance that bordered on threatening. Deja decided to take the seat that would be closest to Sophie and Dare, marking herself as the head of the table.

Awkward silence filled the room.

Emmett didn't know how much Austin knew about Dare, but Austin decided to start the conversation. "How are you settling in, Dare?"

"Fine."

Austin rested his elbows on the table and nodded. "Good."

More awkwardness. Deja kept darting her head back and forth, probably wondering when the other shoe would drop. Emmett wasn't planning to start a fight. He said he'd stay out of her business and he would—unless he saw something that warranted him to step in. Then no way in hell he'd stay out of it. But for now, he wouldn't even ask questions. He'd leave it up to Austin to look like the idiot.

"Oh, do you need me to look at the washer still, Deja? I forgot about that."

Deja grinned—a genuine one—at Austin. Why couldn't she ever look at him like that? "When you get a chance. It's still making that clanking sound. Sounds like a moose is dying or something."

Austin laughed. "You've heard a moose like that before? I'll look at it, but honestly, I don't know anything about fixing a washing machine. Might just have to buy a new one."

Deja cocked a brow. "You're going to buy it?"

Austin squirmed and slowly replied, "Yes."

A throat cleared. Austin jerked his attention to the right. "I'll buy the new washer." Sophie set the pan of lasagna in the center of the table. She then took a seat next to Austin.

"You do realize in a few months we'll be married and

what's mine is yours, what's yours is mine, right? Why can't I buy the washer?" Austin's tone was light, but Emmett heard the frustration mingled in.

Since the moment he met her, Sophie never, not once, let Austin buy her things. She liked taking care of herself. It had been an uphill battle for him. Still was. They didn't fight, per se, but the topic of money did come up frequently. All his cousin wanted to do was take care of the woman he loved. All Sophie wanted to do was keep her independence, the knowledge she could do it all on her own. They'd survive these little arguments. Emmett knew it.

Sophie cut into the lasagna slowly. "It's my house. My responsibility. If it needs a new washer, I'll buy one. Not you." She pointed a stern gaze at him.

"I want to buy it." Austin snapped his fingers as a slow smile emerged. "You know, I'd like a new washer. We'll put mine in your house and I'll buy a new washer here."

Sophie frowned. "It's the same thing. Don't try to fool me."

"It's not the same thing."

"It is."

"No, it's—"

"Austin, just concede the fact you're not buying a washing machine," Deja piped in as she scooped some lasagna on her plate.

"I don't want to."

Deja laughed and pointed at him. "You don't do the pouty face as well as Emmett. You know Sophie will win this argument."

Austin and him shared a look. Half the time they pouted on purpose just to make them smile. Clearly, it worked. Deja laughed, the sound, as always, beautiful.

"I'll buy the washer." All heads turned toward him as he took his turn scooping lasagna onto his plate.

"How do you even factor into this conversation, E-man?" Deja raised a brow, her lips in a thin line.

"That look says you're thinking about grabbing your tire iron. Will it make you feel better to take a swing at me? I'll let you."

"Don't tempt me, E-man. I might actually do it." Her lips slowly tilted into a devious grin.

Damn, she was the sexiest woman alive. Her lips looked so kissable right now.

"Enough talk about the washer. I'll buy a new one tomorrow." Sophie took a bite of her food.

"At least let me look at it first," Austin insisted.

She brushed a hand across his cheek. "What do you know about washers?"

"I'll look at it."

Silence descended. Emmett almost forgot Dare was in the room, he had been so quiet next to him. Everyone turned their attention to him.

Sophie lightly smiled. "Do you know anything about washers?"

Dare shrugged. "Not really. I used to fix shit around the house all the time. I even tinkered with shit in..." He pushed some lasagna around his plate. "In prison."

"Thank you, Dare. I would appreciate it if you looked at the washer for me." Sophie's smile beamed with happiness as she cast a glance at Deja, then looked Dare directly in the eyes. "Swearing is bad for you, you know."

Emmett coughed a little to hide the laugh that wanted to escape. How would Dare handle this? If he disrespected Sophie, even in the tiniest of ways, he might punch him in the face. Nobody, and he meant nobody, disrespected

Sophie. If he didn't get the first jab in, he knew Austin would step in just as fast.

To Emmett's surprise, Dare's neck up to his cheeks turned a slight shade of red. The man was blushing. Emmett cleared his throat, hiding another laugh. Yeah, Sophie had that effect on people.

"My apologies, Sophie. I'll try to watch my language." Dare shoved a bite of lasagna in his mouth.

"Thank you." She stood up. "I forgot the Parmesan cheese. I'll be right back." She walked out of the room, Axel trailing behind her. Axel was never far from Sophie. He was almost like her personal doggie bodyguard.

Deja grinned and chuckled. "Told ya, Dare." She glanced at Austin, not even looking at Emmett. "I warned Dare Sophie didn't like swearing."

"Yeah, she's a stickler about that. Zane likes to test her. He still has a hard time. I appreciate you trying, Dare," Austin said.

"She's sweet, but I'd rather not test that hard glint I saw in her eyes." The tip of his lip lifted. Not quite a smile, but close enough to anything Emmett saw from him so far.

"Good idea. Wish I could follow through with that. Let me know if the washer isn't fixable." Austin took a sip of his beer and rolled his eyes as Deja gave him a look. "What?"

"If you buy her a washer without asking or telling or informing her in some way, well, you know she won't be happy."

Austin leaned back and ran his hands over his face. "I just want to take care of her. I don't want her to worry about shit like this. She has enough to worry about."

Emmett paused, his fork dangling. His voice became low as he said, "What's going on?"

Austin glanced at the entryway, obviously making sure

Sophie wasn't on her way back. "Kevin's trial is coming up. Bastard hired a damn good attorney. She's afraid he's going to get off. Some nights..." Austin ran his hands through his hair. "Some nights are bad."

Deja's voice was low and edged with steel. "If he comes around, he'll wish he were dead. You should've kicked his ass a little harder, Austin."

"Trust me, Deja, I wish I did, too. Zane couldn't even pry me off without the help of another officer."

"Security system still working decent?" Emmett asked, glancing behind him. What was taking Sophie so long?

"It is. Deja, are you setting the alarm at your house? I don't want to worry about you as well. Kevin may or may not know Sophie's living with me. The last thing I want is for him to attack you."

Deja pinned a stern look at Austin. "I'm setting it every night. Don't worry about me. I can take care of myself."

Austin chuckled and winked at her. "Never doubted that for a minute. But Kevin's dangerous. You didn't see him that day. Not like I did. The evil in his eyes. I'll never let anything happen to Sophie again. I'm buying her a damn washing machine, whether she likes it or not."

Deja laughed and shook her head. "You know what, Austin? You're right. If Dare can't fix it, I'll try to smooth a nice path for you to buy a washer."

"Miracles do come true." Austin laughed a little, then frowned as he glanced behind Emmett. "It doesn't take that long to get cheese, does it?"

"Nope, it doesn't." Emmett scooted back his chair as Austin stood up.

"I got this, Emmett. I probably upset her with my insistence on the washer. Why can't she see I just want to help, to take care of her?"

Deja grabbed Austin's arm as he walked past her. "She knows. I know you understand the reasoning behind it, and it's hard to let go, but be patient, Austin."

He squeezed her hand. "You're a good friend. It's about damn time you're on my side for once. I'm not letting you forget you're gonna help me persuade her to buy a washer."

"Just this once." Deja let his hand go.

Austin walked out of the room.

Emmett sat perched on his chair, ready, waiting, on edge. He had no idea why. He just felt like he needed to be ready for something.

"Eat up, E-man. You know how lovey-dovey they get. Austin's going to take his time apologizing." Deja tilted her eyes his way, a softness in them he wished he saw more often.

He started to scoot his chair in when Austin roared from the kitchen. "Shit, Emmett!"

Emmett stood up so fast the chair fell backward. Austin came rushing into the room. "She's gone. The kitchen door is wide open. She's gone."

6

Deja dropped her fork as Emmett rushed out of the room with Austin toward the kitchen. Terror started to bubble up through her veins as she thought of the last time Sophie was injured. The blood, the bruises that covered her body almost made her sick to her stomach. She never had the urge to kill someone before. But that day, she had wanted to rip Kevin to pieces for laying one hand on her.

"She can't be missing just like that, can she?"

Deja forced herself to look at Dare, who looked confused by everything. "Kevin...he's a dangerous man. I wouldn't put it past him to try and hurt Sophie again."

"Who's Kevin?"

The front door swung open before Deja could respond. Sophie walked in, her face covered in fright, her entire body shaking as she walked unsteadily.

"Sophie, what happened?" Deja rushed to her side, grabbed her around the waist, and headed for the couch. "Austin, Sophie's in here!"

Dare stood up from the table and slowly walked toward

the living room as Austin and Emmett ran back into the room.

Austin pulled Sophie into his arms and held her tightly. Deja stepped back and took a spot next to Emmett. Dare still stood off to the side, observing everything.

"What happened? Is that bastard outside? Did he hurt you?" Austin pulled her slightly away, cupping her cheeks gently. "I'll kill him. I will never let him hurt you again."

"Austin..." Emmett said lightly, warning him to watch his words.

Deja agreed with Austin. She'd be more than happy to get rid of Kevin.

Sophie grabbed his hands. "It's not him. I let Axel outside because he started to claw at the door so furiously. You know he always goes quickly, then comes right back. He didn't come back. I called his name, and he just didn't come back. I can't find him." A tear slid down her cheek.

Deja found it hard to believe Axel would run away. He was attached to Sophie at the hip. He followed her every-where. He wouldn't run away.

"That's why the door was wide open? You went outside looking for Axel?" Austin intertwined their fingers together as they dropped their hands to the side.

Sophie nodded, obviously upset that Axel ran away.

"We'll go look for him. We'll find him, Soph. Don't worry." Emmett smiled.

Deja knew he was reassuring Sophie as best as he could. That smile of his managed to reassure *her* a little. Or maybe she just loved when he smiled. She had been surprised to see him when they walked into the kitchen. Her surprise turned into happiness, then immediately into anxiety. No matter how much she wanted and liked Emmett, she was all wrong for him.

"What Emmett said. We'll all search for him." Austin looked at Emmett. "You, Sophie, and I will search the back-yard." Austin turned toward her. "Can you and Dare search the front?"

"Of course." Deja glanced at her brother, who merely nodded.

Austin, Emmett, and Sophie walked out of the room toward the kitchen. Dare met Deja by the front door and stepped outside. They hollered for Axel a few times, then started to walk down the sidewalk.

"So, who's this Kevin guy?"

Deja kept her eyes peeled for any white blur of fluffiness, although, grabbing a flashlight would've been helpful. The night made it difficult to see, especially in the dark corners of houses, trees, and behind cars.

Dare nudged her. "Ignoring me? I'm not good enough to know what's going on."

Deja halted, shocked. He actually thought that. There was no teasing tone in his voice. "Of course you're good enough. I'm just worried about Sophie. She's had it rough. Axel means everything to her."

Dare's eyes glowed a brilliant blue in the night air. They sparkled with a tortured pain, something she saw all the time when she looked in the mirror. They truly did have the same eyes.

"Kevin is her ex-boyfriend. He was abusive. Sophie fled from New York and got as far away from him as she could. She met Austin and they fell in love."

Deja started to walk again, hoping against hope that Axel didn't run away. Or worse. That Kevin hid in the shadows and nabbed Axel as soon as he could. Seemed something devious that asshole would do.

"That's clearly not the end of the story."

Deja tossed her hair behind her ear as a light breeze tried to blow it in her face. "It's my fault she got hurt."

Dare grabbed her arm and forced her to look at him. "I doubt that."

"You've been away ten years. What do you know?"

The pressure on her arm went from light to intense, but not enough to hurt her. All she felt was his pain. "I know my sister. Inside and out. Ten years doesn't change that. Whatever happened, it wasn't your fault. So, tell me what did happen?"

"Do you honestly care?"

Dare dropped her arm and whipped around. "Damn it, Deja. I care. Why do you think I want to leave? Because I care. You're better off without me in your life."

She touched his shoulder, his entire body taut with tension. "I'm better with you in my life."

He refused to speak or to release the tension that had him coiled tighter than a boa constrictor on a mission.

"I needed a new job. Emmett offered me one and I turned him down. I should've taken it. Nothing would've happened if I had taken the job. Instead, that day, I left to fill out an application." Her hand dropped, her insides turning to mush as the horror of that day crushed her to pieces. "Kevin showed up and beat her so badly...if I had only... it's my—"

Dare turned around and shoved her into his embrace, hugging her fiercely. A big bear hug. Just like old times. "Shut up, Deja. Don't say shit like that again. A man beating a woman is not your fault. He probably watched and waited for the perfect opportunity. I don't need to know the man to know that for a fact."

She buried her face into his chest, breathing in the

safety, the feeling of home. She had missed her brother so much.

"I can't believe anyone would harm such a beautiful woman. She seems so nice."

"Sophie's the best. The sweetest woman in the world."

"Is he sitting in jail waiting for trial?"

Deja shook her head. Dare let her go, rubbing his hands up and down her arms to halt the chill that passed through her body. How had he known she needed that? Simple. Her brother knew her that well.

"He has a lot of money. He barely sat in jail before they released him on bail. The one stipulation the judge gave him was he had to stay in Minnesota until the trial. Sophie's been on edge since then. She hides it well, though. He could honestly get off with just a slap on the wrist, no jail time whatsoever. As long as he runs back to New York, I say good riddance."

Dare's mouth slowly tipped up into an evil grin. "Well, if he sees the inside of a jail cell, I'll be sure to let my friends know to give him a warm welcoming."

"Dare..." She bit her lip, knowing exactly what he meant. "Just how would you let your friends know? I don't want you going back there for any reason."

He threw his arm around her shoulder and started to walk back toward the house. "I have my ways, D. Don't you worry about a thing. I don't know Sophie well, but what I do know, no man gets away with harming a woman like that. And she's your best friend. Enough said."

Deja couldn't help but smile. "She is my best friend."

"There you go then."

As soon as they walked back into the house, Dare's smile fled. It instantly made her sad. For a moment there, they almost acted like old times, like brother and sister. Now his wall was firmly back in place. Would she ever get her brother back?

They found Emmett, Austin, and Sophie in the kitchen. Deja took a seat next to Sophie at the small table. "Any sign of him?"

Sophie timidly shook her head, wiping a tear away. "He wouldn't run away."

"We'll find him. I swear we will." Austin said it with such conviction that Deja didn't doubt him for a second. The small grin on Sophie's face said as much as well.

The front door opened and slammed just as quickly. Zane's voice with the little pitter-patter of feet echoed to the kitchen. Axel came running through the kitchen, jumping into Sophie's lap before she could even stand up.

"Oh, Axel, baby, I was so worried. Please tell me you didn't go to the farm. You can't do that, boy." Sophie hugged him tightly.

"I have a feeling that's exactly where he was headed. Nearly hit the little guy halfway here. He has a crazy sixth sense," Zane said as he walked into the kitchen, holding a baby car seat.

"Everything okay?" Austin's frown became worse as he eyed his brother.

"I wish. I need you on the farm. There's a fire." Zane set the car seat to the floor, rubbing his hand over his face.

Silence descended in the house. Emmett was the first to find his voice. "Anyone hurt? Where's Ava? Eleanor?"

"Eleanor left for the weekend to visit her family up north. Ava's being Ava, already jumping into the fray to do her job, no matter how many times I yelled at her." Zane seemed to age right in front of them. The worry lines increased as his frown became deeper. "Some idiot was driving drunk with his girlfriend in the passenger seat. He had a bottle of moonshine, and she grabbed it from him and started to pour it out of the window. He ran through our fence onto our field and crashed near the corral. Don't know how it happened, but a fire started, lighting up the path she created with the moonshine. It's damn close to the white barn. We can't lose all of our stock, Austin. We won't be able to afford...I couldn't find my damn phone...Jimmy..."

Emmett stood closest to Zane. He clapped him on the shoulder. "Is the fire out yet? We're here to help. Jimmy's fine."

"Ava called the chief of police wanting the fire chief there ASAP." Zane laughed. It came out strangled. "Why does my wife have to be in the middle of everything?"

Austin chuckled as he lightly squeezed Sophie's shoulders. "Because she wouldn't be the Ava we love. You didn't answer Emmett. How bad is the fire?"

"It wasn't too bad when I left. I guess we should be thankful the ground's still wet from winter somewhat. It shouldn't hit the barn. Regardless, they wouldn't let me in there to get the pigs out just in case. Ethan had to restrain me a bit. Anyone else and I probably would've decked them." Zane bent down and unbuckled the tiny baby sitting so peacefully in the car seat. "I need you at the farm, Austin. You, too, Emmett. That fence needs to be fixed right, away as soon as it's safe. We can't have all the cows getting loose."

Zane stood up, cradling the baby perfectly in his arms. "Will you watch little Jimmy, Sophie? I forgot the damn diaper bag, but he's not due to eat for another hour at least."

Sophie nodded and gently set Axel on the ground. She stood up and took Jimmy from Zane. "You know we have diapers, formula, and whatever else he needs here. I'd love to watch him. Thank you for bringing Axel back. I had a mini meltdown there."

Sophie had gotten used to everyone in the McCord family. Comfortable with all the men. When Zane pulled her closer for a small hug, not one hesitation or shiver occurred. Deja sat close enough to them that she heard him whisper, "Sorry for swearing."

"Let's go." Austin kissed Sophie quickly on the lips and walked out of the kitchen. Sophie followed. Deja figured she wanted one more kiss, a little more thorough than the chaste one displayed in front of them.

Zane started to follow when he noticed Dare on the opposite side of the kitchen near the back door. "You must be Dare, Deja's brother. We could use all the help we can get. Let's go."

Deja had to stifle a laugh that wanted to burst out at Dare's shocked expression. Not much took him by surprise. Zane wasn't one to hold back on his words or actions. If he thought something, he said it. If he wanted something done, he did it. He rarely asked. He just expected people to listen.

"Not sure I'd be useful. I don't know anything about fixing a fence. You don't want me there." Dare almost looked like he was ready to bolt out the kitchen door.

Zane's stance became rigid. "I would've never said it if I didn't mean it." He glanced at Deja, then back to Dare. "Deja's practically part of the family. You're her brother, which, in turn, makes you part of the family. Family always helps out. So let's go. We could use your help."

Deja wasn't sure who was more shocked, her, Dare, or Emmett, who stood silently in the kitchen. Tears suddenly wanted to fall down in crashing waves at the words Zane just spoke, but she held them back. She'd fall apart later, alone, in her room. She'd sort out the heavy emotions he just unleashed. Part of the family? She had no idea he thought that.

Zane nodded, as if his words wouldn't be disobeyed, and walked out of the kitchen. Emmett turned to Dare. "You can ride with me." Then he disappeared as well.

"They're quite a family, the McCords." Dare said it quietly. Whether out of awe or fear they would hear him, she wasn't sure.

"Best house I ever broke into." Deja couldn't help but grin. Because it was seriously the best house she could've ever picked. She now had food, a roof over her head, a best friend, and a family that accepted her as one of their own.

Dare gave a small snort, almost like he chuckled, and pointed a finger at her as he started to walk past her. "You ever try breaking into another house and we're gonna have issues."

"I have no need to anymore." She swatted his finger away playfully. "Acting like a big brother. Careful, I might get used to it."

He ruffled the top of her head like he did in the old days and smiled. "Shit, me, too." His smile dipped. "It'd be better if I left."

"No, Dare, it'd be better if you started to let me in." She tossed her head toward the living room. "You should go. Zane's not the most patient man."

"Damn McCords. Strangest, nicest bunch of people I've ever met."

"Damn right. They're the best." Deja watched him walk out. She meant every word she said. She was far from the best. Far from perfect. Which was exactly why Emmett would always be unattainable.

7

THE DRIVE to the farm was silent—and awkward. Emmett had no idea what to say to Dare. The tension ran thick in the truck. Emmett didn't want to hate the man, because he was Deja's brother, but he didn't appreciate the way he spoke to her at the precinct.

He appeared decent enough at Austin's house. When they weren't around was he still treating his sister like shit? That's what he wanted to know. He wasn't going to ask, though. A fistfight, in closed quarters, while driving, didn't seem like the greatest idea.

And Zane. Out of everyone in the family, he never expected Zane to see Deja as part of the family, let alone say it about Dare. He'd probably change his opinion soon. Just a little taste of how Dare really was would have him regretting his words.

That wasn't fair. Emmett barely knew the guy to dislike him so much. He did spend the last ten years in prison. It'd take time to assimilate himself back into society. He had to give him a chance. For Deja. Especially for her.

"What are your intentions toward my sister?"

The wheel jerked as he stiffened. He looked at Dare. "Excuse me?"

Dare cleared his throat, his hands fisted, resting on his lap. "I said, what are your intentions toward my sister?"

Emmett forced himself to keep his eyes on the road. It wouldn't do well for Dare to see the lie. "I don't know what you mean. She's my employee, a good friend of the family."

"Bullshit."

Clearly, Dare didn't need to see his eyes to know a lie when he heard one. Emmett wasn't having a conversation about his feelings for Deja. Especially with her brother.

"You suddenly care about your sister? Didn't look that way at the precinct."

"Wow. You got balls, I'll give you that." Dare laughed, or more like grunted. "Deja's the only bright spot in my life. I'd do anything for her, including what I think is the best thing for her."

"By treating her like shit and shoving her away? Yeah, that's totally the best thing for her."

"What the hell do you know? You don't know anything."

Emmett gripped the steering wheel tighter, then whipped the truck to the side of the road, tires squealing as the truck jerked to a stop. He faced Dare. "I know your sister hurts. I see it every single day. I know she's the toughest woman I know, besides Sophie. Sophie has so much grit, only she doesn't realize it, but Deja, she's got just a little more grit. I know..."

Emmett relaxed his hands and drew a deep breath. "I don't know much about her life because she keeps it locked tightly inside. I know the important things, like what makes her smile, what makes her laugh with delight, what makes her tick, what makes her want to grab her tire iron. I know she wants you in her life. It's easy to see. So, I'd say I know a lot. I know what's important. I wish I could say the same about you."

"That just confirms what I thought. You like her, yet you won't tell me your intentions toward her. You can get in the face of a murderer, but you can't tell one tiny little woman how you feel. Coward." The smirk on his face grew as the words sunk in.

Emmett was no coward. "Takes one to know one." Geez, he was reverting to grade school talk like they were having a beef on the playground. He couldn't help himself.

"I'm no coward." Dare's hands fisted again.

"Sure you are. You keep pushing Deja away instead of embracing her. You keep calling yourself a murderer when I don't think you are."

"I killed my parents. What would you call that?"

Emmett leaned back, gauging him. His hands were still fisted, ready to pounce, but Emmett didn't think he'd throw a punch. His body language suggested it, but he wouldn't do it. "Did you shoot them? Stab them? Burn them alive? How did you kill them? Tell me, because I'd love to know."

Dare looked away, his hands squeezing tighter. Emmett felt sorry for him. No, not sorry. Empathetic. He could see the internal struggle, the anguish that rolled off him in waves. The silence engulfed the truck. Emmett pushed too far. So had Dare. He felt like a jackass for pushing his emotions like that. What did he know? Who was he to judge?

He started to lift his foot off the brake when Dare spoke softly. "My mom thought my dad was having a heart attack. They forgot to pay the phone bill, like usual. Or, more like, they used the money on booze instead."

Emmett's foot pressed the brake harder, waiting patiently for Dare to continue. He wanted to ask questions.

A ton of them flooded his mind, but he said nothing. He just waited in silence.

"It was my job to take care of Deja. My parents didn't give two shits about us. They loved each other so much it's like they forgot how to give us some of that love. I was reckless, hurting, selfish. I knew how much it affected Deja as well, but I guess I just didn't care enough. She shouldn't care about me. I don't deserve it."

"I'd say she would disagree with that."

Dare turned toward him. "I liked to pop pills, smoke weed. I always told myself it was okay because I wasn't doing hard shit like meth or coke or heroin. If I cared about her, I wouldn't have touched shit. What do you have to say about that?"

Emmett shrugged, honestly unsure what to say. He just wanted to hear the rest of the story, what happened to his parents. Did he kill them in a fit of rage? Drugs made people do the craziest things sometimes.

"I told my parents I'd drive them to the hospital. The phone wasn't working, so we couldn't call for an ambulance, and we lived in a shitty-ass neighborhood. I didn't trust any of our neighbors to help. I was high as a kite. I felt mellow, calm enough to deal with them, because I tried my hardest to stay clear of them as much as possible."

Shit. Emmett didn't like where this was headed. "You crashed the car, didn't you?"

Dare nodded. "It started raining, just buckets of water pouring down. My mom was in the backseat and refused to buckle up, even after I told her several times she should. My dad finally said something and she sat back. I assumed she immediately buckled up. She didn't. A dog came out of nowhere, and I swerved, slamming on the brakes. The rain...just everything...we hit a tree. My mom was thrown from the car and died instantly, so they say. My dad *was* having a heart attack and died before help arrived. I walked away with a gash to my head. That's it."

Emmett frowned, the confusion clear. "It was an accident."

Dare gave a hollow laugh. "So everyone keeps saying. The courts disagreed. It was criminal vehicular homicide. Want the full definition of what that means? The prosecution even claimed the dog was a figment of my imagination. The drugs created it. They never found a trace of evidence that a dog ran into my path."

"The dog was real." Emmett said it as a statement, not a question. He heard the conviction in Dare's voice. He believed him that the dog was real.

"Doesn't matter anymore. I served my time, and my parents are still dead. Sad part is I'm not really sad. I had planned to hightail it out of that hellhole as soon as Deja turned eighteen, taking her with me. I never wanted them to die. I just wanted to be rid of them. The only thing I hate, that I can't stand, is I hurt Deja. I left her alone. I didn't take care of her like I promised I would." He rubbed his jaw. "I have no idea why I just shared all of that. Shouldn't we be getting to your family's house?"

"Yeah, we should. Although, we'll probably need to wait, especially if the fire isn't out yet." Emmett rubbed his jaw as well, contemplating what to say, how to say it. "I like your sister."

That was *not* what he intended to say. It just slipped out.

Dare chuckled, the sound lifting the depressing mood that had filled the truck. "No shit. You look at her like a lost little puppy."

"I do not."

Dare raised a brow as if he couldn't believe Emmett tried to deny it. "And your intentions toward her?"

Shrugging, he glanced away as he smoothed his hand over the steering wheel. "Deja doesn't like me like that. I don't want to ruin the nice working relationship we have by asking her out."

"So, in other words, you're a coward."

Emmett snapped his head to Dare again. His eyes flashed a warning. "I'm not a damn coward."

"Prove it."

"I thought you didn't like me. You're practically shoving me toward your sister. Makes no sense."

This time Dare looked away. "Someone needs to take care of her."

"You're going to leave her? That'll break her heart. Is that what you really want to do?"

"I already broke her heart, and it'll just get worse if I stay."

Emmett started to ease his foot off the brake. "Yeah, she needs a brother who doesn't go running away from his problems. Talk to her like you talked to me. It would help." Emmett pressed the gas, the truck jerking slightly.

Dare chose not to respond. The rest of the drive was made in silence. Emmett parked on the side of the road near the driveway when he noticed all the fire trucks lining the driveway. No bright fire lit the night sky. They must've taken care of it. Good. Now they had to wait for clearance to tackle the fence that was mangled in pieces.

Bordering the road, a white wooden fence recently painted last year sat broken in pieces. Emmett guesstimated about twenty feet worth of fencing needed to be fixed. Austin liked to give Sophie wood all the time for her crafts. She created beautiful works of art that she sold online. She made good money. No surprise there because she had such talent. It made Emmett wonder if there was any wood on the property to repair the fence until they could properly fix it.

Emmett started walking down the long driveway, Dare next to him. Neither spoke. There wasn't much left to say. Emmett could probably say more, but it wouldn't be wise. He couldn't believe the words they exchanged to begin with.

Stopping next to Austin near the porch steps to the house, he tried to ignore the question in his eyes. What had taken them so long?

"So, what's going on?"

Austin pointed to the barn and the corral. "They just got the fire out. Thankfully, it didn't touch the barn, but it torched half of the corral. We'll need to replace that. Zane's talking to the fire chief with Ava. I didn't want to...I'm so..."

Emmett put a hand on his shoulder. "This isn't like the last fire that happened. This isn't your fault, and neither was the last one."

Austin grimaced. "It kinda was. I'm the one who dated a crazy-ass woman, who then had her lunatic of a brother set fire to the farm."

"Are you still bothered about the washer issue? Because I never see you get down like this."

"The last few nights have been...rough, like I said. She's worried about Deja and—" Austin looked at Dare and gingerly smiled. "Sorry."

"Sophie doesn't need to worry about my sister. She's fine." Dare became rigid, his face hard with emotions that Emmett figured was a lot of guilt.

"We just met, but I'm not going to lie to your face. I would say she's not fine. Deja hides her emotions well, but all it takes is one look into her eyes and you can see fear." Austin squared his shoulders.

"Are you saying my sister is scared of me?"

Emmett took a step, standing between them. He didn't think Dare would attack Austin or that Austin would throw a punch either, but just in case, he wanted to be prepared. "Deja loves you. She's not scared of you harming her. I would say she's just scared you're going to leave, which sounds exactly like what you're going to do."

Austin scoffed. "Which is why Sophie's worried about her." He started to walk away.

"Where are you going?" Emmett hadn't realized Austin was so stressed lately. Normally, Austin was the happy one, the fun one, the one who made everyone else forget why they weren't feeling like themselves.

"To check out the barn. I need to see what we have for supplies to repair the fence near the road. We need to do something for the night. Tomorrow we can fix it properly." Austin kept walking.

"I thought I was family." Dare's sarcasm wasn't lost on him.

Emmett chuckled, not even wanting to touch that subject. But what the hell. "Welcome to the family. We get in each other's face, but it doesn't mean we don't care about each other. If you can't take the heat, then do everyone a favor, especially Deja, and leave."

"You're still an asshole."

"So are you."

They stood there, staring each other down, wondering who would make the first move. Emmett wasn't going to back down. He saw three scenarios in his head. He'd either watch Dare walk away, have to shove him from throwing a punch, or wait for him to help repair the fence.

"Yo, Emmett, I've got good news."

Emmett turned away from Dare to see Ethan walking toward him.

"Amidst all this chaos, I can't wait to hear it."

Ethan's smile widened as he winked deviously. "I found you the perfect woman so you can forget all about Deja. I know you'll never make a move on her, so I'm gonna help you move on. Already got you a date for Wednesday with a nice lovely school teacher."

Emmett stiffened. Could the day get any worse? "I don't want your help. I'm not going out with one of your women."

"Oh, I've never dated her. Gabe and I had drinks the other night, and she was there with Beth. You remember Beth, right? I dated her a few years ago when...well, none of that matters. It didn't occur to me then that she'd be perfect for you, but after you left last night, it did. So I called Beth this afternoon to get her number and I got you a date."

Rubbing his hand over his face to hide the embarrassment, he sighed. "Ethan, I'm—"

"You gonna ask out Deja?"

"Don't we have a fire to deal with?" Emmett pointed behind his brother. The commotion near the barn and corral was still hopping.

Ethan shoved his thumbs under his suspenders and smiled with delight. He had already taken off his turnout jacket and tossed it somewhere. "Fire's extinguished. We took care of that beast without breaking a sweat. This issue with Deja...move on, bro. I'm helping you."

"My sister isn't good enough for your brother?" Emmett almost forgot Dare was standing there until he spoke.

Ethan's brow rose in surprise as he glanced at Dare. "Sister?"

Emmett cleared his throat, almost giddy inside that his

brother just made an ass of himself. Served him right for trying to meddle in his life. "This is Dare, Deja's brother."

"Nice to meet you, Dare. Your sister is good enough, but I'm not so sure my brother is." Ethan grinned at Emmett, it slightly mimicking one of his smirks that said he was up to no good. Which he clearly was. "If he doesn't have the balls to ask her out, then he doesn't deserve her. Now, about this date I set up for you. Her name's Debbie. Cute as a button. She's a teacher, very soft-spoken. You'll love her."

"I'm not going out with her. I'm not a damn coward." Emmett started to walk away, ignoring the laughter ringing around the farm. He refused to be baited by his brother like that. He liked Deja. End of discussion. He whipped around. "Watch me ask her out. Tomorrow. Tell your teacher thanks, but no thanks. I like Deja. And if you got a problem with that, Dare, come throw a punch."

DARE WATCHED as Emmett stalked away, wondering what the hell just happened. So much shit happened within the space of twenty minutes. He basically spilled his guts to a stranger. He almost got into a fistfight from words he didn't want to hear. He was accepted into a family, then tossed out like he was a piece of shit. Now he wanted to punch someone again. Maybe himself.

"Well, that worked better than I thought."

Dare averted his eyes from Emmett to his brother still standing by him. "What?"

"My plan. It worked better than I thought it would. Debbie's not my type, but I don't want her to feel bad Emmett won't be showing up, so I'll have to take his place. Unless you wanna go out with her."

Dare puckered his brows as he tried to assess what the hell he was talking about. "You do realize I just got out of prison."

Ethan nodded. "What's your point? You haven't had a woman in a long time. Although, Debbie's not the type to sleep with you on the first date. Just saying."

"Are you messing with me right now?"

"No. Do you want me to?"

"What the hell is going on?" Dare didn't like how confused this entire conversation was going. He was two seconds away from saying screw it all and walking away. Because if he didn't, he'd be sorely tempted to knock a fist into this guy's face. He needed to punch something.

Ethan laughed and clapped him on the shoulder, making him flinch. "Lighten up, Dare. Let me work my magic, and I'll find you a woman who'll be willing to release some of that tension for you a lot sooner."

"I don't want a woman."

Ethan dropped his hand and winced. "Oh, you're gay. My bad."

Dare rubbed his hand over his face and groaned. "I'm not gay." He pointed toward the direction Emmett walked off. "What did you mean your plan worked? I'm not about to let any of you assholes hurt my sister."

"I'm not gonna take offense to you calling me an asshole, but be warned, it's the only time I'll allow it. Emmett needed a little nudge to get his head out of his ass concerning Deja. If I bug him about other women, it'll motivate him a lot faster. I didn't realize it would work right away. You got a problem with my brother dating your sister?"

Dare noticed how Ethan's good-humored nature slowly disappeared and was replaced with an underlying wrath. "Maybe."

Ethan's face suddenly brightened. "Honesty. I like it." He swung his arm around Dare and forced him to walk with him. "Now, let's talk about what sort of woman you want. I know lots of people."

Dare was too shocked to do anything but follow him and listen. Then he realized it would be kind of nice to hook up with a woman. Release some of the tension swirling in his veins. But what woman would want to sleep with a criminal?

8

EMMETT PAUSED. His fist hung in the air. He normally wasn't afraid to approach someone. And he certainly wasn't afraid of Dare. No way in hell.

Then why couldn't he knock on the door?

Because he'd probably ask questions he wasn't ready to answer.

He hadn't received a phone call from Gabe yet, but he knew it was coming. Ethan hadn't wasted any time last night spreading the word to Zane and Austin that he was finally going to ask out Deja. It only seemed reasonable that Ethan would call Gabe to blab to him as well.

Hearing that news, Austin's mood had lifted, clapping Emmett on the back in an "attaboy" gesture. He still couldn't believe Austin seemed so stressed. He knew the fire could've potentially set them back, losing money they couldn't afford to lose. But Austin was the lighthearted one, the one who always saw the glass half-full, not empty. Zane was the opposite. Last night, it was like their roles were reversed. The issue concerning Sophie bothered him. He'd have to talk to Austin to see how he could help. He didn't like seeing his cousin upset, and he didn't like knowing Sophie was struggling, even for a moment.

Thankfully, they had enough wood to make a makeshift fence last night. He figured Austin and Zane were busy this morning already properly fixing the fence. He debated going over there to help, even called to offer his help, but Zane declined, saying they had it all well in hand.

A new corral needed to be built. Regardless of what they said, he'd help with that task. The car had hit the corral. The woman who poured the moonshine out of the car had dropped a cigarette she was smoking. That's what started the fire. The cigarette had lit up the moonshine like a fuse on a stick of dynamite.

He still had no idea why she poured the stuff out of the window. Ava would get to the bottom of it and then probably push for the stiffest penalty. Nobody messed with their family.

Zane had gotten scared at the possibilities the fire could create, and rightly so. Although, it hadn't been necessary for him, Austin, and Dare to all go to the farm last night. He didn't mind helping. Dare didn't appear to mind either. He had revealed a little of his personality last night, not by much, but enough to see he wasn't that bad of a guy. He just made a mistake. A deadly one, but a mistake, none-theless.

He paid for his crime. Emmett figured he continued to pay for his crime every single day, and would until he died. It couldn't be easy living with the fact he killed his parents.

Which was why he was standing on Deja's porch, his fist ready to connect with the wooden door. He wanted to help him out, even if he was an asshole on occasion. It had nothing to do with the fact he wanted to impress Deja or get into her good graces. Absolutely not.

At least he kept telling himself that as he finally knocked on the door.

The door swung open. Dare's hair was disheveled, his eyes little slits, as if he just woke up. Emmett chuckled.

"Something funny, McCord?" Dare grumbled as he wiped a hand over his eyes.

"Did I wake you, Sleeping Beauty?"

"Deja's not here. Piss off." Dare started to close the door.

Emmett slapped his hand to stop the door and jammed his foot in the doorframe. "I came here to talk to you."

Dare stared at him with a critical eye, then must've decided it wasn't worth it to argue with him. He shoved the door open wider and gestured Emmett inside.

"I need coffee. I got used to drinking that sludge they call coffee in the slammer. Deja buys much better stuff." Dare walked away, clearly caring less if Emmett followed or not.

Emmett took a seat at the table while Dare quickly started a pot of coffee. While the coffee pot started to work its magic, Dare turned around and leaned against the counter. "So, to what do I owe this pleasure?"

"I'm here to offer you a job."

Emmett figured not much surprised Dare, and if something did, he hid it well. Not this time. His jaw dropped as the questions in his eyes blazed fiercely.

"What for? To get into my sister's panties a little easier?"

He rubbed a hand over his face to calm the irritation at Dare talking about Deja like that. Sure, he wanted to look good in her eyes, like he cared about her brother. Not that he didn't care about Dare. He had no opinion about the guy other than the fact he could treat her a little nicer. He wasn't sure why he was offering him a job. Maybe because it felt like the right thing to do. And he needed someone to fill the position. His last employee he recently hired just decided not to show up anymore. Business was booming right now. If he didn't want to lose the good paying customers he currently had, he needed to find a replacement immediately.

Emmett lowered his hand and gently set it down on the table instead of slamming it like he wanted to. "Do you want a job or not?"

"Did you ask my sister out yet?"

"Do we need to talk about Deja right now? This has nothing to do with her. Maybe I'm just trying to be a nice guy here. Is that so hard to believe?"

Dare's lips thinned into a tight line, then he abruptly turned around and poured some coffee into a mug. Being the classic jerk he liked to be, Dare didn't offer any coffee to him. He stood with his back to Emmett for the longest time, figuring that was his answer. That he should just get up and leave.

Finally, just as Emmett was about to stand up, Dare turned around. "What do you do? Own some kind of landscaping business?"

Emmett nodded. "One of my employees recently just stopped showing up, and I need someone to fill the position quickly. Like, today. You need a job. I need an employee. That's all there is to it."

"What's the catch?"

Standing up, he tried his hardest not to clench his fists, to appear calm and collected when he was anything but. "There is no catch. Are you always so cynical?"

Dare shrugged. "To be honest, even before prison, most people weren't nice to us. They always got something out of it."

Like sister, like brother. Deja and Dare were so much alike. Obviously molded by the childhood they had. Emmett couldn't imagine what it was like growing up in a household where their parents didn't care about them. Worrying about what people thought about them. Suspicious and wary of anyone who tried to offer help.

He grew up in a loving environment. The only truly tragic thing that ever occurred was when Jimmy, Zane and Austin's brother, died in the line of duty in New York City saving Ava's life.

"Look, Dare, I'm not going to lie. I like your sister, which you already know. Part of me is offering you a job because of her. Part of me is offering because of you. I don't judge people. At least, I try not to. If you came to me, without me knowing Deja, and I saw you had a record, I'd still treat you fairly. I'm not sure how many other people would say that. Do you want a job or not?"

Dare nodded to the coffee pot. "Help yourself. I'll go change." He walked out of the kitchen.

Emmett poured a cup, draining its contents by the time Dare came back downstairs. He was wearing a plain black T-shirt with a pair of jeans.

"This okay to wear?"

"Yep. As long as you don't care it gets dirty."

"Not really."

Dare locked the door and followed Emmett to his truck. "So, am I gonna be mowing lawns and shit?"

"Pretty much. Can you handle that?"

"It doesn't take much brains to mow a lawn," Dare said with a laugh as he hopped into the passenger seat.

Emmett chuckled and started the truck. "You'd be surprised. I can tell you some really funny stories."

"I'd like to hear them."

That sounded as if he was being sincere. Moments like this, he almost thought the two of them could be good friends. When Dare wasn't sulking and thinking the worst about life, he was a decent guy.

"Your brother Ethan is something else. He's trying to hook me up with some women to...you know...hook up."

"Unless you give him the evil eye that you've mastered so well, he'll have you hooked up in no time. He normally gets his way because he's a pest and doesn't know how to back off."

A low rumble left Dare's mouth as his lips curled into a smile. "Can't say I'm offended by his pestering. It's been a long time for me."

Grinning, Emmett shook his head and laughed. "You'll be regretting those words when he won't stop pestering you."

"Is that why you gave in so easily to ask out Deja? Are you going to do it?"

Emmett shot a glance at Dare, surprised to see no anger or distrust on his face. Just indifference. Maybe a little wariness. "Do I have your blessing?"

"Would you leave her alone if I said no?"

He gave that question some thought. Serious thought. "No. I like your sister. There's something about her. Before I met her, I had this impression of her. A woman with no morals, someone who had no respect. Then I met her. Her eyes...there was a pain hidden in the depths, and a ferocity that couldn't be mistaken. She nearly knocked me on my ass from one simple look."

Dare was silent. Emmett glanced at him again. He was staring out the window as if ignoring every word Emmett just uttered. Talk about looking like a fool. Although his hands weren't clenched like they normally were when they talked about Deja, he still appeared pissed by what he said. Emmett turned his attention back to the road.

"Why haven't you asked her out yet?"

"Scared shitless. That about sums it up. She's...she's just unattainable."

"You seem to tackle everything head on. Yet, you're scared to ask out my sister." Dare chuckled as if it was the craziest thing he'd ever heard.

"Honestly, I'm scared I'll lose her altogether. I like the friendship we have. I don't want to ruin that. If she turns me down, which she probably will, then I risk losing her even as a friend."

"I could tell you liked my sister right away." Dare paused. Emmett glanced at him, knowing there was more he wanted to say.

"And?"

Dare met his stare, his eyes twinkling with mischief. "And my sister looks at you the same way you look at her. Ask her out, Emmett. You might get the answer you want."

Deja slammed the front door closed, threw her purse on the little table near the closet, and headed for the kitchen. She almost wished she had some wine lingering in the house. But since Dare was released, she didn't buy any kind of alcohol. She didn't think it would be a good idea to have any around.

He wasn't drunk that deadly night, but she wasn't positive if it would be healthy for him. He needed to get on the right path. Get a job. Insert himself back into society before he tasted a drop of alcohol. He had a drug problem back then. She didn't want him to have a drinking problem now. Maybe it wouldn't make sense to other people, but it made sense to her.

Pulling open the fridge, the cool air tickled her skin, some of her hair standing on end. She grabbed the pitcher of iced tea and poured a glass.

She hadn't seen Emmett the entire day. Not in the morning. Not in the afternoon. He didn't even stop in before the day ended. Talk about strange. He was always busy. If he wasn't completing a job himself, then he oversaw one of his workers at a job site. No matter how busy he got, he stopped by the office. He didn't need to. Part of her thought he did it just to see her. Which was bad of her to want or even think about. But she enjoyed seeing him, talking with him.

It was a good thing he didn't stop by. She shouldn't torture herself so much.

After downing the entire glass of tea, wishing it was wine instead, she poured herself another glass and opened the fridge to put the pitcher away.

What should she make for supper? Last night's dinner was ruined because of the fire. Thank goodness, it hadn't turned out worse. It'd be great to try dinner again with Sophie and Austin. She wanted Dare to fit in with them, to make friends. Maybe it would help him see how life could be better if he just stopped shoving everyone away. Mostly her. It hurt just thinking about it.

Shoving the fridge door shut, unsure of what to make, she realized it was way too quiet in the house.

Where was Dare?

She nearly dropped her glass of tea as she set it on the counter and raced for the stairs.

Please. Tell me he didn't leave without a word good-bye.

Yesterday, when she got home from work, Dare had been lounging on the couch channel surfing. It took her almost an hour of schmoozing to get him to agree to go over to Sophie's for supper. He didn't appear too happy to go with

Emmett last night to the farm. When he got home, he barely uttered a word good night. She left the house this morning before he even woke up.

She should've said good-bye. She should've said something to make him stay longer. The signs were all there that he would leave. That he didn't care.

Nearly tripping on a few stairs as she ran two at a time, she halted to a stop in front of his closed bedroom door.

"He didn't leave. I have faith he didn't leave."

Pep talk done, she grabbed the handle and turned it. She sank against the doorframe at the sight of his clothes scattered around the floor. Not even three full days out and he already managed to make a mess of his room. He never could keep a clean room. Not that their parents cared about much, but their mother always wanted them to keep their rooms cleaned. She still couldn't figure out why. Maybe so it seemed like she cared when she really didn't.

She needed to take Dare shopping or, at least, give him money to buy new clothes. He was wearing clothes she had found at a few garage sales, stocking up his closet a little bit before he was released. She tried to get sizes she thought would fit, but without seeing him for ten years, she had no idea what his size was. The clothes he wore yesterday said she didn't do too badly.

His messy room gave her hope he hadn't left her for good. So, where was he?

Walking back downstairs, taking the stairs at a snail's pace, her thoughts tumbling in a million different directions, she almost tripped on the last step when a knock sounded on the door.

The door swung open before she reached it. Emmett stepped through the threshold, his face a myriad of anger. What was he upset about?

"What are you doing, E-man?"

He whipped his hand toward the door. "I should ask you the same thing. What are you doing? Why isn't the door locked? Austin's really worried lately, and I wanted to make sure you were being safe. We can't trust Kevin. You need to keep your doors locked."

Rolling her eyes, she bypassed him and shut the door, then flipped the lock. "Better?"

A slow grin emerged. "Actually, it is."

She wasn't sure what to make of the look on his face. Why was he staring at her like that? "Why are you here, Emmett?"

"I needed to find out."

"Find out what?" Her brows dipped as the confusion took hold. She wanted to take a step back. A very big step. The look on his face—was that desire? No. She already flung herself at him once and he shoved her away. That's all people liked to do to her. Push her away.

Taking one large step, he was in her face, his mouth inches from hers. "Find out if you want me as much as I want you." He cupped her cheeks and pressed his lips to hers.

She couldn't resist the softness of his lips or the gentleness in his touch. She moved closer, at the same time wondering what the hell she was doing. He took her movement as acceptance and dropped his hands to wrap around her waist. She felt the heat of his arousal immediately. He wanted her. He wanted so much more than a kiss.

It scared the hell out of her.

She shifted her arms between their bodies and pushed him away. Despite the kiss being gentle and soft, they were breathing heavily, as if they had attacked each other with intense passion.

"Why are you kissing me?"

"Why did you kiss me the other night?" he countered.

"I...it was a mistake." She walked around him and took a seat on the couch.

Where was a glass of wine when she needed it? Or better yet, a shot of whiskey. Something strong to drown out the hurt. The worry.

The couch dipped as Emmett took a seat next to her. He grabbed her hand before she could move away. His touch was still gentle and soft.

"I should've asked you a question before I kissed you. I couldn't stop myself. I couldn't get our last kiss out of my mind."

She yearned for him to pull her into his arms. She also yearned to yank her hand out of his. She wasn't good enough for him. Why couldn't he see that? Why did he kiss her? What did he want to ask?

"What are you doing? We shouldn't kiss. We shouldn't—"

His lips silenced her words. She enjoyed the subtle taste of mint that touched her lips from his. Did he pop in a mint before coming over? Was it his intention to kiss her no matter what?

He slowly pulled away from her, his hand still locked around hers. "Can I take you to dinner?"

Her mind was still enjoying his latest kiss. Until he spoke. "What?"

"I'd like to take you to dinner."

"Why? Why are you kissing me?"

"I'll point out that you kissed me first. Now, I want to kiss you whenever I want, and I want to take you to dinner because I can. Because I like you...more than a friend."

His hand trembled within hers. He was nervous. She

couldn't believe it. Emmett didn't get nervous. Sure, he said some silly, crazy things at times, but that was just Emmett being, well, Emmett.

"It's not a good idea if we date, E-man. We shouldn't."

"Why not? Give me one good reason why."

"Employee." She pointed to herself. "Employer." She poked him in the chest with her free hand.

He grabbed that hand before she could pull it away. "There's no office rule that says we can't date. Try again."

"We'll ruin a good friendship."

"Any great relationship starts out as good friends. Take Sophie and Austin, for example." He grinned.

She couldn't help but return a smile. It was all wrong. Why couldn't he see that? Kissing him two days ago had been a moment of weakness. She had been dying to kiss him for ages and she used any excuse she could. But he pushed her away. Why was he doing this now?

"We're not compatible. We're doomed to not work out."

Laughing, he snatched a kiss. She couldn't help but lean toward him as he did.

"Wrong. We fit together perfectly. We have tons in common. The most important thing is we're both huge baseball fans. Doesn't get more compatible than that. You can't come up with a good reason."

She sighed and tried to extract her hands from his. He wouldn't budge, although, she didn't try too hard. "I don't deserve a good man like you."

She whispered it so softly he had to lean closer to hear her words. She knew he heard, too, because his face became hard as stone. His eyes suddenly blazed with fire. Not the color of desire either.

"I wish you'd open up to me. I wish you'd tell me what would make you say something like that, let alone think it.

You have no idea how beautiful you are, inside and out. You could have any man you want, and picking me might seem like you're settling. So, maybe that says I don't think I deserve you. But I want you. You have so much love and kindness to give, and I want some of that."

"Emmett..."

He drew her closer. She didn't resist. His lips hovered next to hers as he whispered, "I love the sound of my name on your lips. Say you'll go out with me. Let me take you to dinner."

"Dare needs me right now. I don't think starting anything would be good. I don't even know where he is. I should try to find him."

Surprisingly, he backed away. "He's with Ethan."

"Why is my brother with your brother?"

Emmett cracked a grin. "They bonded last night. Go figure. I dropped him off at Ethan's after work when Ethan called and they decided to get a drink. Meet women or something like that."

"After work? Women? What's going on?" This time she managed to yank her hands out of his and stood up. She took a few steps away from the couch, needing some distance.

Emmett slowly stood up. "He's not a bad guy once the orneriness wears off. I offered him a job and he accepted. Worked his ass off today, too. Ethan, for whatever reason, is determined to find him a woman and...you know...yeah." He glanced away, almost embarrassed by what he said.

Deja shoved her hands to her hips. Oh, she knew. "To have sex. Did you think this dinner invitation would go much smoother if you gave my brother a job? What kind of sick game are you playing? I refuse to be made fun of and look like a fool."

She stalked over to him and poked him hard in the chest. Her finger almost hurt from it. Emmett worked hard during the day and his body showed the signs. She could just imagine the hard ridges and plains of his chest that hid beneath his shirt. She poked him again just to feel it once more. Oh, what she'd give to run her hands up and down his chest.

No. He was obviously playing her for a fool. She wouldn't allow it.

"You can take your kisses and date and shove it where the sun don't shine, E-man. I don't want you and never will."

He snatched her hand that kept poking his chest and rubbed his thumb over the top, soothing her anger somewhat. "Your body says otherwise. What are you afraid of? You wanted me a few days ago. You were willing to go further than a kiss."

She brought her body next to his and almost purred with contentment. "You're right. You want me, E-man. Then take me."

He dropped her hand and stepped away. "I hate it when you talk like that. I want you, damn it, but not like that. I won't let you use sex as a shield."

Crisis averted. She knew that exact reaction would occur if she acted like that. "I won't let you make me look like a fool." Her face went rigid as she jerked her hand toward the front door. "Get the hell out."

He hesitated, his features displaying how torturous a decision it was for him. Would he leave? He'd better, or she might give in to her desires. She might actually take his offer of more than friendship. Even knowing he was playing her. What would it be like to go further than a kiss with Emmett? She wanted to know.

But she had pride. She had respect for herself. She

wouldn't bow down to any man in that way. If he didn't simply like her for her, she wouldn't give in.

"I offered your brother a job because it was the right thing to do, not because you'd sleep with me. Why can't you see my true feelings? I—forget it. If that's your opinion of me, that I would do something so despicable, then that's on you."

He turned around and left. No hesitation in his steps. No jerky movements as he unlocked the door. Just utter calmness.

Perhaps he did care for her. Maybe she blew everything out of proportion. It was hard to think any man, or any person, would want her simply for her. She had yet to meet one person who treated her that way.

Except Emmett.

Shit!

Sinking down onto the couch, tears soaked her face as she realized what she had just done. She shoved away the best man to ever step into her life. Why?

Because she was scared. Because the thought he'd want someone like her seemed ludicrous.

If it wasn't prominent before, it was now.

She didn't deserve him.

9

EMMETT LET the brisk air wash over his skin before he pulled open the door to Chico's Bar and Grill. He should've headed home. To his empty house. To the loneliness. To the quiet. To lick his wounds and wish the night hadn't turned out the way it had.

Instead, he headed to where Ethan and Dare were hanging out. More punishment. What would Dare say about Deja turning him down? Probably nothing good.

He was starting to realize—and picture—just what kind of childhood Deja had. She didn't know love when she saw it.

Love?

He froze at the bar as the word flowed around his mind. Was that what he was feeling? Was that why he kept torturing himself? Was that why he put himself out there tonight, saying the things he did, because he loved Deja?

Yep.

And she thought he only wanted to screw her, and he'd do anything in his power to get his way. Hell, why couldn't she see if that were the case, he would've slept with her days ago when she flung herself at him. He refused to let her bury her emotions with sex. If he ever had the chance with her, it'd be because they wanted the same thing. Not because she wanted to use sex to shield her emotions.

Damn her.

He loved her.

Women were not his forte. He had never told a woman he loved her before. Probably why he was mucking everything up with her. Well, he did try to tell a woman he loved her once and she—

He wasn't going to think about that right now.

He ordered two beers, chugging one down before he walked away from the bar to find Ethan and Dare sitting at a high-top table near the back of the bar, close to the pool tables.

"Didn't think we'd see you here. Why aren't you wooing Deja? Or are you still a chickenshit? I haven't canceled the date with Debbie yet." Ethan grinned as he took a swig of his beer.

"Having fun, Dare? Is my brother annoying you to no end like he does with me?" Emmett sat down, wishing he'd ordered three beers. He could've chugged two before joining them. Why did he come here again?

"Na, he's actually got a wry sense of humor. And he has a keen eye for beautiful women."

Emmett glanced around the bar, noting for a Thursday night that it had a decent crowd. A few tables held several women, a mixture of them with couples, and the rest filled with men, just like their table.

"Aiming to ask one of these women out tonight?" Emmett asked as he fiddled with his beer bottle.

"Not likely." Dare eyed him critically, then smirked. "Did you ask anyone out tonight?"

"She thinks I gave you a job just to get in her pants. She doesn't believe me when I say I like her. That there wasn't an ulterior motive." Emmett slammed his beer back and almost drained the entire bottle.

"Whoa there, bro." Ethan laid a hand on his shoulder, then made him set the bottle down. "Drowning your sorrows, remember, that doesn't solve shit."

Emmett looked at Ethan and shrugged. "There was a reason I never tried to ask her out. I knew she'd never say yes."

"You know, a few days before getting released, I pictured in my head what the outside would be like. How lonely I'd be because I didn't want to taint Deja with my presence." Dare stopped talking as both of them turned toward him. "I never pictured meeting a family like you guys. I never pictured my sister hurting at the thought I wanted to leave."

Dare took a drink of his beer. Emmett recalled the way Deja declined to have either of them drink last night. She must not want Dare to drink. It made Emmett want to snatch the beer out of his hands. Even with his heart hurting like mad, he wanted to please Deja in any way possible. What a sucker. Would that feeling ever go away?

"But you're gonna stick around." Ethan phrased it as a statement rather than a question. His brother always had the ability to lay down the law without being overbearing. Why couldn't Emmett manage to express his true feelings to Deja without being overbearing? So she could really believe him when he said he cared about her.

Dare nodded. "Yeah, I am. Deja needs me. I need her." Dare tossed his wary eyes to Emmett. "Strangely, I think she needs you, too."

Emmett couldn't help but grin. "Gosh, was that your stamp of approval, Dare?"

He cracked a smile and laughed. "Damn right. Enjoy it while it lasts, because if you hurt my sister, you'll be the sorriest man alive." Dare suddenly turned serious, his eyes heavy with wariness. "You gotta understand something. Growing up, it wasn't easy. Our parents were clueless. It was just Deja and I. My sister has always been beautiful. People...kids...can be cruel. She's not pushing you away because you're an asshole. She's pushing you away because she's scared."

"It's there in her eyes. She hides it well, but her eyes are so expressive," Ethan said pensively.

"It didn't go well tonight. What do you suggest I do?"

"Don't give up. She's worth it. Just don't give up." Dare chugged the rest of his beer. "She's never given up on me. She needs someone who'll do the same."

Sound advice. Emmett could do that. Would do that. He stood up.

"Where you going, bro?" Ethan eyed his bottle he didn't finish, then glanced at him.

"Not giving up. Have fun, gentlemen." Emmett tossed a twenty on the table.

Dare looked at the money. "What's that for?"

"Things might get a little volatile because I'm not leaving until she listens to me." Emmett stared him down, then said slowly, "So have fun."

In other words, he didn't want Dare walking in and potentially ruining anything.

Dare grabbed the twenty and waved it with a smile. "Thanks. Don't back down. Her bark is worse than her bite."

Emmett left, Dare's last words resonating with him. She'd put up a fight for sure. But he wasn't giving up, just like Dare said. Oddly enough, he had his approval. That made everything much better. He felt a little lighter inside because of it.

Deja would be his sooner or later. Because he loved her. Maybe that's what he had to do. He just had to tell her.

Tell her that? He could barely ask her out on a date. He'd probably never get the words *I love you* out.

Driving back to Deja's, his mind tumbled into a million different scenarios. None of them sounded like a great idea. Even going back to her house seemed like a terrible idea. Yet he found himself standing on her porch ready to knock on her door.

Did she lock her door? He should check again. Regardless of what she thought, Kevin was a dangerous man and could hurt Sophie by hurting the people she cared about.

Twisting the knob, he met resistance. Well, at least she locked the door. On one hand, he was happy she did. On the other trembling hand, he was annoyed as hell. Would she answer the door when he knocked? She wasn't too happy with him when he left. He should've never left.

Saying a silent prayer everything would turn out well, he knocked on the door and waited.

And waited.

Almost pulling his phone out of his pocket to check the time, he forced himself to be patient. Why was it taking her so long to open the door? Did she know it was him knocking? Did she even hear the knock?

He knocked again, waiting what felt like minutes instead of seconds. He started to raise his fist to knock again, refusing to be beaten that quickly, when the door swung open.

Her eyes were red-rimmed, her lips molded into a frown. She looked so sad it broke his heart. He put that look there.

He'd obviously made her cry, and that was the last thing he ever wanted.

"What do you want?"

He stared for a moment, taking in her forlorn expression, the distrust in her eyes. What did he want? He wanted a lot of things. Her thoughts. Her feelings. Her heart. Her love. The better question was what didn't he want? Because he wanted everything.

"You."

Her bottom lip quivered, then steeled like a tightrope. There was no way he could witness her cry. Once was enough to last him a lifetime.

Without waiting for an invitation, or for her to speak, since she didn't appear as if she was going to respond to his one-worded answer, he stepped inside, pushing her lightly to the side. She stared at him quizzically but made no move to stop him. He shut the door and locked it, then turned toward her. She started to open her mouth to speak, but he stopped her with one swift kiss.

He didn't want her to use sex as a shield. He wanted her to want him for him, except his words didn't seem to work. She didn't believe him when he said he cared. Perhaps he could show her. She would learn the truth from his touch. This wasn't sex. This was passion. He would make sure she understood the difference.

Turning the kiss from soft to insistent, he swooped in with his tongue, demanding she follow suit. She matched him every step of the way. Wrapping his arms around her, he pulled her closer as the kiss kept a steady pace, their tongues swaying to a delicious beat. His hands worked their way up and down her back, soothing her, caressing, and making her body anticipate more. At least, that was the hope.

She moaned into his mouth, encouraging him further. She wanted him. He knew none of their fighting words earlier were between them at the moment. It was in every tiny movement she made, inching closer to him, pressing her lithe body to his. Her sweet moans as he devoured her mouth. He wanted to kiss other unseen areas. This wasn't enough anymore.

Cupping her ass with his hands, he lifted her up. She quickly wrapped her legs around his waist. He broke the kiss, murmuring against her mouth, "I'm going upstairs, unless you say no. What do you want?"

She nuzzled her head between his neck and shoulder, shuddering. He waited patiently for her response, dying to rush up the stairs, but refusing to move a muscle until she answered. He wouldn't go any further with her unless he had her complete blessing. They hadn't settled anything between them. Right now, none of it mattered. Later they could talk it out. Right now, all he wanted was her body naked next to his.

He started to worry when she didn't respond—with words or with a touch. Her head just stayed cocooned between his neck. Her hot breath flowed down his back, making him wish her lips would touch him, just for a brief moment. Anything.

"Deja?" he whispered, his soft words echoing quietly between them. "What do you want?"

Ever so quietly, she whispered back, "You."

That's all he needed to hear. He headed for the stairs with her wrapped safely in his arms. As he started to climb, her lips started moving. Tiny kisses peppered around his neck, up his jaw, across his cheek, to a short path to his ear where she took a nibble. He trembled from each touch, almost tripping on the top step. He couldn't wait to get to her bed.

"Which room?"

He hated asking. He didn't want to waste any more time than was necessary. Having her under him, kissing, touching, lighting her body on fire was all he wanted to do, not wait for her to answer a simple question.

"First door on the left." Her lips trailed down his jaw and then across his neck and shoulder.

He shuddered again at the touch, then swung her bedroom door closed with a quick kick. In so many words, he told Dare to stay away. Just in case he didn't listen, which he could see him doing. He didn't need Dare to walk past and see what they were doing.

He laid her on the bed, covering his body completely over her. Without missing a beat, he drew her T-shirt up and over her head, unclasped her bra, and took a tight nipple into his mouth.

Heaven. Her body, the way she arched to meet his kiss, made him ache for her even more.

Deja wasn't sure what she should be doing. With all her talk about sex and men, she was sadly a novice. Could Emmett tell? Would he stand up and look at her with disgust? She always, so easily, rebuffed men. Pretending that she was a sex vixen worked well. Acting confident spoke louder than anything.

She loved his mouth on her breast. She suddenly wanted to feel his chest. Learn and memorize every hard contour of his body. Grabbing the hem of his shirt, she pulled up, almost crying out in dismay when he had to let go of her nipple to allow her to take his shirt off. She whipped the shirt to the floor as he resumed his tender strokes on her other breast.

His hand trailed down the side of her body, the light caress sending waves of desire straight to her core. When his hand met the snap of her jeans, she knew she should speak up before he went any further. She should've spoken up downstairs. She should've shoved him out the door.

It occurred to her downstairs, why did he suddenly want to sleep with her? He kept saying she couldn't hide behind sex. What was this then?

Did he truly care?

Of course he did. Why couldn't she just believe that?

As he started to shove her pants down, she helped him with the task, at the same time wondering if she should speak up yet.

She wanted him. She wanted him so much that she didn't care what reasons he had for bringing her up here. This just proved even more why she wasn't worthy of his affections. Taking pleasure from him even when she shouldn't.

Cold air hit her skin, tiny goose bumps popping up. Some from the cold, some from the desire as his hand dipped inside her panties. She arched up as he started doing delicious things no man had ever done before. Nothing else mattered. Not the issues between them. Not the reason he was here. Not the fact she wasn't good enough for him. Nothing mattered other than his soft, tender touch.

"Deja, you're so beautiful," Emmett whispered as he kissed his way across her chest to her lips.

She locked lips with him as he continued to work magic with his fingers. She wanted so much more.

Her hands stroked his back, his body trembling with

hers. She snaked her hands from his back to the front of his pants. With a quickness she didn't know she possessed, she unbuckled his pants and started to shove them down.

"Let me." He lifted and removed his pants and boxers, stopping for a moment to dig into one of his pockets. A condom landed on the bed near her thigh.

The sight of that had her panicking. This was really happening. She was about to have sex with Emmett. If she wanted to speak up, now would be a great time. There would be no going back if she didn't.

She froze. She could feel him removing her panties, his hands roaming around her body delicately. It all felt so wonderful. Her body had never felt so alive. So ready for more.

No words reached her lips.

Then he covered her lips with his, making speaking that much more difficult.

As much as she considered herself brave, strong, and in control of her life, she was none of that right now. She was weak. Taking when she should be honest.

His kiss became light as he positioned himself over her body. He quickly donned the condom and nestled his hard cock perfectly between her legs.

His soft caress across her lips, down her jaw, and to the side of her neck made her forget what was about to happen.

"I need you so badly." Emmett nibbled her ear and then slid inside her without restraint.

The moment of pain almost blinded her, made her immobile. Then slowly, nothing but a complete sense of rightness settled over her. He felt so large inside her. So right. So perfect. By the feel of him, she couldn't believe he fit.

She was enjoying the sensations all around her that it

took her a moment to realize he had stiffened, ramrod straight, not moving an inch. Why wasn't he moving?

This was worse than she thought. She should've said something. But would he have believed her? Nobody ever did. Not one person had ever believed her.

She slowly opened her eyes, unaware she had shut them, to see his face blank of any emotion. What was he thinking?

Bringing a hand to his cheek, she lightly rubbed it and laughed. A sexy laugh. Or, at least, she tried to make it sound like one. "What are you doing, Emmett?"

His brows dipped as his lips fell into a frown. She supposed that troubled look was better than anger. Although, he could still be horribly angry with her.

"Deja...God, why didn't you say something?" He dropped his head next to hers on the pillow.

She didn't want him to look away. That just confirmed everything she always believed. He hated her. He was ashamed, disgusted, revolted.

She should've made him leave.

He lifted his head, yet wouldn't meet her eyes. "Why didn't you tell me you were a virgin?"

10

HER WORDS from the other day resounded in his head.

This is who I am. I'm a slut. I sleep with any man, for any reason.

Why would she say that? It was a lie. Nothing but complete bullshit. He knew it was bullshit when she said it because she rarely dated and her personality just didn't speak that she was a slut. But this. This was beyond bullshit. Unbelievable.

He wanted to turn away, bury his head in the pillow again. But he couldn't.

Shit, what did he just do?

She still hadn't answered his question. Why wouldn't she warn him? He could've—should've—shit! This was bad.

He brushed his hand across her cheek. She shied away. Which was funny, although no chuckle left his lips. He was buried deep inside her and she was turning away from a light touch to her face.

"Did I hurt you?"

He would die inside if she said yes. In all likelihood, he

did. His stomach gurgled in agony. He never wanted to hurt her in any way, especially this way.

"What are you talking about?"

He frowned, then brushed her cheek again. This time she didn't move away from his touch. "I wasn't gentle. I'm afraid to move right now in fear I'll hurt you more. I would've never—"

"Never had sex with me if you had known. Well, news flash, I'm just using you."

He leaned into her face, his lips mere inches from hers. "This isn't sex. This is so much more. I would've never went so fast if I had known. That's what I was going to say. I wanted you so badly, but I would've taken it all slower if I had known. I feel sick inside that I probably hurt you. Why can't you see how much I care? Why do you hide behind this tough persona with me? Admit it. You care about me. You're just scared."

"Emmett...just...shut up. It didn't hurt. Either get on with it or get off me."

Her lips spread into a thin line, yet her eyes were thick with torture. He hated seeing that. Instead of her brother putting it there, it was him. She didn't want to talk? Fine. He wouldn't talk. Clearly, he wasn't doing a good enough job showing her with his touch how much he cared about her.

What would she say if he blurted out he loved her? Would she shove him off? He couldn't believe she hadn't done that yet.

He pulled out slowly, her eyes round with shock. She thought he was going to walk away. Well, he'd show her. He'd show her just how much he truly cared. With the grace he should've shown in the beginning, he pushed back in. His lips were still a breath away from hers. Her face softened. The fear that he wasn't going anywhere left. Her eyes dilated with pleasure as he repeated the same action. So, she wasn't lying about this. It didn't hurt. He could see the delight every time he slowly pulled out and back in.

"You're beautiful."

A slow pull out, with a sweet thrust in.

"Don't say that."

He brushed her lips with a soft kiss.

"You feel so good. I've waited forever to have you in my arms."

"This is just—"

Silencing her words with a hard kiss, he started to move faster. The kissed turn frantic with passion as she met him thrust for thrust. He couldn't get enough of the way she moved beneath him. He should've realized from the beginning all her bravado and talk about sex was just a shield from the truth. He'd never forgive himself for how he started this, but he'd be damn sure it ended with ecstasy.

Her tongue swirled with his as they kept in perfect rhythm together. She was made for him. This moment said everything he needed to know. He never connected this powerfully with a woman. He never would either. Only Deja. Why couldn't she see that?

Perhaps she did. Perhaps it was her fear holding her back. That had to be the problem. How could he get her to talk?

Never mind that now. He deepened the kiss as deep as it could go, then picked up the pace. She moaned, the beautiful sound telling him just how much she was enjoying it. That's all that mattered to him.

Her hands, which had been gripping his shoulders, slid down his back, her nails scratching a delicious path. She grabbed a hold of his ass and held on tight as a powerful orgasm attacked her senses. He couldn't take the pleasure squeezing around him. He couldn't hold back. He let go and came with her.

He broke the kiss slowly, then rested his head to the side. He rolled slightly, taking her with him, then he stroked a hand down her hair and across her back. Up and down. Smooth skin. Such beauty in his arms.

What did he say now? What did he do? This wasn't how he expected the night to go. He just meant to make her see how much he cared—with words. And he goes and takes her virginity instead.

Damn! He still couldn't get over that.

He kissed her neck and then rolled off the bed. "I'll be right back. Gotta throw the condom away."

He disposed of the condom quickly and didn't hesitate to wrap her in his arms as soon as he came back. She didn't hesitate either, wrapping her sweet, naked body to his. He was glad she chose to stay naked. He loved the feeling of being skin to skin with her. He already wanted her again.

Neither spoke. He still didn't know what to say. Nothing sounded good enough. He didn't want to argue with her. Not now. Never again. That would be impossible, though. They enjoyed sparring back and forth too much. She looked so beautiful when she got angry.

He waited for her to speak, but he soon felt her body relax. Her breathing became even as she fell asleep. His last thoughts before he drifted off were how he would never walk away from her. She was his. End of story.

EMMETT ROLLED TO THE SIDE. His hand met coldness where Deja should've been lying. Popping his eyes open one at a time, the sight before him confirmed what he feared. She wasn't in the bed.

Tossing a glance at the clock on her nightstand, he bolted up. Seven thirty in the morning. He never slept that long, or that good. His hand grazed the spot where she should've been lying. He wanted to make love to her right now. Although, he wasn't sure how that would've worked out. He only had the one condom in his wallet. He had no idea if she was on the pill. They'd have to talk about that.

Shit. It was probably a conversation they should've had before they had sex. Maybe she would've confessed she was a virgin. Or maybe she would've kicked him out of the house without him getting the chance to hold her in his arms.

Her missing in the bed didn't bode well. Guess they'd be talking about a few things. Would he be welcome back in her bed? He sure hoped so. He had high hopes he'd be back here soon. Tonight if he had his way.

She was a virgin. Twenty-five years old, and a virgin. He was her first. He still had a hard time believing that. She was gorgeous. Her eyes sucked a man in with one tiny glance. He'd seen it plenty of times when they were together in public or a client was in the office. He hated it every single time they looked at her like she was the most beautiful creature on earth. She was *his*. He wasn't giving up without the fight of his life. Oh, boy, what a fight it would be. He knew she was going to fight him the entire way. So many secrets she kept hidden from him, and it was about time she started talking to him about it. He knew enough to draw a conclusion that most people assumed the worst about her. A slut? Never.

He was almost thirty. He'd had a few steady girlfriends. Only one relationship that almost turned into marriage.

Then she cheated on him. He shied away from women after that, not trusting his instincts. Not that he was ever suave when it came to interacting with women. Then Deja walked into their lives. He was a goner the first time he laid eyes on her.

Hopping out of bed, he threw on his clothes from last night and headed downstairs. He didn't hear the shower going, so there wasn't a need to see if Deja was in the bathroom. He noticed the other two bedroom doors were closed, so Dare was still sleeping. Thank God for that. He didn't want to run into her brother anytime soon. He had to have seen his truck last night when he came home. Whenever that was. Emmett couldn't believe he slept so well that he didn't hear Dare come in. Did he come home last night?

Home? He was already thinking in those terms with her. He didn't care where he was, where he lived. Wherever Deja was would be his home.

He walked toward the kitchen when he heard shuffling sounds as if someone was rummaging in the cupboards, and nearly made a one-eighty degree turn to walk back out when he saw who it was.

"Did I wake you, Sleeping Beauty?" Dare said with a smirk, mimicking the words Emmett said to him yesterday morning when he knocked on the door.

"Morning, Dare." Emmett's heart sunk when he noticed Deja wasn't in the kitchen. Did she leave the house?

Dare grabbed another cup from the cupboard and started to pour two cups of coffee. "You know, when I said don't give up on my sister, I didn't necessarily mean you should sleep with her right away." He handed one of the mugs to Emmett, his face impassive, yet his lips pressed tightly together.

Emmett was surprised he didn't throw the hot coffee in

his face. He looked pissed. "It wasn't my intention. It just... sorta happened. Would you like to hit me now?"

Dare bypassed him and sat at the table. "There's cereal, bagels, or if you're really hungry, you could make us some bacon and eggs."

"Is that my punishment instead of a fist to the face? Making you breakfast?" Emmett sat across from him. "Where's Deja?"

Dare took a sip of coffee before responding. "She left a little bit ago and said she had lots to do in the office. Did you two argue this morning? I kinda expected you to walk out with her."

"How'd you know I was here?"

Chuckling, Dare raised a brow. "Do I look like an idiot? Your truck is parked outside."

Emmett rubbed his thumb across the curved handle of the coffee cup, debating what to say. This was her brother. Talking about sex wasn't the kind of conversation he wanted to have. Did Dare know she was a virgin? Probably not. He couldn't imagine Deja talking to him about those things. And she wasn't a virgin anymore. He still couldn't believe it.

"What'd you do?"

Emmett glanced up from the cup and made himself look Dare in the eye. "I just tried to show her how much I care. I have no idea why she left. She didn't even wake me up."

"When we were kids, some of the girls used to tease her that she stuffed her bra because she developed so young. She didn't have many friends. Neither did I. We were a team. I don't tell you this shit to make you feel sorry for us. I just need you to know to handle her carefully. My sister acts tough, but she's far from it. I don't think you'd intentionally hurt her and I'll still kill you if you do."

Emmett grinned, then finally took a sip of his coffee.

"That threat's getting old. Find a new one." He took a larger gulp of coffee and stood up. "Come on. I normally don't sleep this late. We have a busy day and I have to run home to shower and change. Are you going to get weird if I sleep over more nights?"

Dare laughed like that was the funniest thing he heard in years. "Dude, she left this morning without waking you up. What makes you think you get to sleep over again?"

"Because I'm not giving up."

Last night, besides the horrible part where he probably hurt her, was the best night of his life. He wanted to sleep next to her every night. He'd be okay with just sleeping, too. If she didn't want to make love again, he'd wait until she was ready. She was too important to screw anything up.

Problem was he probably already screwed up.

DEJA GLANCED up when the office door opened. Her heart beat erratically for a second before she realized it was only Sophie. She left this morning, easing out of bed like a snail. She didn't want to risk waking up Emmett. She slipped out so well, he never even heard the front door close behind her, and she had closed it pretty hard, expecting, or more like wishing, he'd run out of the house and stop her, wondering why she was leaving without a good morning kiss. That didn't happen. Of course, she could've acted a little stronger and woken him up before leaving the bedroom.

Scared. Nothing but a little scaredy cat. They had both fallen asleep last night without talking about anything. She wanted to avoid all talk. She wanted to forget anything ever happened. Except she found it extremely difficult to forget how wonderful it felt to be with Emmett. She wanted to spend the night with him again.

"Hey, Soph. How's it going?"

Sophie grabbed a chair against the wall and scooted it closer to her desk. "Okay. Just checking on you. I just left the mechanics."

Ugh. Another conversation Deja didn't want to have. She was no coward. She reminded herself of that daily. Especially this morning, staring in the mirror for so long, she was surprised her eyes didn't fall out.

"What's the damage? I'll pay you back every cent. It'll take me some time, though. I hope that's okay."

Sophie reached across the table and squeezed Deja's hand. "I don't want your money. The insurance is paying for it. It was an accident. The front end was pretty banged up. Too much work for a car that isn't worth it. Austin's going to go shopping with me this weekend. Well, whenever they get done with building a new corral. Are you coming over to the farm tomorrow to help?"

What a loaded question. Emmett would be there. It was already mid-afternoon. She was surprised he hadn't stopped by already. She'd been on edge the entire day, waiting for him to walk in. He still hadn't. If she didn't speak to him tonight, tomorrow could get awkward. This morning had been awkward with Dare, who didn't say a word that he knew Emmett was still in the house. She didn't talk about it either. She *really* didn't want to talk to Emmett.

"Is everything okay, Deja? You look far away right now."

She blinked a few times and then smiled. "I'm fine. I feel horrible about your car. Are you sure the insurance is paying for everything?"

"Yes. Don't worry about my car. You don't have to come over tomorrow if you don't want to."

"I'll be there. I know nothing about building a fence, though." She chuckled to loosen the terror running through her body. It didn't help one bit.

Sophie smiled. "Me neither. Knowing those McCord men, they won't let us help anyway. I figured I could make them some pies, lunch, snacks, that sort of thing. You can help me in the kitchen. Eleanor is still visiting family."

"Perfect. They do like their pie."

Sophie softly laughed and stood up. "They do. You can ride with us tomorrow, if you'd like."

Deja figured that was the best plan; otherwise, she'd have to call a cab. "Can I bring Dare?"

"Of course. I'd love to get to know him better. I'm so sorry the fire ever happened and ruined our supper the other night. How's he settling in?"

"Good. He's working for Emmett. It's a load off my shoulders wondering if Dare would find a job. Emmett took that worry away by offering him a job."

She had accused him of doing it out of selfish reasons. A reason to get in her pants. So wrong of her. She knew better than that. Yet, she didn't know how to apologize.

"That's because he's a wonderful man. He cares about you, Deja. You know that, right?"

Her eyes widened that Sophie would say that. They never talked about things like this. She figured Sophie had an inkling she had feelings for Emmett, but she never brought it to light. Sophie respected her privacy the most, because she was private herself.

"I know you care for him. Austin is the most patient man I have ever met. I have a lot of baggage that still needs sifting through, and he just takes every day with the utmost patience. I love him even more for it. I imagine Emmett would do the same."

"I slept with him last night."

Did she just blurt that out?

She did. And she felt so much lighter. It had been weighing on her, on her conscience, on her heart.

Instead of looking horrified or shocked, Sophie offered a small smile. "I know."

"But how?" Did Emmett go blabbing his mouth to Austin, who then told Sophie? Just like high school, spreading the word she was an easy lay. Except this time, she couldn't dispute it. She'd be the liar if she tried to deny it.

Sophie sat down with a soft chuckle. "Deja, his truck was sitting outside your house. I just kind of figured something finally happened between you two. You've both been skirting around your feelings for a long time. I'm so happy you two are together. You make a beautiful couple."

Deja couldn't help but roll her eyes. "We're not together, Sophie."

A frown marred her delicate features. "I don't understand. He spent the night. There's no way Emmett would treat you like a one-night stand. He's not that kind of man. I know he cares about you."

"I...we...it's complicated."

Sophie nodded, letting it go just like that. She knew Deja didn't want to talk about it. Sophie would never pressure her to talk. She loved Sophie even more for that wonderful trait. She knew talking about things was hard, and when Deja was ready, she'd come talk to her about it. Deja was the same way.

Sophie stood up again, then moved the chair against the wall. "I just wanted to stop by and say hi and tell you about my car, which you're not to worry about." She pierced her with a hard stare that meant business. Deja had no intention of making her mad. She wouldn't worry about the car if she said not to. "Austin and I will pick you and Dare up around eight tomorrow."

Deja nodded. They said their good-byes and Sophie was gone soon after. The day dragged on. Deja found the dumbest things to do, afraid to leave. Afraid to go home to an empty house.

It wasn't empty anymore. Dare was there now. Or was he? Did he still want to leave? Would he hang out with Ethan again? She had no idea. They didn't talk about things like that. This morning would've been a good time to talk. Or not. Emmett was in the house. She didn't want to talk to anyone. She made that abundantly clear when she whisked out of the house without a word good-bye.

Her head jerked up as the office door opened. Her heart froze in her chest as she stared into Emmett's eyes. He finally came looking for her. What took him so long? Why did he look like he didn't want to see her, let alone talk to her?

"Did you talk to Taylor yet about that form? He still hasn't turned it in."

"We need to talk."

He waited all day to come see her and that was the first thing he had to say. She didn't like how he said it either. He said it so awkwardly, in a tone of voice that suggested she was about to be dumped. Not that he could really dump her. They weren't in that kind of relationship. He was definitely about to say there wouldn't be a repeat of last night. Which made her heart hurt even more. She wanted to lie in his arms again. She had felt so safe and loved in his arms.

Love? No. A man like Emmett would never love a woman like her—a thief, a burglar, a slut. Well, the last one was a lie, but still, people believed it about her.

"I'm not sure we have anything to talk about."

"Really? I thought we'd talk about a few things over dinner. Grab your coat. I made reservations. You work too hard. It's time to call it a night."

Her body tingled at his words. "Are you asking me out on a date?"

The corner of his lip turned up in a delicious grin. "I meant to do that last night, but I'm not complaining how it all turned out. After dinner, I plan to explore your body a little more thoroughly than what I did last night." His grin slowly died. "That's part of what we need to talk about."

Her skin prickled with desire at his words, then slowly morphed into terrifying goose bumps. Having sex again was one thing. Talking about last night was entirely something else.

"Take your dinner and shove it. We had sex. End of story."

He stalked over to her and pulled her into his arms before she could protest. His arms snaked around her body and wrapped her tightly against him. His mouth hovered over hers. "You're mine. End of story." His lips silenced any protest she would've made. Not that she wanted to. Being in Emmett's arms was finally finding a real home.

11

EMMETT PULLED out a chair for Deja, then took a seat himself. He kissed her senseless in the office and then ushered her out of the building without letting her say a word. She didn't try too hard to speak or protest that he was taking her to dinner. He took it as a good sign.

All day, pushing his body to the limit with hard work, he tried to figure out how to handle her. How to show her what he said and did was real. Dare said to handle her carefully. Well, that's what he'd been doing since he met her. Maybe that was part of the problem. Last night, he exerted a bit of dominance by walking into her house and pulling her into his arms without waiting for her invitation. Just a little bit ago, he did the same thing. Here she sat, looking detached. Not fearful, not sad. Maybe she wanted—needed—him to take charge. Because being careful for almost an entire year had gotten him nowhere.

He picked up his menu the waiter had placed in front of him and opened it. "I read a review that this place has great chicken Alfredo."

She glanced at him over the rim of her menu. "I don't feel like pasta."

Okay. In terms of trying to start a conversation, that was pretty lame. Talking would be harder than he imagined. He was starting to doubt the brilliant plan to talk about their issues in a restaurant. When he made the reservations, he requested a table in a quiet, secluded part of the restaurant. They were tucked away in a corner. A few people sat near them, but not close enough to hear anything. Of course, if the conversation turned heated it could turn into a different story.

Now what did he say? He wanted to be thankful she didn't have any sorrow in her eyes. But when it came to Deja, she rarely displayed that heartbreaking emotion. Only recently, since her brother was released, had she let the pain show. Generally, she hid her feelings well. Behind a huge barrier she had erected probably early on in childhood. How did he break that barrier down? Slowly could take forever. Tearing it down with a wrecking ball might be his best option. It made him nervous as shit to do it.

He made these reservations to show her what they had was more than sex. He wanted everything. Her companionship. Her friendship. Her love. He went about it all backwards last night, letting his body speak louder than his mind. He didn't regret last night. He just wished it had turned out a little differently. Mainly, he wished she would've told him the truth.

He lowered the menu. "I heard the steak's pretty good, too." Still lame, but that's all the bravery he had at the moment.

Her eyes peeked over the menu again. "I don't feel like steak."

Nodding, he pretended to look at the menu once more.

Food wasn't a priority. He wasn't sure he would be able to take one bite. Why did he think this was a good idea?

EMMETT PUSHED in Sara's chair and took a seat across from her. The ring in his pocket was starting to burn a hole. He could do this. He loved her. She loved him. Two years of dating was almost overkill. Time to pop the question. At least, that's what Ethan and Gabe told him. He couldn't explain it to them, or even to himself, why he kept putting it off. He just wanted it to be right. To be perfect.

Ethan bulldozed over all his reasons and forced him to buy a ring. His exact words were, "Marry her or dump her. Two years is ridiculous, man. Mom and Dad barely waited five months before getting engaged. She's either the one or she's not. Time to decide."

Sara was the best. She worked as a receptionist at a doctor's office. Everyone loved her there. She was sweet, kind, friendly. Perfect for him.

She was twenty-three. He was twenty-seven. Ethan was right. It was time. He just wanted to be sure. He just wanted the moment to be right. Decisions like this shouldn't be made lightly. Once he married, it'd be forever. He wouldn't have it any other way.

Ethan was one to talk. He was almost like Austin—a player. A man who needed a woman on his arms at all times. He went through women so frequently, it was hard to keep up with whom he was dating at any given time. Maybe that made him more knowledgeable about women. Emmett wasn't a novice, but he floundered at times when it came to women.

He loved Sara. That's all that mattered.

They ordered food. Emmett asked for the best bottle of wine

they had. Sara smiled at him and rested her arms on the table. "*The best bottle of wine, Emmett? What's the occasion?*"

"*What, I can't buy my beautiful girlfriend the best there is.*" He smiled as he reached for her hand. His other hand hid under the table, tapping the box in his pocket.

A smile graced her face, but there was no happiness in her eyes. She slowly pulled her hand away. "*We should talk.*"

Talk? That didn't sound good the way she said it. Why did she pull away? His hand slowly moved away from his pocket. "*What do you want to talk about?*"

"*I slept with my boss.*"

Emmett's smile froze. To anyone, it would probably look like he was smiling at his girlfriend with adoration. Far from it. He just couldn't move a muscle from the shock coursing through him. The ring now felt like heavy lead, weighing him down. Weren't they supposed to love each other? This didn't sound like she loved him at all. Not that they used the "L" word yet. It was just sort of assumed. Or, at least, he thought so.

"*It was one time and a total mistake. I'm sorry, Emmett. Please forgive me.*" Her hand lingered on the table, just in reach of his. It looked like she wanted to reach for him.

"*Forgive you?*" His smile finally vanished as confusion took its place. "*Why?*"

She bit the bottom of her lip. "*I don't know. I didn't mean to do it. It happened at the office after hours.*" She touched the tips of his fingers. "*I want to work through this. I don't want to lose you. I didn't want to hide this from you. It'll never happen again. I swear.*"

He moved his hand away. "*You cheated on me, Sara. For no good reason, apparently. How am I supposed to trust you now? You say it won't happen again, but how can I be sure?*"

Tears formed in the corner of her eyes. "*Because I love you. We can work through this.*"

Now she finally said she loved him. All this time, he had assumed, not really needing to hear it. She obviously didn't know what love meant.

Before he could respond, the waiter approached the table with their food and the wine meant to celebrate their engagement. Now, it would just dull his emotions. Without missing a beat, Sara started to eat, talking to him as if he had forgiven her. Hell, no, he wouldn't be forgiving her. But he wasn't one to make a scene. He'd survive this dinner and then wipe her from his life.

SHIT. He hated how Sara told him in a crowded restaurant that she cheated on him. He had wanted to shout, release his anger for the way she had broken his heart. But ever the gentleman, he finished the meal, took her home, and told her they were through with little fanfare. She tried to put up a fight, spewing words of love, but he shut her down with little effort. He couldn't continue to love a woman who did something like that to him. He never felt more relieved that he hadn't professed his love like he had planned. He didn't end up being a complete fool. Just a partial one. He still couldn't understand why she cheated on him. What did he do to make her do that? Or, what didn't he do?

Here he was, in love with another woman, trying to do what he hated Sara for doing. Having a serious conversation should take place in private. What had he been thinking? Deja could potentially cause a scene. She wasn't one to hold back. One of the many reasons he loved her.

Simple way to solve that problem. He'd enjoy this meal. Hopefully, anyway. Then take her home and talk to her there. He wouldn't bring anything up about last night yet. Besides, she wasn't responding too well to his simple talk.

He glanced at her, her eyes glued to the menu. More like, actively trying to ignore him. Her long blonde hair was pulled back in a ponytail. Nothing dramatic, just simple and cute. She never had to do anything special. He always found her so beautiful.

He should've skipped the restaurant and went straight home. His house, preferably, to avoid Dare. The things he wanted to talk about needed to be said without any interruption. He wanted to talk about these things. Now. What would she say if he said he wanted to leave?

"Deja, I—"

"Oh, my. Emmett McCord, is that you?"

Emmett glanced to his right to see the last person he ever wanted to deal with. Did his thoughts about Sara conjure up this woman? He never cared for Chelsea Bridget, one of Sara's closest friends. Ethan always laughed at her name. He thought it was so funny she had two first names.

"Hello, Chelsea."

She walked right up to him, not once glancing toward Deja, and placed a hand on his shoulder. "It's been ages. How are you?" Before he could answer, her eyes trailed to Deja. "Holy shit, Deja Wilson. How in the world do you know Emmett?"

Deja's brow rose, then she smiled so innocently. Emmett knew better. There was nothing innocent in her look. "I was wondering the same thing about you."

Not good. At. All. There was history between these two, and Emmett wasn't getting the good kind of vibe. Was Chelsea one of the people who hurt Deja with her words? He wouldn't be surprised. While Sara had been sweet and caring, Chelsea was the exact opposite. He always got the impression she wanted to hook up with him. Not that he ever implied he wanted her sexually or encouraged anything of the sort. Her hand on his shoulder was telling him she still wanted him. He lightly shrugged her hand off. She backed up a step.

"Emmett dated Sara. You remember Sara Bergen? They were practically engaged." Chelsea smiled wide, then turned to him. "What are you doing with Deja? I don't mean to sound rude or anything, but her brother is bad news. A very dangerous guy." She glanced at Deja. "You have to admit that. I'm still shocked at what he did."

Deja's face turned hard. The look in her eyes said she wanted to grab her tire iron and bash Chelsea over the head. Emmett was tempted himself. He knew Chelsea could act like a bitch, but to this extent? Blatantly say that to Deja. How dare anyone speak to her that way.

"Dare has more courtesy than you, Chelsea. That was uncalled for." Emmett pierced her with a stare that said she would do well not to say anything else. "You owe Deja an apology."

Chelsea bristled as if he'd slapped her. Deja just stared at him as if he'd lost his mind. Maybe he did. And he was about to really lose it if she didn't leave. What was he thinking? Chelsea was the last person to ever offer an apology. He'd die holding his breath waiting for one.

When Chelsea continued to stand there and say nothing, Emmett said, "I'd appreciate it if you left us alone. We're trying to enjoy our meal."

Clucking her tongue in distaste, she pursed her lips. "I always respected you, Emmett. Thought you were such a catch. I guess you decided to lower your standards if you're with someone like Deja. Dumping Sara for someone like her." Chelsea waved a hand in Deja's direction.

Emmett stared at Deja for a moment, her face difficult to read now. The anger was gone, replaced with indifference.

More of her shield erected. Damn Chelsea for just making his job even harder. Well, screw that.

"Sara doesn't even compare to a woman like Deja. Or you, for that matter." Emmett grinned as Chelsea's face fell into a frown. "Which is why I'm the happiest man on earth that she agreed to marry me. So, please let me eat dinner with my fiancée in peace before I have you removed."

Chelsea huffed in indignation and walked away. Wow. That was easier than he thought. She didn't put up a fight at all. Shocking, really.

Unsure of what Deja would think of him for saying that, he stared at the menu instead of looking at her. He was honestly surprised Chelsea walked away without more of a fight. "I guess that paints quite a picture of your childhood. What a bitch."

"You were engaged to Sara Bergen?"

He looked up. She still looked indifferent. Like nothing bothered her with what just happened, even him calling her his fiancée. "No."

"But she said—"

"She said practically engaged. We dated for two years. I never asked her. I thought about it, especially with Ethan bugging me, but then she opened my eyes. She cheated on me."

Her shock was swift as she leaned toward him. "She didn't? I know she could be ditzy, but dumb? She was an idiot for losing a great guy like you. Wow."

A smile touched his face as he leaned closer, getting near her lips. "How do you know them?"

She sunk back in her chair. "I went to high school with them. I'm surprised you know them."

"I'm sorry to say I do now. I wish I would've met you first. Now that we're getting married, I'm the happiest man on earth. They don't matter." His smile grew as he stayed leaning over the table, her eyes round with shock again.

"You were just playing with her, calling me...saying that...it's not real."

"Sure it is. I love you. I'm ready for that step. I think I never asked Sara without Ethan prodding me because I must've known I didn't *love* love her. But you, I know I *love* love you. I'll get you the most gorgeous ring there is. I promise." He winked as he finally sat back.

Her mouth opened and closed like a fish. Clearly, he rendered her speechless. Yep. The way to show Deja how he felt was to exert his dominance so she had no reason to doubt him. Marriage? He never thought about it before, but now the idea was planted firmly in his mind. He had no doubts or reservations whatsoever. Not like he had with Sara.

"You didn't even ask me, Emmett. You can't just assume I'll marry you. Stop joking around. That's all this is. I'm not the type of woman—"

He stood up, leaning over the table without a thought or care about anything in his way and silenced her words with a kiss. He kept it short and brief, but long enough to let her know, hopefully anyway, that he wasn't kidding. "I wouldn't lie or joke around about something like this. I love you."

He sat back down with a smug grin on his face. He could see the protest on her lips when the waiter stopped at their table.

"Have you decided what you'd like?"

Emmett tapped the menu. "The chicken Alfredo. I hear it's delicious. We'll also have the best bottle of champagne you have. We're celebrating our engagement."

The waiter smiled. "Congratulations." He beamed his thousand-watt smile toward Deja. "Your fiancé is a lucky man to have snagged such a beautiful woman. What can I get for you?"

Emmett thought Deja was about to argue and throw a fit that his words were all lies when a slow smile crept over her face. "Thank you so much. I'll have the most expensive steak you have. I hear it's the best."

The waiter nodded and walked away.

"I don't like games, Emmett. But I'll play along and empty your wallet."

He set his elbows on the table, folded his hands together, and grinned. "I'm not playing games. You'll figure it out soon enough. You can have anything you want from me. What are you so afraid of? Is it so hard to imagine that someone might actually love you for you? Because I do. With every breath in my body. I see I have a lot of work ahead of me to prove it."

12

DEJA LOOKED at all the ingredients covering the counter. What did Sophie want her to do? Because she needed something to occupy her mind. Thinking about what happened last night and this morning wasn't helping to calm her down.

Dinner had been...wonderful. Surprisingly. Once the shock of seeing Chelsea after so many years, and Emmett boldly saying they were getting married, they had morphed into a comfortable conversation. She had decided it was best to ignore what he said. He was only kidding, and making a scene in the middle of a restaurant wasn't on her to-do list. So, she changed the topic.

She figured once the meal was over, Emmett would insist on coming inside her house like the night before. He didn't. He walked her to the door, kissed her with a kiss that had her wishing he followed her inside, and left. He didn't even wait for an invitation. He just left.

Which confirmed he was only messing with her. Playing some sick mind games. It pissed her off. Dare had been lounging on the couch watching something on TV when she got home. She didn't glance once at it, barely even said good night to him. She had rushed to her room and locked the door. Not that she worried Dare would bug her, but who knew. She had hoped he would, like when they were younger. He didn't. That hurt almost as much as Emmett playing games with her did.

Then the morning came. She forced Dare out of bed, telling him they were helping on the farm today. She didn't give him a choice in the matter. Another surprise again, he didn't argue too much. When a knock sounded on the door, she opened it expecting to see Sophie and Austin. Nope. Standing tall and proud, with the sexiest smile yet, was Emmett.

He gave her a kiss that spoke of such promises for later, flashed a shy smile, and then slipped a ring onto her finger. Too shocked to speak, she let him usher her out of the house without arguing. Dare had glanced at the ring, but didn't say anything. The ride to the farm had been awkward.

Of course, not as awkward as Emmett announcing their engagement once they arrived at the farm. Hugs and congratulations went rampant until Zane finally said it was time to get to work.

Engaged. This ring. He was either still playing this game to the extreme, or he actually wanted to marry her.

She fingered the ring with her thumb, watching as it sparkled, connecting with the sunlight streaming through the window over the sink. It didn't look like a cheap ring. At least two carats, a princess cut, with tiny diamonds trailing down the band. It was gorgeous, more than she would've ever imagined when she dreamed as a little girl of getting whisked away by a knight in shining armor.

She had no idea what to do. Part of her still thought he was joking. He had to be. They didn't match at all. She was nothing compared to him. Trailer trash as some of the kids used to tease. A criminal, even though her record didn't display it. She wasn't good enough for a man as sweet, caring, and handsome as Emmett.

"Are you okay, Deja?"

She tore her gaze away from the ring, dropping her hand to her side. Gabe stood near the fridge. "I'm fine. How's the corral coming along?"

"Good. The drinks Sophie passed out were a lifesaver, but not enough. We're all a little more parched than we realized. I'm just grabbing some more water bottles."

Deja nodded, then looked away. She should start measuring out flour or something. Do anything to make it look like she wasn't scared or a chicken or anything. She should've walked outside with Sophie and helped pass out drinks instead of staying hidden in the kitchen. Not that Sophie gave her a choice. Her words had been, "Get the dough started for the pies. I can handle the drinks."

Sophie just knew she didn't want to go out there and face everybody—face Emmett. She had been extremely uncomfortable when congratulations circled her. Sophie knew. She saw it right away, whisking her inside the house as soon as Zane spoke. Dare still hadn't said much. Not even a quick word of congrats.

She looked at the recipe before her and grabbed a measuring cup. Sophie better hurry because she was bound to screw this recipe up. She was not a baker, not like Sophie.

"You don't look happy."

The measuring cup nearly slipped through her fingers, sending flour everywhere. Almost afraid to look at Gabe, she steeled her spine and met his gaze. "I'm fine."

He set the few water bottles he grabbed from the fridge

onto the counter next to him. "You keep saying that, but I'm not seeing it."

Strange. She didn't have conversations like this with Gabe. He normally hung out in the background, speaking occasionally. He was shy, or more like, soft-spoken. He usually only spoke when something needed to be said. Apparently, he felt like this was one of those times. She liked Gabe. He could be funny and always a gentleman, no matter the occasion. Although, what was she thinking? All the McCord men were gentlemen.

"I get it. You don't want to talk about it. I hate it when my brothers goad me into talking. I didn't mean to be so bold." He smiled softly and started to grab the water bottles. "Emmett's the happiest I've seen him in a long time. I just wished you matched his happiness."

"It's not real, Gabe. This is a mistake."

His hand paused, a slight quiver as he did. "Then why are you wearing the ring?"

Deja looked at the ring adorning her finger. Why *was* she wearing it? Because it looked good on her hand. Because she wanted to believe it was real. Because she loved Emmett. Those words would never come out of her mouth, though. He didn't mean what he said last night. He couldn't.

"We all make mistakes, Deja. I'm sorry you think being engaged to my brother is one of them."

Her eyes popped up to Gabe. He didn't look mad, but she didn't miss the flicker of disappointment.

"He didn't even ask me. He just shoved the ring on my finger."

"Again, then why are you wearing it?" He took a few steps toward her. "You've made mistakes in your life. Things happen. You're scared to open yourself up. I get it. But this isn't one of them."

Was she that easy to read? Even Gabe, someone she rarely saw, could tell she was scared. That wasn't good. She lightly laughed. It sounded haughtier than she intended. "Like you've made mistakes like me. Get real."

Gabe glanced around, his eyes darting to the door as if he didn't want anyone to hear what he was about to say. "I have, actually. Do you want to know the colossal mistake I made? You have to promise to keep it to yourself."

Intrigued by this, positive he had never made the kind of mistakes she had, she nodded.

"When I went to Vegas with my buddies a few months ago, I got really wasted. I mean, it's Vegas, right? You're supposed to have fun." He laughed and shook his head. "I guess I had a little too much fun. I woke up the next morning next to...she was beautiful. Long strawberry-blonde hair. I had no idea who she was."

"Wait a minute. Are you telling me, Gabe the shy goose, had a one-night stand?"

His cheeks burned bright red. "I hate that nickname. I wish Ethan had never told you that." His eyes darted to the floor. "It was a little worse than that. I married her."

"You're lying. Give me a break. I see you're trying to make me feel better, but that's kind of a stretch, even for you." Deja dumped the flour into the bowl and scooped up another cup.

She refused to be made a fool of. Out of everyone in the McCord family, she never expected Gabe to act this way.

Her head jerked up when she realized Gabe stood right next to her. His cheeks were still a rosy red, mismatching with the frown and wrinkles covering his forehead. "I'm not lying. I have the paperwork to prove it."

Her eyes narrowed. "Are you still married?"

"Yeah. I kind of freaked out when I saw a naked woman

in the bed next to me, no matter how beautiful she was. I slipped out of bed, took a shower, and by the time I got out, she was gone."

"Did she wipe you clean? Did you call the cops?"

He shook his head, then ran a hand through his shaggy black locks of hair. "She didn't steal from me. I found the marriage license. I tried to track her down but had no luck. All I have is her name and little snippets of memories. I'll never drink that much again. I might have to hire a PI to find her. I mean, I need to get this fixed. I can't stay married to a woman I don't know."

"You haven't told anyone?"

He laughed, although she heard no humor in it. "You know my brothers. They'll just tease me up and down for doing something so idiotic. I don't want to hear it. It was dumb. Married to a woman and I don't even remember it." He grinned. "See, we all make mistakes. Is marrying my brother really one of yours?"

Deja glanced at the ring again.

"It's okay to be scared. It's okay to feel like you're alone. But, the thing is," he gently smiled, "you're not. You have us. You have Emmett. He loves you. It's been obvious to all of us for a very long time."

Gabe walked back to the water bottles and stacked them in his arms. He started to walk out.

"Hey, Gabe."

He stopped and glanced over his shoulder. "Yeah?"

"Your secret's safe with me. Thanks for the talk."

"Thanks for listening. I feel better someone else knows. I guess I must've ditched my friends that night because they don't even know what happened." He smiled, reminding her instantly of Emmett. "I'm glad you'll be a part of the family officially. You're good for Emmett."

Deja had to wipe a stray tear away as soon as Gabe walked out. Could Emmett really want to marry her? The ring on her finger said he was serious.

Opening herself to another person would take more courage than she possessed. Could she do it? If it was anyone else, probably not. But Emmett? She just didn't know.

───

HE PULLED the truck into the garage and hit the button. The loud crunching noise of the garage door descending awakened Deja in the passenger seat.

"What's that noise? Are we home?" She blinked a few times, glancing around.

Emmett grabbed her hand and kissed it lightly. "We're home."

Her eyes narrowed. She pulled her hand from his grasp. "This isn't my house. Why are we at your house?"

"Because we should talk, and I don't want Dare to interrupt us."

"Oh, now you wanna talk. Don't you think talking would've been good before you shoved this thing onto my finger?"

The diamond twinkled before his eyes as she held her hand up. It looked good on her. He paid a pretty penny for it. Nearly drained half his savings, but it was so worth it. She was worth it. Just like she was worth this ensuing fight sure to begin.

He was a little surprised they didn't have this fight earlier this morning when he, as she put it, shoved the ring on her finger. Giving her time to think about his actions always made her react in the wrong way—fleeing as far away from him as she could possibly get. That's why he slipped the ring on her finger without asking. That's why he said they were getting married without asking. He was still waiting for her to argue about it. Apparently, it was time.

"It looks good on you." He stepped out of the truck.

"Emmett, don't you walk away from me."

Of course, that's what he did anyway, chuckling beneath his breath as he heard her angry footsteps trailing him. He tossed his keys on the counter near the door that led from the garage and headed for the fridge. They ate supper before leaving the farm, but he needed something to drink. Not to drown his sorrows as Ethan loved to say. He was just thirsty, that's all.

He turned toward her with a beer dangling from his hand. "Want one?"

Her hands were poised on her hips, her lips in a tight line, and her hair flowed down her back, a little resting on her chest hiding her cleavage, making him itch to cross the kitchen and brush it back. Probably not what she wanted him to do. Or maybe he should just kiss her. Show her without words just how much he loved her. He had a feeling this conversation still wouldn't convince her.

"What's going on?"

"We're having a beer. You wanna watch a movie?" He flashed her a smile, but it did nothing to deter the hard look on her face or relax the rigidness of her stance.

"You said we were going to talk."

"Did I? We can watch a movie first."

"I don't want to watch a movie. I want to talk."

A slow grin crept onto his face. "Great. Let's talk."

"You tricked me." She threw her finger out, pointing at him like he was the last man standing. Which he probably was. "You knew I didn't want to talk, then made it seem like I do. I don't."

"Now you're just confusing me, Deja." He couldn't help but chuckle. It was wrong to make her mad like this. He wasn't even sure why he was. Perhaps because she looked so adorable when she got upset. "Here, have a beer." He grabbed another beer from the fridge, holding one out for her to take.

She fiddled with her finger. The ring went flying across the island standing between them. "Here, have a ring."

Okay. He might've gone a little too far. That was the last thing he wanted her to do. He set both beers down and picked up the ring. "I know the owner of the jewelry store. I had to wake her up and have her open the store early this morning just so I'd be there on time to pick you guys up. I wanted you to have a ring, not just think it was a bunch of talk on my part."

"Emmett, you can't just say you're going to marry me and not ask. This has gotten out of hand. Your entire family thinks we're getting married and we're not."

Toying with the ring, he kept his eyes trained on that instead of her. "Why wouldn't you just tell me you were a virgin? Why would you call yourself a slut when it's not true?" He lifted his head. "Why can't you love me?"

Her face turned to sorrow for a brief moment before disappearing as if it never happened. "It's just something people love to call me."

Okay, so she wanted to ignore the statement about love. Fine. He'd let her for now. "But it's not true. Even if I wouldn't have been the first guy, it's not true."

"You don't know me."

He clenched his fists. "I know you. I may not know the secrets you hide inside, but I know everything I need to know. You're beautiful. You're kind. You're there for your friends and family. You're human. Sure, you've made some dumb mistakes, but we all have. Why are you so hard on yourself? Why am I like a broken record telling you how much I care about you?"

She bit her lip as her mouth started to break apart into a frown. "We're very different people. I come from the wrong side of town. You could do better than me."

He stalked to her in three long strides. Cupping her right cheek, his thumb soothed the worry from her face. "I hate it when you put yourself down. Did I hurt you? If I would've known, I would've been more gentle."

"It was beautiful, Emmett. You could never hurt me. Unlike me, who continues to hurt you. I'm not ready for marriage."

He slipped the ring into his pocket, then grasped her face between his hands. "I jumped the gun. I'm sorry. You know how I feel now. That's what I want. I want you as my wife. I love you. How can I show you what I say is real? What will make you believe me?"

"I don't know."

He brushed his lips with hers. She slowly opened her mouth to him. Taking cue from her that she wanted to kiss him, he dove in, savoring everything about her. Her sweet taste. The way her body fit perfectly with his. The tiny sounds she made as they kissed. God, he loved her. Why did he hide his feelings for her for so long? He could be such an idiot at times.

Wrapping his arms around her waist, he pulled her closer. A small moan escaped from her as her arms circled around him. Needing more, knowing no amount of talking was going to convince her of anything, he lifted her up, cupping her ass as she tangled her legs around his waist.

Hoping not to run into anything, he made his way to his bedroom while kissing her the entire time.

Laying her down on the soft brown comforter, he broke the kiss long enough to remove her shirt. She looked perfect lying there. Like she belonged there.

He lowered his mouth, kissing her lightly as he worked the clasp on her bra. "Tell me to stop now if you don't want to go any further. Otherwise, I'm going to explore this beautiful body from head to toe."

"What happened to talking?" she whispered as he slipped her bra off and cupped one of her breasts.

"I'll talk myself blue trying to convince you how I feel. I guess showing you will have to suffice. If I have to make love to you over and over until you understand, that's just a cross I will have to bear."

Giggling, she lightly swatted his chest. "Stop. You think you're so funny."

Nibbling her neck, trailing a path down to a succulent nipple, he laughed with her. "Just speaking the truth, sweetheart. I love you, and I'll show you every day of my life just how much."

DEJA WILLED HERSELF not to move, not to brush her hand across Emmett's chest in any way. He was sleeping and she didn't want to wake him. Observing him like this, looking so handsome in his sleep, was all she wanted to do.

She knew she didn't have the greatest childhood. Dare was her only bright spot in life. She didn't even have any great friends growing up. Just Dare. So many years of listening to put-downs, name-calling, accusations, judgments. It should be easy to believe everything Emmett said. And she did. She knew he wasn't a man to lie. Everything he said was true. But letting those words into her heart, holding them as true, that's what she had a problem with.

Nobody ever said such things to her. It wasn't like she could treat it like a light switch. Simply flicking the switch up and magically feel happy, believe in happily ever after. Those types of fairytale endings only happened in the books she used to read as a teenager. Not in her life. Her life never once displayed any sort of happiness.

Sure, she had Sophie's friendship, and she supposed the friendship of the McCords. But true happiness? She didn't know what that felt like.

Emmett's easy breathing, the way his chest lifted up and down so smoothly told her how relaxed he was. No worries. Or did he worry? Did he think by her sleeping in his bed she was suddenly going to marry him? He hadn't pulled the ring back out, but they had also fallen asleep after making love twice.

Twice. She still couldn't believe how tenderly he had moved over her body, placing kisses in so many spots, she knew he didn't leave one part of her body untouched. After loving her so sweetly, the passion in the room had spiked. The hunger took over. He had rocked her body with such intensity, she still tingled from the aftermath how many hours later.

Twenty-five years old and she finally slept with a man. She wanted to say it was because she was waiting for the right man. Nothing but a lie. The truth was she had been scared. Scared to open herself up to another person. Scared of how it would end. Scared how they'd react after the fact.

Here was Emmett, saying he loved her. Saying he wanted to marry her. Saying so many things and she still held him at an arm's length. What was wrong with her? She had no idea. No idea whatsoever.

Simple truth—nothing but a scaredy cat. How pathetic. When would Emmett give up? That's what scared her the most. He'd eventually get sick of trying. That should push her to give in to her feelings and tell him she loved him back. Instead, it made her want to pull away even more.

Letting the fear win. Like always.

She rolled away from him, sick inside for wanting what she couldn't have, even knowing she could have everything with little effort.

Even in sleep, Emmett knew when to comfort her. He instinctively moved with her, wrapping an arm around her stomach and pulling her close. Giving in, loving the way his arm held her close, she knew in the morning she'd just pull away again. She didn't know how to stop acting that way. She hated herself for it.

13

DEJA PULLED the blanket around her shoulders and positioned herself a little better on the couch. A nice Sunday afternoon watching baseball was just what she needed. She wished Emmett could enjoy it with her, but after spending all day yesterday helping rebuild part of the corral, he needed to work today for a client who didn't mind he rescheduled yesterday for today.

Of course, most people didn't mind. Not when Emmett called and used his sweet, charming voice to persuade them. Kind of like what he was doing with her.

When he dropped her off at home, kissing her like it was the last time he would see her, she almost asked for the ring back. Almost. The fear held her back. Like always. She wanted to kick herself repeatedly for even taking the thing off. Served her right for acting like an idiot. He loved her. She saw it in everything he said and did. She just had to accept it. Believe it wholeheartedly.

A loud thump sounded.

Turning toward the foyer, her eyes darted immediately to the bag lying by Dare's feet. Slowly trailing upward, she met his gaze. No words came to mind. What could she say? Her brother was abandoning her. She didn't think he'd actually do it. The bag lying on the floor said otherwise.

"It's not what you think."

"Really? Because it looks like you're leaving." She turned away, her eyes glued to the TV like she cared. Suddenly, she didn't anymore. Minnesota was winning, but all she felt was heartbreak.

The couch dipped.

"D, listen to me."

"Just leave, Dare."

Deja tried to pull away when he wrapped an arm around her shoulder. Using his free hand, he rubbed his knuckles over her head, laughing. "Don't laugh. I know you don't wanna."

Swatting at his hand, she pressed her lips together to hold back her laughter, refusing to let him lighten the mood. "Knock it off, you butthead."

He ruffled her head again. "Tell me you love me."

Unable to hold in the giggles, she let loose. "You're a moron."

Squeezing her tightly into his side, he sighed. "Yeah, but you love me, right?"

"I do." Gazing at him, her smile turned into a frown. "Why is your bag on the floor?"

"You're my sister. I love you. I will until the day I die...but I need to work through my shit. I don't think I can do it living here."

"Where are you going? Please don't leave, Dare. I won't bother you. I promise."

"I'm not going far, D. Don't worry. Ethan offered me his spare room."

Deja leaned away, raising a brow. "Seriously? You're going to live with Ethan."

"He's not so bad. The McCords seem like decent people. Emmett loves you. I see you're not wearing the ring he gave you."

She lifted her hand, fingering the bare spot. "I gave it back. I...I need to work through my shit, too." She tipped her lips up into a lopsided grin. "We're something else, uh?"

"He's good for you. I can't believe you broke into someone's home, but I guess you hit the right one." Dare chuckled, shaking his head. "Don't do anything that stupid again, do you hear me?"

Resting her head on his shoulder, she laughed with him. "I like when you act like a big brother. I missed this. Promise you won't leave for good? I don't think I'd be able to handle it."

He kissed the top of her head. "You have my word."

"Are you leaving now?"

"Na, I thought I'd watch the game with you first. What do you say?"

"I like that idea."

Deja wasn't thrilled about him leaving, but she understood. He needed time to himself. To assimilate back into society. Back into her life. Pushing her away the last ten years had taken its toll. He obviously needed to ease his way back in. As long as he didn't leave for good, she'd take whatever he was willing to offer.

She didn't want to lose her brother again.

EMMETT SHOWERED AS QUICKLY as he could, then hopped out and dressed. He grabbed his duffle bag from the top shelf in his closet and shoved a couple sets of clothes inside with some toiletries.

Maybe he was being a little too presumptuous, but oh well. When it came to Deja, he needed to continue to stay strong and in her face. If he gave her too much time to think, she'd pull away from him even more.

He was slowly making progress, even after his fumbling by insisting she marry him without asking. He had no idea what possessed him to do that, but he didn't regret it. Although, a little planning would've been helpful. He couldn't change anything now. He'd just have to convince her to put the ring back on her finger. Which meant he couldn't give her too much space.

He zipped the duffle bag closed and locked up his house, the ring nestled snugly in his pocket. He wanted to be prepared for the moment when she changed her mind. She had to change her mind. He loved her too much to lose her.

After a long day of hard work clearing out a client's yard that was overgrown with too many weeds, he was ready for some fun with Deja. The client neglected their property for too long. Those jobs were the worst, but he always found peace in that kind of work. Especially today. The more he exerted himself, the easier it was to get his frustration out.

Dare also eased some of it. He called an hour ago explaining he'd be staying with Ethan for a while. Deja needed him. Emmett had every intention of seeing Deja tonight regardless, but Dare's phone call made it even better. They'd have the house to themselves. It would've been a little awkward spending the night with Dare in the house, but he would've done it.

He didn't ask why Dare decided to stay with his brother, but thanked him for the heads up. They didn't get along when they first met, but now it was like they were friends.

He preferred it that way. If—no—*when* he married Deja, he wanted Dare to accept him. Getting on his bad side would be the worst thing.

Thirty minutes later, Emmett parked in her driveway. With a quick knock, he repositioned the containers in his hand while he waited for her to answer.

The door swung open.

Sadness mingled with happiness shined at him. He grinned as he lifted the Chinese food in his hands. "I bought your favorites."

She nodded to the duffle bag. "And what's that?"

"Well, we haven't had a sleepover in a long time..."

"We had one last night." Her brow rose in defiance.

"Not really. We didn't even play spin the bottle." He produced a pout, his signature one, and tried his hardest not to laugh when a hand went to her hip to go with her stern look.

"Are we going to play truth or dare as well?"

"Of course. We're going to stay up late, too. It's not a sleepover unless you do." He poured a little more poutiness into his expression until she finally cracked a grin.

"Get in here. I'm starving." She held open the door.

Emmett stepped in, tossed his bag near the stairs, and headed for the kitchen where he laid the containers on the table. He grabbed some plates from the cupboard while she grabbed some drinks for them.

Converging to the table at the same time, Emmett set the plates down and quickly pulled her into his arms before she could walk away.

"I missed you."

She rolled her eyes. "It hasn't been that long."

Kissing her lips, lingering for a deep one, he pulled her against his body. She always fit so perfectly.

"Long enough." He placed a light kiss upon her nose. "Dare called me. How are you?"

"Fine."

Brushing a hand down her hair and onto her back, he kissed her lips one more time. "Let's try that again. How are you?"

Biting her bottom lip, she said nothing. Just as suddenly, she tucked her head between his neck and shoulder. A shudder rippled through her. "I know he needs his space. I honestly get it. It still hurts."

Rubbing her back up and down, he tried to soothe her as best as he could. "Kinda how you need your space from me. Am I coming on too strong? I don't mean to."

Tightening her arms around him, she placed a soft kiss against his neck. "I like you right where you are."

"Good." He kissed the side of her head and then gently pulled her back. "Let's eat before I toss the food to the floor and have my wicked way with you on the table."

A dangerous gleam entered her eyes. "I like the sound of that."

He laughed. "Me, too. A little too much. Food first, ravishing second. Because I know how much you hate cold Chinese food. I'll never forget the tantrum you threw when we worked late that one night and the food got cold."

Taking a seat across from him, she pursed her lips. "I do not throw tantrums. I don't pout like you do."

"You do throw tantrums. And you're oh so adorable when you do." He winked, earning a death glare worthy of a threat to get her tire iron. "Like now. So damn beautiful."

"Sock it, E-man. Eat your food."

He started to scoop some food onto his plate, debating his words. If they were going to have a relationship, one that would last, they needed to be honest with each other. They had to work through their issues.

"Why do you always deflect compliments? You're beautiful. I'm going to say it as often as I can."

Her brows dipped, yet she didn't say anything.

Nodding at her silence, he knew when to retreat. For now, anyway. "We're playing truth or dare later."

Lifting her eyes, she stared at him questioningly. "Oh, yeah? Why's that?"

"Because you have to at a sleepover." He grinned—a sweet grin. "And maybe you'll actually talk to me."

She dropped her eyes to the food on her plate, tossing the fork around, yet scooping none of it up. "I'm scared, Emmett. I don't do talking well."

Reaching for her hand, he lifted it gently and kissed her. "Me neither. But I hate the pain in your eyes. Let me take it away."

She slowly raised her gaze. "I'm not sure it's possible."

Kissing her hand again, he smiled tenderly. "Yes, it is. I'm going to prove it to you. Because I love you."

Her frown slowly turned into a small smile. Hope, for the first time, rose within his heart. Before now, he had been deathly afraid she'd never open up to him. The look in her eyes said otherwise.

That's all that mattered. He'd do anything to take that tormented look in her eyes away. Anything.

THE BAG DROPPED to the floor with a loud thud. Dare glanced around the room, appreciating the simplicity of it. A big queen-size bed took up the middle of the room. A plain brown dresser stood against the wall near the window. The

closet door stood open, a few large jackets hanging, otherwise empty. No knickknacks. No pictures on the walls. Just
simple. The way he liked it. Wanted it. It reminded him of
his cell.

Wasn't that interesting? Shit. Not what he wanted to
think about, yet here he was thinking how he missed the
simplicity of his cell. He didn't hang shit on the wall there.
Didn't keep anything in his cell. On a rare occasion, he
sometimes left a book in the room, reading it at a leisurely
pace. Even then, it felt like too much clutter.

Clutter. He could never keep his room clean. His mother
had always nagged him about it. "Why can't you be like your
sister and keep your room clean?" He couldn't count how
many times he heard that from her.

Well, why couldn't she act like a mother? Now she never
could. Not anymore. Because of him.

It's funny how he resorted to his bad habit in Deja's
house, leaving his clothes lying wherever he felt like tossing
them. But here, he would keep it neat and clean. Just like he
had the last ten years. He needed that structure. Otherwise,
he'd go out of his mind.

He needed space. Telling Deja today he was leaving tore
his heart out just like the first time he left her ten years ago.
Seeing that look of devastation on her face—he couldn't
stand it. He also couldn't stop it. Explaining why he needed
his space was impossible. How did he explain he felt guilty
as hell? That he could hurt her. He was nothing but a
danger to her.

He killed their parents. Who knew when he'd end up
hurting his sister? He couldn't allow that to happen. Trying
to explain that to her wouldn't go well. She wouldn't understand. He knew it. She'd just argue with him and tell him he
didn't know what he was talking about. It was an accident.

It was no damn accident. More like idiocy and selfishness. Plain and simple.

A knock sounded behind him.

"Yo, want a beer?"

Dare turned toward Ethan and nodded. "Yeah, I'll be right out there."

"Take your time." Ethan grinned and walked away.

Dare had been surprised as hell when Ethan offered him one of his rooms. One minute he was half pouring his heart out about hurting his sister, the next minute Ethan was offering him a place to stay. Ethan just knew. He just knew he needed his space.

He knew his sister didn't want him to drink. He saw the way she looked at him when they were at the farm yesterday. The piercing glare from her bore a hole in his stomach from the guilt of having a simple beer. What did she think would happen? He'd drink, get behind the wheel, and hurt someone else?

He laughed at the lunacy of it. Hell, he hadn't been drunk that night. He had been high. Perhaps she thought drinking would lead him down the path of drugs. It wouldn't. He'd kill himself before he touched one little drug ever again. Never again.

At least at Ethan's house he could have a drink and not feel guilty as hell about it. He might feel an ounce of regret with the first swallow, but after that, he'd feel nothing but numbness.

Numb felt like a good feeling to him. Just wash all these horrible emotions away.

Dare walked out to the living room and swiped the extra beer from the coffee table before taking a seat on the couch.

"Get settled in?"

"Dude, I had one bag."

Ethan touched the tip of the beer bottle to his lips. "True."

"Thanks, man. I appreciate you letting me stay here for a while."

"No prob. How'd Deja take it?" Ethan reached for his phone on the coffee table. "Maybe I should call Emmett to check on her."

Dare smiled. His sister sure found a great family that cared about her. If he ever left for good—no. He wouldn't leave. He told her he wouldn't. He just had to work through this shit.

"I called him. He should be over there already." He fiddled with the label on the bottle. "She wasn't wearing the ring this morning. I felt bad for calling him, thinking maybe they got into a fight or something, but I did anyway. He's good for her...even if he is an asshole sometimes."

Ethan chuckled. "Aren't we all assholes at some point?" His face fell somber. "Maybe I scared him into rushing things. Emmett was burned by a woman once, and I rushed him into asking her to marry him. The same night he almost does, she confesses she cheated on him. Maybe I should stop trying to mess with his love life."

Dare laughed, slapping his knee a little. "Shit, man. Maybe you should."

Ethan gave him a cocky grin and shrugged. "Na, I don't think I could if I tried." His finger hovered over the phone. "You sure he was going over there? I know she's your sister, but she feels like mine, too. I just want to make sure she's okay. I hope she doesn't hate me for offering you a room. I just—she wasn't pissed at me, was she?"

"She wasn't pissed. Emmett said he was planning to go over there regardless. She never made it home last night, so I imagine your brother is happy as a clam I won't be there so he can spend the night. I didn't ask why she didn't have the ring. I don't think she'd talk to me about it."

"Too weird of a conversation, huh?"

Dare grinned deviously. "No. I'd kick Emmett's ass if he hurt her. So if he did, she wouldn't tell me, because she wouldn't want me to hurt him."

"Then I'd have to kick your ass for kicking his ass...could get awkward around here."

Dare tapped his beer bottle with Ethan's as they laughed together. "Better hope your brother doesn't hurt my sister then."

"Or the other way around. Not that I'd hit a girl...but Deja could end up hurting Emmett."

"Yeah, we're both messed up. It might happen."

Ethan frowned as he eyed his phone again. "That's what I'm afraid of."

14

"TRUTH OR DARE?"

"Stop."

His hand slid down her arm, circling her stomach, before resting just below her breast. "Truth or dare?"

"Emmett, honestly, we're not playing that game. It's late. We should go to bed."

His tongue grazed her nipple playfully, then blew a soft breath against it. "We're playing the game. I insist. You promised."

Scoffing, she playfully swatted his hand away from attacking her other breast. "I never promised any such thing."

"Are you sure?" He cocked a brow, a devilish grin playing on his face.

"Stop."

Snatching a kiss, he shook his head. "I can't help it. I like having sleepovers with you."

He loved them, actually. His very first sleepover he ever had with her was not a happy memory. Almost a year ago, they had their first one. While he had fun with Deja and

Sophie, the reason for staying with them wasn't a good one.

Austin had been in New York on vacation and found out Sophie's ex was hell-bent on coming to find Sophie and hurt her. Emmett had stepped in, reassuring Austin no one would harm Sophie. It had been the first time he had the opportunity to get to know Deja.

The first time he laid eyes on her, he almost lost his breath. Spending the night, even as platonic as it had been, with Sophie in attendance as well, it had driven his emotions home with clarity. He was pretty sure he fell in love with her back then. That quick. Hiding it was impossible. He wouldn't. Not anymore.

Trailing kisses down her chin to her neck to her breast and slowly to her belly button, he swirled his tongue a few times before lifting his head. "Truth or dare?"

Deja rolled her eyes. "Fine. Dare."

A slow grin grew. "I dare you to put the ring back on your finger."

She froze, her body suddenly taut with tension. He almost cursed himself for making her feel that way when she began to relax as quickly as she had tensed up. "I changed my mind. Truth."

His grin refused to disappear, even knowing she'd hate truth just as much. "Why are you afraid of what's happening between us?"

She turned away, her breaths deep and harsh. "Why are you doing this, Emmett? Why can't we just enjoy each other?"

He sat up, trying his damndest not to get pissed. It was useless. And his own damn fault for bringing it up. "This isn't just a fun time between the sheets for me, Deja. This is real. What's between us is real. I love you."

"Stop saying that."

He leaned down into her face, inches from her sweet lips. "Make me."

"What are we, a child? Make me? Seriously."

Cracking a grin, he moved his mouth a little closer. "Naner naner boo boo. I love you."

She couldn't suppress a laugh, no matter how hard she tried to keep it in. "You're not funny, you know."

He brushed his lips with hers. "Then why are you laughing?"

"I don't want to play this game anymore."

He kissed her hard, demanding she release the passion lingering within. She obediently listened as she wrapped her arms around him, then slowly brushed her hands up his back and through his hair. Without breaking contact, the kiss deepening stronger than ever before, his hand fumbled near her nightstand. With a quickness he never knew was possible, he donned on the condom and entered her with one swift thrust, thankful they had been lying in bed naked.

She moaned into his mouth, the kiss never stopping as he started to move in and out of her with complete abandon. She didn't want to play that game. Fine. He'd play a totally different one. A game of love. He would show her at every available opportunity what she meant to him. She would eventually see what they had was real. They were real. Meant to be together. Forever.

Grasping her cheeks, he kept the pace slow and steady. She met every deep thrust with just as much enthusiasm as she did with their sweet kissing. Her fingers threaded through his hair, down his back, and grabbed his ass, holding on tightly. Nothing felt better than her hands anywhere, everywhere on him.

The pace picked up. Her moans became louder between

their kisses. He let go of her cheeks and her lips and grabbed her legs, lifting them to his shoulders, getting as deep as he could while thrusting as hard as he could.

"I love you, Deja. Forever. Believe it. Believe this. If it takes doing this every single night to prove it, I will."

"Shut up, Emmett." She closed her eyes as pure bliss crossed over her face, her hands clenching the sheets.

His body tightened in pleasure as they both came together in ecstasy. The beautiful feeling of loving her washed over him. She was perfect in every possible way. Even when she told him to shut up.

Which she liked to do a lot.

He collapsed on top of her, snuggling his face into the crook of her neck. He smiled, then placed tiny kisses while they both tried to come down from the high.

"You tell me to shut up a lot."

"That's because you talk too much."

He pressed a tender kiss close to her ear. "Or that's your way of saying I love you."

She tensed briefly. There it was. Enough to convince him what he said was true. She loved him. She was just too scared to say the words.

"Don't worry, honey. I won't rush you into saying it. You just keep telling me to shut up. I hear it every time you say those words."

"Emmett, shut up."

He grinned at Sophie, who chuckled at their byplay. "Don't worry, Soph, she's not mad at me. That's just her way of saying I love you."

Deja turned away from the kitchen sink, and with her

soapy hands, pushed Emmett toward the exit. "Get out. Leave us to clean up the dishes."

"Tell me one more time to shut up."

She rolled her eyes. "Shut up."

He snatched a kiss, winked, and walked out. Deja sighed, then turned back toward the sink. Ignoring Sophie and the questioning look on her face was hard to do. Impossible, in fact. Especially when she stood so close to her and grabbed a clean plate from the drip-dry and started to wipe it dry with a white dish towel.

"Just ask already."

Sophie softly laughed. "I'm the last person who'd make you talk if you don't want to, you know that. Is this you wanting to talk?"

"Thanks for making supper again tonight. I think Dare's starting to fit in with everyone. Surprisingly, I think it's Ethan who's helping a lot. Who would've thought?"

Sophie's brow rose slowly at her dodging the real talk she should be doing, but didn't say anything about it. "I don't mind cooking. I'm glad Dare's sticking around for you. I know you were worried about that."

"I was worried. Still am, a little." She stopped washing the plate. "He honestly thinks when I tell him to shut up that I mean to say I love you. Ridiculous."

"Do you? Love him, I mean."

"I'm not sure I know how to love. Growing up...my life wasn't filled with a lot of love. My parents were so involved in themselves, they rarely paid attention to Dare and I. What does Emmett even see in me? I'm a criminal. A complete mess."

"You're someone who made a mistake, nothing more. I know he hates it when you put yourself down, and so do I." Deja turned to look at Sophie when her voice held a lot more sternness than normal, then she continued, "Austin's not fond of it when I put myself down. We all have insecurities, Deja. It's not easy overcoming them, but it's possible. Emmett won't give up on you. So don't give up on yourself."

"I don't know what I did to ever deserve such a wonderful guy."

"I think the same thing every day. We're just two lucky women, and that's that." Sophie smiled brightly as she grabbed another plate to dry.

"Any word on that douche bastard?"

Sophie pierced her with a hard look. "Language, please."

"Not when it comes to that asshat. I'm sorry, Soph. I have a few more dirty words to say about him."

Sighing, Sophie nodded. "The prosecutor wants me to testify. I don't want to. Austin and I have...sort of argued about it. I'm not sure why they need me to. Of course, Kevin is trying to twist it that I hurt myself before Austin walked into the room. And then is insisting that Austin attacked him for no reason."

"The jury actually believes that shit?"

Sophie shrugged. "The prosecutor must be a little nervous if she wants me to testify." Her breath hitched. "I can't. I just can't, Deja. I already relive what he did to me in my nightmares. I can't relive it in front of a bunch of people. I just want him to leave me alone. Leave the state. That's all I want."

Deja placed a soapy hand on her shoulder. "Then you do what you're comfortable with. Nobody, especially Austin, is going to let that bastard get his hands on you again. He'll get his just reward one day. Trust me." She lifted her hand and laughed. "Whoops. Sorry about the sudsy mess."

Sophie laughed with her and pulled her into a hug. "You're the best friend anyone could ask for."

"Ditto, Soph."

Sophie let her go and picked up another plate. "I love you, Deja. You're like a sister to me."

Deja willed herself not to cry. "I love you, too. I always wanted a sister."

"That wasn't so hard to say."

"What?"

"I love you."

Deja crinkled her brows in confusion. "Of course not. I do love you. I even tell Dare that."

Sophie looked at her with a perplexed expression. "I know you love Emmett. He knows it, too. Why is it hard to say it to him?"

Her mouth opened, then closed just as quickly. Why was it hard? She honestly couldn't say. Perhaps because no man had ever loved her. They always saw her as a warm body good for one thing—sex. Emmett saw her as so much more. She knew this. Yet letting him in was difficult. What happened if he took her love and broke her heart? He had the power to do it.

She pressed her lips together and shook her finger in a naughty gesture. "You tricked me."

Sophie's lips tipped up into a sweet grin. "Just showing you that you can say the words. You know how to love." A slow breath left her body. "I'm scared every day. That's what Kevin did to me. But I fight that emotion every day. I let Austin in. I let him love me, and I love him back. It's okay to be scared. There's nothing wrong with that. And it's okay to let the love in. Austin taught me that."

"And if he breaks my heart?" Deja bit her lip, shocked she said that.

"That's what best friends are for." Sophie grinned

wickedly, then tossed her head toward the living room. "And brothers."

"Brothers? I only have one."

Sophie shook her head with such animation. "You have five. Dare, Austin, Zane, Ethan, and Gabe. They might be Emmett's family, but you know they'd let Emmett know just how dumb he was if he hurt you. Trust me."

Deja never thought of it that way. She knew Dare would be on Emmett in a heartbeat if he hurt her. That's one reason she didn't like to mention anything to him concerning Emmett. But the others? Would they stick up for her? Sophie seemed so convinced they would.

"Let the love in. If Austin hadn't captured my heart, I probably would've fallen for Emmett. He's the sweetest, kindest man I ever met besides Austin."

Deja pulled the plug and watched the water run down the drain in a slow, dizzying manner. She could picture Sophie and Emmett together. Emmett adored Sophie so much. At the start of Sophie and Austin's relationship, she almost thought Emmett liked Sophie a little too much, but he swore he didn't. After a while, she believed him. Trusted him. So it shouldn't be hard to say the words I love you and ask for the ring back.

Oh, but it was.

Folding the rag over the middle portion of the sink, Deja looked at Sophie and grinned a very devious grin. "I need to go tell Emmett to shut up."

Sophie giggled. "You go do that. He'll love to hear it."

She might not be able to say the actual words, but if he thought two simple words—shut up—meant she loved him, then she would say it at every available opportunity until the real words could pass through her lips. Until she overcame her fear.

One day she'd stop being scared. Today wasn't that day. But soon. Because she was no coward.

DARE PROPPED his foot over his knee, leaning leisurely into the couch as Austin, Emmett, and Ethan all chatted together. He didn't have much to add. The things he did want to add probably wouldn't go over well with these guys.

He couldn't stand to hear Austin talking about the way Sophie was hurt by this Kevin guy. Such a sweet woman, it was difficult to imagine anyone laying a finger on her.

He wouldn't call himself a violent man, not even being locked up ten years for killing his parents. That was an— shit. He wasn't going there, thinking such things that everyone had been telling him recently. He refused to believe it was an accident.

Still, he wasn't a violent man. But for Sophie, he'd be one. He wanted to track down this Kevin guy for hurting her, for making her terrified every day of her life. He didn't need to know her to feel the rage flowing through his veins. No man should hit a woman. Plain and simple.

He may not be violent, but he did spend the last ten years in prison. He made friends. Some of those friends were violent. One little word from him and they'd do whatever he asked. Two of his friends immediately came to mind. He saved both their asses from a serious beating. They owed him. Yet he knew these gentlemen surrounding him wouldn't go for it. They weren't evil men like him.

No matter how much he wanted to deny it. That's what he was. Evil. A danger to others.

"You know, Austin, I know you want to see that bastard

behind bars, but putting Sophie on the stand—I don't know, man." Emmett rubbed his face to suppress a groan.

"I know. I don't know why I'm arguing with her about it. I don't want to put her through that pain. I deal with it enough at night. I just...he can't walk. I told the prosecutor I'd take the stand and swear under oath that I saw him with his foot against her throat. She thinks with the way Kevin's attorney has been portraying me that it won't sway the jury much."

Ethan swore under his breath at Austin's words. "Well, shit. He's portraying Sophie like she has mental issues and hurt herself. Is putting her on the stand really going to sway the jury? I mean, come on. Is he paying some of the jurors? I wouldn't put it past him. He has tons of money."

"I never thought of that," Emmett said, then glanced at Austin. "Do you think that's possible? Maybe he's even bribing the prosecutor. She doesn't need Sophie on the stand. There are plenty of photos to show how badly he beat her." Emmett rubbed his face again. "I can still see it in my mind."

"Me, too, Emmett. Me, too. I could throw up just thinking about it." Austin rested his head against the couch and sighed. "It's possible he's using his money to get off. I never thought of it that way. This is just another way for Kevin to torture Sophie. Will it ever stop?"

"I can make it stop."

Dare couldn't believe he just said that. But damn it. He couldn't stand to hear any more. He was willing to beat the shit out of Kevin himself. Be damned the consequences. It'd be worth going back to prison.

Three sets of eyes turned to him in unison. All of them stared at him with confusion until a light bulb must've gone off in Emmett's head. He leaned forward on the recliner, jabbing a finger in his direction as his face morphed into anger.

"Don't you do anything stupid, Dare. Deja would crawl into a hole and never come out if you went back to prison. She's already almost climbing into a damn hole."

Ethan nodded. "She'd never survive—emotionally—if you got sent back. Emmett's right. Stay clean."

Dare shrugged. "I never said I would do anything, just that I could make it stop. He'd learn his lesson. I can get the case to turn in your favor. That's all."

Austin sat next to him, tense, his facial expression giving nothing away of what he was thinking. He glanced toward the kitchen, then leaned closer to him as he whispered, "I don't know you well yet, Dare, but I know Deja. What my cousins are saying is true. She wouldn't take it well, and she'd be pissed at you." Austin sighed. "That being said, I don't want Sophie living in fear."

"Austin..." Emmett warned.

Austin whipped his head toward Emmett, whispering harshly, "You don't hear her scream at night in terror. It breaks my heart."

"Come on, man. Do you think teaching Kevin a lesson, as Dare put it, will stop her nightmares?" Ethan asked honestly.

Rubbing his jaw, as if contemplating the question with earnest, Austin shrugged. "No, but if the prospect of having to testify would disappear and he's sent away to prison, maybe then they would. That bastard deserves it. He should be six feet under."

Emmett cleared his throat. "We're not having this conversation. Dare isn't a killer, no matter how much he believes it."

Dare cocked a grin. "Your faith in me astounds me."

"Don't be a dickhead," Emmett snapped.

He laughed heartily, but not too loud. "Don't call me names."

"All right, enough." Ethan glanced between the two, eyeing them both with a look that said he'd pop one of them with a fist if they didn't stop. "Austin never meant he wanted to kill him. Right, Austin?"

"Yeah. I'm a lover, not a fighter." Austin gave a wicked smile, yet his eyes reflected so much anguish.

"I never said the guy would die, just be taught a lesson. One he would never forget." Dare set his foot to the ground and leaned forward, resting his elbows on his knees. "I wasn't going to say anything, but I couldn't take it anymore. I don't know Sophie. I barely know you guys. But Deja has accepted you as her family, which, like Zane said the other day, makes you my family, too. I protect my family. I protected Deja all the way until I couldn't anymore. I regret that every damn day."

Dare flicked a glance toward the kitchen, then his eyes landed on Austin. "I have friends on the outside. I haven't said hi to them yet. I'm sure they'd be more than happy to give Kevin a little advice."

"Advice?" Austin raised a brow questioningly, although the look in his eyes said he knew what Dare meant. "Why would they give anyone *advice* for you?"

"Saved their asses a few times in prison. That's why we're friends. Sophie's sweet. She's been kind to me since the moment we met. I don't like to hear these things about her. It pisses me off."

Austin grinned. "Pisses me off, too. I can't keep secrets from her. Trust is very important between us. I...I want nothing more than to teach Kevin a lesson, but I can't ask you to do that. I could never lie to Sophie about it. Although she hates him, she wouldn't like knowing we had a hand in something like that."

Dare nodded and sat back. "Offer stands if you change your mind."

"Now that we settled that little issue, let's not bring it up again." Emmett glared at him.

He nodded, assuring Emmett he wouldn't do anything stupid. His two friends could be discreet. Austin didn't want to lie to Sophie. Well, Dare would make it so he wouldn't have to. What Austin didn't know wouldn't hurt him, and he wouldn't have to lie—not even a tiny little lie.

He never planned to contact his friends once he hit the outside world, wanting to separate that life with his new one. Not anymore. For Sophie, he'd contact them. Kevin would soon learn a lesson he'd never forget.

15

EMMETT RUBBED HIS JAW, the numbers blurring like crazy in front of him. Trying to concentrate on work while the woman of his dreams sat on the opposite side of the wall was hard. She was wearing a simple white blouse that hugged her chest nicely and a sweet skirt that came just above her knees. A little too sexy for his tastes. Completely work appropriate, but for his imagination, not good at all.

The last two weeks had been the best two weeks of his life. Deja still hadn't said I love you or taken his ring back, but it didn't matter. Still the best two weeks ever. If she didn't spend the night at his house, he was at hers. They were inseparable. She loved to tell him to shut up—a lot. One of these days, she'd express her love in a different way. With the real words.

He was a patient man. He'd wait forever if he had to. She was worth the wait.

"Wanna grab a pizza and head to my house tonight?"

Emmett looked up from his paperwork that he hadn't been focusing on for the last five minutes and smiled at

Deja, who stood in his doorway looking even sexier than she had this morning.

She had taken her hair out of her ponytail, her long tresses hanging beautifully down her back with a few curls lying gently on her shoulders. Gorgeous. He loved when she wore her hair down, which wasn't often. She enjoyed pulling it back in a simple ponytail for work, and a messy bun on her off time. Maybe if he told her how he loved it long and loose, she'd wear it down more often.

"Emmett?" She grinned sweetly. "Did you hear me?"

Nodding slowly, he stood up. "Your beauty leaves me speechless sometimes."

She rolled her eyes. "Shut up. Are you ready to go? I'm starving."

"I love you, too." He chuckled as he grabbed his light coat slung across the back of his chair. "Your plan sounds great."

Looping her arm through his, they walked out together and hopped in his truck. He had gotten in the habit of bringing her to work every day. Most days, he dropped her off at work, then headed off to whatever location he was needed at. At the end of the day, either he'd swing by to pick her up right away, or stop in the office and do paperwork, then leave with her. Life would be even better if they moved in together.

Bringing that up would be a huge no-no. Although, the words lingered on the tip of his tongue almost every day.

She threw the ring back at him. Refused to say the actual words of love. Moving in? Yeah, that would never happen. Not even if he exerted his dominance, which she always responded well to in the moment. Once she had time to think, that's when it all went downhill. He could only throw her off for a brief moment. There's no way he'd want her to move into his house, then move out the next day.

When should he bring it up? Losing her wasn't an option. Life had been great the last two weeks. He didn't want to do anything to ruin that. Asking her to move in with him could potentially ruin everything.

Thirty minutes later, they made it to Deja's house with a large pepperoni pizza with extra onions. Deja flipped the baseball game on as Emmett grabbed some plates and napkins from the kitchen. Plopping down next to her, he filled her plate up and then handed it to her.

"Always a gentleman. Stop spoiling me."

Kissing the corner of her mouth with a chaste kiss, he grinned. "Never, my beautiful. I enjoy spoiling you too much. You're lucky I love driving you around. I might spoil you by buying you a car."

She dropped the pizza and gave him a serious glare, the kind that said he better be joking. "Don't you dare."

Grabbing another small kiss, he laughed. "I did say I love driving you around."

"Emmett..."

"Eat your pizza, honey."

"Promise me you won't buy me a car. I'm like Sophie in that regard. I can take care of myself."

"The pizza's getting cold."

"I'll hurt you with my tire iron if you buy me a car."

"I love it when you talk dirty to me."

"I'm not joking here. Tire iron, in my hand, bashing commence."

He cocked a sexy grin. "Tell me more."

Suddenly laughing uncontrollably, she playfully slapped his shoulder. "How do you do that?"

"Do what?"

"Make me laugh when I'm trying to be serious."

"Because I love you. It just comes easy to me."

She opened her mouth, hesitated, then sighed as she muttered softly, "Shut up."

"It'll come out real one of these days." He winked, then loaded up his own plate full of pizza.

He started to take a bite when a knock sounded on the door. Before he could set his plate down, the door swung open.

"Hey, Austin. What's the matter? Is Sophie okay?" Deja stood up as soon as Austin rushed into the living room with quick steps.

Emmett slowly set his plate down. His cousin looked pale and frightened. "What's the matter, man?"

"Kevin...he...Sophie..."

Deja fisted her hands as her lips turned harsh. "Did he hurt her again?"

Austin ran a hand through his hair as he shook his head.

"Shit." Emmett leaned into the couch cushion, afraid to look at her.

"What happened? What's going on?" Deja's head jerked back and forth between them. "Emmett?"

He looked at her, not wanting to voice what he figured had happened. He turned toward Austin as he stood up. "Is Sophie okay? Just spit it out."

"She's fine. She's crying of all things, but she's okay." Austin rubbed his jaw, so much so that it started to turn red.

"Damn it, Austin! Quit messing around. What the hell happened? She's okay, but she's crying? That makes no sense." Deja walked around the coffee table and got into his face. "I'll beat it out of you."

"You know what's amazing, Deja. You threaten that a lot, but I know you'll never do anything about it. It's all talk. A few weeks ago, I thought the same about Da—" Austin stopped talking, clearly regretting the few words he just said.

Emmett moved closer and pulled Deja into his side. "What happened to Kevin? How bad is it?"

Austin sighed. "He's dead."

Deja gasped, her eyes round with shock. Emmett rubbed her arms to soothe her. Soothe himself a little. Not good. At. All.

Without any warning, she ripped herself out of his arms.

"A few weeks ago? Please, finish your sentence, Austin." Her eyes spewed with venom. "You think Dare killed Kevin. How did he die? Because my brother is not a killer!"

Austin opened his mouth, hesitated, then blurted, "I'm not saying he did. Officer Dorscher stopped by to tell us. He said it was a robbery gone bad. Two people mugged Kevin as he was getting out of his car and they shot him. Right now, they don't have any suspects."

"Why would Sophie cry over him?" Deja's expression was still hard with anger. "Why do I get the feeling you still think Dare had something to do with this?"

Austin pressed his lips together like he didn't want to say anything, yet his eyes said he did. Emmett decided to give him a reprieve. "He told me, Austin, and Ethan he could teach Kevin a lesson. That he had two friends who'd be more than willing to do that. Two people just mugged him. It's a little difficult to think he didn't have something to do with it. Although, he said he didn't want the guy dead."

"Get out. Both of you. My brother would never do something like that. It was just talk. He wouldn't do something so stupid." Deja pushed past Austin and swung the door open. "Get out!"

Austin eyed him with a mixture of guilt and sorrow, then

he turned around and stepped outside without a word. Emmett wasn't about to do the same thing.

"Let's talk about this. Let's finish our pizza and talk—"

"If you think I'm joking about getting my tire iron like Austin seems to believe, you're going to soon learn a lesson of your own, Emmett. Get out. I'm done talking. My brother is not a bad person. He's not a dangerous, violent man. He made a mistake with my parents, but he isn't a murderer."

Emmett saw the fierceness in her eyes. The truth in her posture. She wasn't about to budge and let him stay. Damn Austin! He could've called him to talk about the possibility of Dare being involved. Why did he have to bust into the house like he had?

He walked to the door and stopped in front of her. "Fine. I'll leave, but this is far from over. I love you, and if you think I'm just going to walk away because you're a little upset right now, you're wrong."

He stepped outside, wanting to grab a kiss before he did, but didn't want to test her. She had a distinct look in her eyes that said she wanted to hit him.

The door slammed behind him. A loud clicking of the lock right after.

"I'm sorry, Emmett. I didn't think. I just reacted."

He swung his attention to the porch swing. Austin sat there, lightly pushing the swing with the tip of his foot. Emmett took a seat next to him.

"We should go talk to Dare. Did you say anything to Officer Dorscher?"

"I didn't say a thing. I didn't even say anything to Sophie about the possibility. She'll be so mad at me if she finds out I was hiding something like this from her. Is it horrible to not feel bad he's dead?"

"I don't know. I honestly don't. Because I don't feel bad either."

"I can't leave Sophie alone right now."

Emmett nodded. "I'll go talk to him."

They stood up together. Austin walked down the porch steps first. Emmett slowly trailed behind him. Austin turned slightly. "I'm sorry. Now Deja's pissed at you. I didn't mean for that to happen."

"It'll be fine."

Austin gave him a look as if he didn't believe that.

"Don't worry about it, Austin. We'll be fine."

With a quick nod, Austin hustled back to his house as Emmett headed for his truck. What would happen when he confronted Dare about Kevin? Was he involved?

As much as he believed it, he wanted to look the other way. Kevin was a dangerous man. He hurt Sophie so badly he didn't deserve to live anymore. Yet, they weren't judge and executioner. Dare didn't have the right to make that kind of decision. Emmett couldn't let it slide. He'd have to tell the police. Dare would go back to prison. No doubt about that.

Deja would never forgive him.

DARE STRETCHED HIS LEGS, crossing them at the ankles as the dude on the TV droned on about the Minnesotas' latest games and how they needed to keep up the momentum if they wanted to have a great season. Shit, they needed a good season for once. Losing too many seasons in a row put a diehard fan down. And he was a diehard fan, just like his sister. Although, she only loved them because of him.

When they were kids, he would sit in front of the TV for

hours, every single day, and watch baseball. His parents would be doing whatever they did, barely paying attention to them. Deja, too young to be alone, would bring her toys and sit by him. She'd be playing dolls and he'd be watching the game, screaming occasionally at the TV.

He didn't know when it happened, but one day he realized she sat next to him, the dolls not in attendance, and was screaming with him. Those were the memories he liked to relive. The happy ones.

A loud knock sounded on the door.

"Yo, it's open." Ethan sat up.

Emmett stepped into the house, glanced at Ethan and Gabe, who sat together on the couch, then his eyes landed on him. The look of wariness made his skin crawl. Why did he look at him like that? Dare uncrossed his legs, yet made no other move to sit up. Whatever was on Emmett's mind couldn't be good.

"Wanna watch the game with us?" Ethan took a sip of beer, then set it on the coffee table.

Emmett shook his head, then took a seat on the recliner directly opposite of him. He still wouldn't look away.

"You have something to say?" Dare wanted to jump up and get in his face, not sure why he felt compelled to do that. Maybe it was the predatory gleam in Emmett's eyes. He looked pissed.

Gabe and Ethan glanced between them as they stared each other down.

"Kevin's dead. A robbery gone bad." A muscle in Emmett's jaw ticked as if he wanted to say more, but refrained from doing so.

"Shit. You're kidding me. Does Sophie know?" Ethan rested his elbows on his thighs. He flicked a glance at Dare.

Emmett nodded. "Austin told Deja and I."

"Why are you looking at me like I know something about this?" Dare finally sat up a little.

"Gee, I don't know, Dare. Why do you think?" Emmett snapped.

Dare abruptly stood up. Emmett did as well. Ethan, sensing the immediate tension, sprang from the couch and stood between them, almost like a buffer. Gabe stayed in his spot, his eyes darting between everyone.

"Let's all calm down." Ethan held out his hands like it would stop them from advancing at each other. Not that anyone made a move yet. He turned toward Dare. "I think it's a fair question."

"What question, Ethan? I didn't hear a damn question. I just heard an asshole talking." Dare fisted his hands.

Ethan took a deep breath. "Come on, man. You know what we're talking about. You offered to have some of your friends teach Kevin a lesson."

Dare clenched his jaw. Figured. One thing goes sideways and people automatically assumed the worst about him. Shit never changed. To think he thought these people actually liked him, cared about him. Nobody cared but his sister. The one person who shouldn't even care.

"What exactly did you tell my sister?"

For the first time, Emmett's anger slightly dissipated. "Let's just say she kicked us both out of the house. I don't want to believe you were involved, but two people committed the robbery. You said you had two friends...Is this really just all coincidence?"

What was the point? Did anyone ever believe him when he tried to explain shit? No. They always came up with their own conclusions, and anything he said never changed their minds. At least his sister still had faith in him.

Dare cracked a smile and laughed as he loosened his

fists. "You already have it all worked out in your mind. You ain't gonna believe a damn word I say anyway. Well, screw you, Emmett. All of you. You can all go to hell."

"Dare. Yo, man—"

He flipped Ethan the bird as he walked around the couch and down the hallway to his bedroom. He wasn't about to stick around and let them interrogate him. That had happened too much in his life. Dealing with it again, with people he had started to consider his friends, well, shit, he just wasn't sticking around for that.

Tossing his clothes into his bag as quickly as he could, he glanced around the room he had started to think of as home. He had been comfortable here. Ethan was a decent roommate. He didn't pry into his business. After a hard day's work, they would sit around the TV watching the game most nights with a beer or two and unwind. Talk about nothing in particular. He had felt at ease.

Zipping up his bag, he froze. Where would he go now? He didn't want to bother his sister, or deal with the inevitable talk they needed to have. Sure, she kicked out Emmett for thinking something horrible about him. But what did she really think? Did she also think he had some-thing to do with his death? Getting a man killed?

Of course, the bastard deserved it. He didn't know the true extent of how much Kevin hurt Sophie, but even touching one hair on her head warranted a severe beating. Now he was dead. Served him right. Yeah, it had crossed his mind to have his friends give him a little visit, but he changed his mind.

Walking out of the room with the only bag he owned, Dare headed for the front door without looking toward the living room.

"Dare, shit, man, you don't have to leave. No one said

you had anything to do with it." Ethan walked around the couch and stepped into his pathway.

"Get out of my way."

Ethan's face narrowed as if he were going to argue, or even throw a punch first, then stepped to the side. "You don't have to leave."

Dare walked to the door and pulled it open. He finally looked at them. "You know, my whole life I never had anyone believe me about anything. The only person who always stuck by my side was my sister. I guess I just thought you guys might be different. I was wrong. Go to hell."

He slammed the door behind him.

16

———

SOPHIE FIDDLED with the end of the blanket. The tears had finally stopped flowing. She couldn't even understand why she cried. It wasn't sadness that poured out. Relief, maybe.

Definitely relief. Kevin could never hurt her again. He was a dangerous, devious man. He may have displayed nonchalance with everything involved with the case, but she saw the evil in his eyes every time she saw him at the courthouse. He would've eventually done something to her or to someone she loved. She knew it.

Good riddance. The world is a better place without you. God, what a terrible thing to think. What kind of person did that make her? Nobody should have to die the way he had. Or did he? He hurt her so badly.

"Hey, whatever you're thinking, stop. I hate it when you look sad." Austin wrapped his arms around her, pushing her head to rest against his chest. "He's not worth your thoughts."

"It's over. It's surreal. Are you sure he's dead?"

Austin rubbed a hand up and down her arm. "He is. You don't have to worry about him again."

The doorbell rang.

"I'll get it."

Austin stood up before she could argue. Not that she wanted to argue. She had no energy to get the door. She didn't have the energy for anything. Even in death, Kevin controlled her. She didn't want to waste any more time thinking about him, and yet, she couldn't seem to help herself.

"Dare. Hey, man."

Sophie turned her head to see Dare staring at her behind Austin's shoulder. He looked stoic. She stood up and walked to the door.

"I didn't have anything to do with it."

She couldn't stop the confusion from showing. "With what?"

Dare glanced from her to Austin, his lips thinning as he stared at Austin a little too hard. A little too scary for her tastes. She didn't know Dare well, obviously, since they all just met him a few weeks ago. But he was Deja's brother. That's all she needed to know. She trusted him like she trusted everyone in the McCord family. She just wasn't sure she trusted this new look on him right now.

"Austin didn't tell you?"

Sophie turned to Austin, who stiffened beside her. "I guess karma's come to bite me in the ass."

She cleared her throat in warning at Austin's foul language. "What did you do? We don't keep secrets, Austin. You know how I feel about lying."

Austin grabbed her hands, squeezing tightly with reassurance. "Pixie angel, I did not lie about anything." He grimaced with guilt. "Maybe I took my time to tell you something, though."

"Sounds like lying to me."

"I would never lie to you. You know that. I love you."

"Then what's Dare talking about?" She trembled, suddenly afraid to hear what he had to say.

Austin didn't let go of her hands as he looked at Dare, then back at her. "A few weeks ago, Dare offered to teach Kevin a lesson. I declined the offer and that ended the conversation."

Her eyes flew to Dare. "You wouldn't hurt anybody...on purpose."

Dare cracked a smile. "Thanks for believing that. No one else does." He sighed. "I thought about still having my friends doing it after Austin declined, but I didn't."

She slowly brought her eyes back to Austin. He shrugged as he smiled in his sweet, endearing way. "It seemed kinda believable that he had two of his friends do something when he offered it two weeks ago. Two people killed Kevin. It just seemed like a strange coincidence." His eyes rolled to Dare. "I'm sorry. If you say you had nothing to do with it, then I believe you."

"Would've been nice to have that belief without siccing Emmett on me." Dare's frown softened as he looked at Sophie. "I just wanted to say I didn't do anything. Thank you for welcoming me into your home. You're a sweet woman."

Sophie extracted her hands from Austin, ignoring the way his features fell as she did. "Of course. I hope you'll come over still, but I get this feeling you're not going to."

Dare nodded. "I'm hitting the road. Thanks again, Sophie." He turned around.

"Wait." She grabbed his arm, surprising him and herself. Men made her nervous. She'd gotten used to the McCord men, but strangers... It didn't take much for her to break out in a sweat when they got near. Dare was still a stranger, regardless of the fact he was Deja's brother. She only shook his hand when she first met him so she didn't appear rude. "You can't leave Deja. It'll break her heart."

Dare covered her hand with his. "You can't break something that's already broken. Don't worry. I wouldn't hurt my sister any more than she's hurting right now."

"Her heart...it's not broken," Sophie whispered. She knew that was a lie, though, as she stared into Dare's eyes.

"Yeah, it is. Emmett did exactly what she feared he'd do. It's a good thing she kept her distance. It's a good thing I'm leaving peacefully, because once I see her heartache for myself, I'm gonna want to hurt him within an inch of his life." Dare let her hand go and started down the steps, turning slightly when he got to the bottom step. "He failed to realize something. You all did. Love isn't saying it all the time. It's showing it. It's believing in it. Nobody's ever believed in us."

Dare rubbed his jaw, almost as if he were debating his next words. Then he spoke. "A dog ran into the middle of the road the night I was driving. I was high. There's no denying that. But they all swore that dog wasn't real. Everyone. Nobody believed me. Except my sister. Not once did she hesitate about it. She even got into a fistfight at school when someone said I was a damn liar. That's love. An innate ability to believe in that other person without thought. Emmett will never have her love because he doesn't know how to do that."

Dare walked away. Sophie closed the door, unable to watch what way he was planning to go. She sincerely hoped he at least said good-bye to Deja before he disappeared. She'd check on Deja later. Right now, she was so full of different emotions, she wouldn't be useful in any sort of conversation with her.

"Sophie..."

Her head snapped to Austin. She brushed a hand across his cheek. "Stop protecting my feelings. You should've told me right away about that conversation. I don't want to be mad at you, but I can't help it."

He grabbed her hand before she could pull away. "I'll always protect you. No matter what. I didn't tell you because...because thinking about it made me want to find Dare and tell him, 'Yeah, man, teach him a lesson.' That's horrible to even think about."

"No, it's human. Dare has a point. I can see why he's so upset nobody even gave him a chance."

"You don't see our point as well. It's a little strange that happened to Kevin after what he said."

"Maybe. You said karma bit you in the butt. Perhaps karma finally caught up with Kevin. Simple as that."

Austin squeezed her hand tighter when she tried to pull away. "Did karma bite me? It's my fault that Deja's mad at Emmett. I blurted it out in front of her when I should've talked to him alone. How mad are you at me?"

A tear slid down. "I don't want to be mad. I just want this...this weight holding me down to go away."

Austin didn't hesitate. He scooped her into his arms and headed for the stairs. "Let me help with that, my pixie angel. I love you."

"I love you, too, Austin." And she did. With all of her heart. She couldn't be mad at him for keeping what Dare said a secret. She might've been tempted herself to have Dare teach him a lesson. What would Austin say about that? What did that say about her?

Of course, none of that mattered. Kevin was dead. *Good riddance.*

The bedroom door swung closed.

"I THOUGHT you were supposed to keep the door locked."

Deja turned away from the sink and smiled at her brother. "That bastard is dead. No worries anymore. What are you doing here?"

"How pissed are you at Emmett?"

"He confronted you, huh? Well, that just upped my piss-o-meter to dangerous levels."

Dare chuckled as he walked closer to her and leaned against the counter in a nonchalant way. Yet the tension slowly built within the room.

"Thanks for always believing in me."

Deja dried her hands on a towel and then threw it at him with a smile. "You're my brother. I'll always believe in you."

"I'm leaving."

"Dare..."

He put a hand up to stop her from begging him not to leave. And she would beg. She couldn't lose her brother so soon after kicking Emmett out. They both knew what that meant. At least, Emmett should know. She wasn't about to let him back in her house, in her heart, anytime soon after what he insinuated about her brother. Unacceptable. Nobody treated her brother that way.

"I didn't just up and run. I'm saying good-bye. Do I need to pound in Emmett's face for you?"

"What did they say to you?"

He ran a hand through his hair as his brows dipped. "It's what they didn't say. Why is it you're always the only one to believe me? Just once, I'd like other people to give me that chance."

"Well, I guess with your record, paired with what you

said, they just figured it to be true. They don't know you like I do. You're just a big teddy bear. So big and lovable."

"A teddy bear? You're comparing me to a fluffy stuffed animal." He rolled his eyes as he laughed. "That's one for the books."

"I want to come with you."

He glared at her with a stern I'm-not-your-father-but-I'm-acting-like-one look. "You have a good life here. A home. A job. Friends. I don't even know where I'm going. Where I'm going to work. I'll probably bunk down in St. Cloud somewhere. I can't go too far from my parole officer. It's not like I'm leaving for good. I'm just leaving this rinky-dink-ass town."

"This is a house I rent. It's not a home. I have no job because I refuse to work with Emmett anymore. The only real friend I have is Sophie. We're a team. We always have been. Where are we going, partner?"

He shook his head as if he couldn't believe everything she just said. "Where do you wanna go, D?"

She shrugged as a smile crossed her face. "Wherever the adventure takes us, I guess."

"About Emmett—"

"We're not talking about him. Ever. I should've figured he would think the worst about you. You guys never got along when you first met. I can't be with someone who's going to treat you that way. You're my family, and family always comes first. No exceptions. How could a guy like that love someone like me anyway?"

Dare took two steps and pulled her into a hug. A big bear hug. "That's simple. You're amazing. You're beautiful. Any guy would love you. It's his loss. I'm sorry it got screwed up between you two because of me. I'm sorry I act like a jackass half the time."

"Me, too."

Dare let her go with a laugh. "Hey, you're supposed to say there's nothing to be sorry about."

She poked him in the chest. "You do act like a jackass sometimes. But I love you. You did nothing wrong. Emmett and I were never going to work out. We were doomed to fail from the beginning."

He snaked an arm around her shoulder and ruffled her hair. "Love you, too, sis."

"Don't." She shoved him off. "Let me go pack."

"You're okay leaving right away?"

"No time like the present. I do have to say good-bye to Sophie. Other than that, there's nothing left for me here."

And what was left, she didn't want. The memories of Emmett consumed each room. She couldn't walk anywhere in the house without picturing his face. Now, with how it ended, picturing his face would hurt like a knife to the heart each time. She couldn't live like that. Didn't even want to try. Moving on from him was already going to be difficult. Why make it harder on herself?

Part of her wanted to forget what happened today. Rewind the entire night to the moment they were laughing and eating pizza and he made her feel like he honestly cared. She couldn't do that. If Emmett couldn't understand how much Dare meant to her, or believe that he was a good guy, then she couldn't be with him. Because in her mind, believing Dare would do something horrible like that, meant he believed she was just as horrible. That didn't say he loved her at all.

Here she thought all this time she didn't deserve someone great like Emmett. Truth was, he didn't deserve someone like her. She was loyal. She knew true love. She would never turn her back on her brother. Emmett's doubt in him told her he wouldn't hesitate to turn his back on her.

That left her with only one choice. Leaving with Dare. She couldn't look Emmett in the eyes again. She was afraid of what she'd see.

Because she didn't think she'd see the love he always talked about.

Well, she could be glad about one thing. She never caved in to the impulse to ask for the ring back. Or said I love you. Even though she did. She loved Emmett with her whole heart. Too bad he didn't love her the same way.

17

HIS HAND FROZE IN MIDAIR. He didn't want to admit he was almost afraid to find out what happened. Almost. But he needed to know. He didn't sleep well last night, tossing and turning, reaching for the woman he loved, his hand meeting nothing but the coldness of the bed.

Deja was pissed. Beyond pissed. She didn't answer any of his phone calls last night. He called three times. After the third time, he nearly got in his truck and drove to her house, then decided against it. A little time to cool off would be good for her. For them.

It wasn't unreasonable to think Dare had something to do with Kevin's death. He said as much a few weeks ago that he'd teach him a lesson. He also said he wouldn't kill the guy. That right there should've told him that Dare had nothing to do with it. He honestly believed Dare wouldn't do something so dumb that would land him back in prison.

But maybe he didn't know his friends would go that far. Maybe he didn't realize how dangerous his friends were.

Dare left. He was pissed they didn't believe him. He didn't confirm with words that he had nothing to do with it.

His actions, him leaving, said it all. Dare had nothing to do with it. Now, here he was, trying to do some damage control. Except he couldn't find Deja.

This morning, he went to the office first. The darkness that hit his eyes told him right away that something wasn't right. That he screwed up more than he could've ever imagined. Deja didn't even come in to work. She always showed up. Even the time he pissed her off when her brother was first released from prison, she showed up to work. Not today. That scared him more than he cared to admit.

So, he knocked on her door. No answer. The door was locked. The lights were off inside. All he heard when he pressed his ear to the door was silence.

She wasn't home either.

Where did she go?

Sophie would know. He just couldn't find the nerve to knock on her door and find out. Deja left. That's what happened. She left without saying a word to him. That's how badly he screwed up. If he didn't ask Sophie, then he could pretend his whole life wasn't crumbling down around him.

The door swung open. He jerked back.

Austin frowned as he jumped a little himself. "What are you doing? You scared the shit out of me, Emmett."

"Just trying to find the nerve to knock."

"Why?"

"I can't find Deja."

Austin glanced down at his feet. That didn't bode well for him. That confirmed everything Emmett feared. She left. Without a word good-bye.

"Where is she?"

Austin shrugged as he looked at him. "I have no idea. She left last night. She said she was leaving with Dare and nothing Sophie said changed her mind. With what happened with Kevin, added in with Deja leaving, Sophie had a rough night and morning. That's why I'm so late getting to the farm. Zane told me not to worry about anything, but Sophie's finally kicking me out of the house. She claims she's fine now. Of course, I don't believe her, but I thought maybe she just wanted some time alone."

"Does Sophie know what…" Emmett couldn't even finish speaking. He was wrong. They were all wrong for doubting Dare right away. Now look what happened. He lost the woman he loved.

"Dare stopped by before Deja did. I was kinda forced to tell her. Surprisingly, she wasn't too pissed at me. She also didn't doubt Dare. Not like we did. I believe him. I guess it was just coincidence."

"If I would've known Deja was going to leave, I would've never stayed away. I need to talk to her. Are you sure Sophie doesn't know where she went?"

Austin stepped to the side as Sophie lightly pushed him. A small white envelope was pinched between her fingertips. "She wanted you to have this, Emmett. I know you tried your hardest to get behind the walls she built. I don't know where she went, and frankly, I'm not sure I'd tell you if I did know. Dare is everything to her. Doubting him was probably one of the worst things you could've ever done."

Sophie didn't mince her words. They were words he already knew. He screwed up colossally when he voiced his doubt. He nailed the coffin shut when he confronted Dare without thinking about it. The envelope felt like lead in his hand. He didn't know if he could read what she wrote.

"Are you mad at me, Sophie?" Emmett knew he sounded like a lost little child. That's what he felt like at the moment.

He lost so much, especially his heart, in less than twenty-four hours.

"No. You didn't do anything to me. I just feel sad. About everything. I feel like I lost my best friend. I'd like you to leave now, Emmett." She pushed Austin gently. "You, too. Go to the farm. I'll be fine."

Austin grabbed a quick kiss before Sophie basically slammed the door in their faces.

"What just happened?"

Shrugging, Austin slowly made his way down the porch steps. "I got kicked out of my house. You got booted by Sophie, which I thought I'd never see, and you have a letter to read."

Emmett's hand felt hot, as if the letter were burning a hole right through his skin. "I'm not sure I can read it. She left." He squeezed the letter so tightly it crumbled in his hand. "She left without saying a word."

"She didn't even glance my way last night either. Sophie was pretty shaken up about it all, but she understands and respects Deja's decision. It's not like they'll never see each other again."

"And me? Will I ever see her again?"

The look on Austin's face didn't give him much hope. "Don't know, man. I hope so. Read the letter. Maybe it's not that bad. I have to get to the farm."

Emmett said good-bye and dragged his feet as he walked to his truck. Slamming the door shut, he suddenly felt confined. The air in the truck felt thick. Laden with guilt. With regret. He handled everything all wrong yesterday. He knew how Deja felt about Dare. He should've been more sensitive about the issue. Way more supportive than he acted.

"Damn it!" He shook his hand as the aftereffects from

slamming it against the steering wheel vibrated from the tips of his fingers up through his arm.

Taking the crumbled-up envelope, he tore it open. Smoothing out the paper, the words blurred at first.

Emmett,

You can consider this my resignation. I'm sorry for leaving you in the lurch without two weeks notice, but I think it's best we cut ties right away. You know it's best so don't even think about arguing the point. I'm not mad. You probably just laughed at that, but it's not a lie. I'm more sad. It's actually hard to put into words how I really feel. What I do know is we were never meant to be. I had fun. That's about all it was. There wasn't love or happily ever after meant for us. I think you know that. You're a great guy, just not the one for me. Thanks for the good time. Best of luck finding another secretary. I am sorry about that, but there isn't much I can do about it. I will

Deja

What a load of shit! Every single word. She honestly expected him to believe this. Never. He didn't believe one word. The part she crossed out at the end. What was she going to write? He was dying to know.

The way she ended it so abruptly. Just a simple signing of her name. No farewell. No, I'll miss you. No, I'll think of you. No, call me. No, I'll pick up the phone if you call. Nothing. Just—Deja.

The sound of crinkling filled the truck as he squished the paper into a tiny ball and threw it to the floor.

"Bullshit. You don't mean a word of it."

She was scared. Plain and simple. She loved him. He knew this. He felt it every time she looked at him with her bright-blue eyes. They glimmered with love. He felt it every time she touched him. He felt it every time she cradled her sweet body to his, whether in the bed or on the couch.

If she thought he was going to give up just like that because of some lame-ass letter, she was wrong. They were far from over. She wanted to dump him, which she did via a crappy letter, then she'd do it to his face. He'd make her tell him to his face that he was nothing but a good time for her. He'd like to see that happen.

Because it wouldn't. She wouldn't have the guts to say that to his face. Because everything she wrote was a lie.

Now the great question was where would he find her? That might be a little hard to figure out. He didn't have a clue where to begin. Not one.

The truck roared to life.

Ethan might be able to help. He knew a lot of people. Maybe he knew someone who was good at finding people. Like a PI. He'd do whatever it took to find her.

He wasn't about to let her walk away from him without a fight. That's not how he operated. No way in hell he was getting dumped via a letter. Not today.

What they had together, what they felt for each other, was more than just a good time. He'd make her see that.

———

"Hey, Gabe. Have you talked to Ethan today? I can't seem to track him down. I stopped by the fire station and they said he has the day off." Emmett pulled out a chair at the small café table near the front door and sat down.

"Nope. Last time I saw him was last night." Gabe took a sip from the paper cup. "Want a coffee?"

Emmett shook his head. "I suppose you're drinking that frilly kind of coffee with all that sweetener shit in it."

A tiny smirk crossed his face. "Why are you looking for Ethan?"

"Deja left." He ran a hand over his face as he groaned in despair. "She left. She moved, Gabe. She dumped me with a letter. A goddamn letter."

"I guess she was really pissed about that whole thing with Dare. Do you think he had something to do with Kevin's death? Are you going to say something to Ava?"

"No. I shouldn't have doubted him. I can't lose her. Not like this." Emmett dropped his eyes as he swirled his finger in circles on the table. "I need to find her. I have no idea where to begin."

"Yeah, trying to find a person is—so Ethan's not answering his phone?"

His head popped up. Gabe's hands were holding the cup tightly, his eyes looking out the café window. "You okay, Gabe? You seemed a little quiet last night."

"Yeah, there was a lot of tension." He chuckled. "There wasn't much to say."

"So, you're good?"

"Yeah."

For some reason, especially since Gabe wouldn't even look him in the eyes, Emmett didn't believe him. Being self-ish, really selfish, he decided to let it go. He had more pressing concerns. Like finding Deja.

"Where do you think I should begin?"

"To find Deja?" Gabe shrugged, took a sip of coffee, and then pulled out his wallet. "Here, he might be able to help."

Emmett took the business card and read the name on it. "Tom Dornety, Private Investigator." He glanced at his brother. "Why do you have the name of a PI just hanging around in your wallet?"

"Just do."

Definitely something going on with his brother. He wished he had the time to dig it out of him. But he didn't.

Gabe was the worst trying to pry information out of. Of course, they liked to tease and rip on him about anything in a brotherly, loving manner. That probably didn't help. Gabe liked to keep his emotions tightly inside because of it.

"You're sure everything's okay?"

"Call him, Emmett. I'm sure it won't be too difficult to track her down. What are you going to say to her when you find her?"

Okay, Gabe still wanted to ignore his problem. Fine. He'd talk to Ethan and they'd gang up on him together. Emmett stood up, the card pressed firmly between his fingers. "I have no clue. I'm gonna start by telling her I love her and then ream her out for leaving me."

Gabe chuckled. "Doesn't sound like a well-thought-out plan."

"When it comes to Deja, nothing I do is ever thought out."

"Yeah, maybe that's your problem."

———————

HER HAND WAVERED in the air, the weight of the gift not as heavy as the nervousness running through her veins. "Just take it already."

Dare snatched the gift bag from her hand, raising a brow. "What is it? It's not my birthday."

She rolled her eyes. "Just open the dumb thing already. I meant to give it to you when I picked you up that day... but..."

"But I acted like a typical jackass." He threw her a smirk.

"Yeah, you did. It's nothing. It's not a big deal. It's just a small gift."

Dare took his time pulling out the tissue paper, making

her nerves fly higher each second she waited for him to find out what it was. It was killing her. She just wanted him to tear the paper apart and find the gift already.

He held the bag upside down after he took out all the tissue paper and shook it. "It's empty. That was a great gift." His smirk from earlier grew larger.

"It's not empty, you idiot." She started to reach for the paper. He batted her hand away with a light tap.

Digging through the tissue paper some more, two small rectangular pieces of paper fell away, drifting to the floor. His eyes grew wide as he bent to pick them up.

"Deja...this...I can't accept these. It's..."

In his hand, a hand that looked to be trembling slightly, were two seats to a baseball game behind home plate. They had cost her a pretty penny. Last year, being her typical stubborn self, she refused to go when Austin took Sophie, Emmett, Zane, and Ava to a game. They sat behind home plate. The stories they told of that day had made her insanely jealous. She knew then, when her brother was released from prison, she would take him to a game and get him the best seats in the house. According to Ava, those were the best seats.

A sigh escaped.

She needed to stop thinking about them. Thinking about any member of the McCord family was not going to help her move on from Emmett. Two days had already passed and she still couldn't get the obstinate man out of her head. She missed him like crazy.

But she wasn't going to think about him right now. No. Right now was about Dare and making him happy.

"One of my favorite memories growing up was watching baseball with you. I want to go to this game and have fun."

Dare's eyes trailed from the tickets to her, a little misty, if what she saw was correct. Was her big brother on the verge of tears? Not once, never, had she seen her brother cry. Not when they lost their parents. Not once in the courtroom. Not even when they hauled him away to spend ten years behind bars.

"These had to cost..." His hand rubbed his eye with a quick flick of his wrist. "Behind home plate. I always wanted to sit there."

She decided to ignore the fact he almost let a tear slip down. "Well, here's our chance. I almost forgot I had them. The game is tomorrow night. I'll see if Sophie will let me borrow her new car." She shook her head. "Or not. That's a bad idea. I wrecked her car last time I borrowed it."

"I think she'd wanna see you. Call her and ask. Spend the afternoon with her tomorrow, and then we'll hit the road. I can't wait for this."

The smile on her brother's face made the sadness inside a little less difficult to deal with. She made the right decision. Leaving Emmett behind, leaving everything behind was the right thing to do. She needed her brother right now. He needed her. She couldn't be with someone who had no respect for her feelings. Her brother was everything to her. Clearly, Emmett didn't see that.

A knock sounded on the door.

"It's probably housekeeping. That pillow I have sucks. I called a little bit ago to get a new one. I gotta take a piss. Can you grab that?"

Deja nodded and watched as Dare walked through the door that connected their rooms together. They couldn't keep staying at a motel. It was getting too expensive. She had enough money saved to make the first month's rent somewhere. The problem was, most places they looked at the last two days had wanted first *and* last month's rent. She didn't have that much money.

They'd make it through this. She had faith they would. Not to mention their fierce determination to handle anything life threw at them.

Another knock sounded on the door. This time, sounding a little more aggressive.

Great. Dare left her to deal with an annoyed employee. The person on the other side of the door was lucky she was in a good mood; otherwise, she might've bitten their head off for the unprofessional manners.

She knew why Dare suddenly had to use the bathroom. His eyes had still been glossy. He needed a moment to himself. When she bought the tickets, she never expected that reaction. She was doubly glad she'd bought them. His happiness, his surprise had been worth every penny.

She flipped the lock and swung the door open. Her heart stopped beating as all the air left her body.

"Hi, Deja."

Emmett's silky smooth voice slid over her body as if his hands connected with her and made a delicious path everywhere. How did he find her? What did he want? Why did he look angry?

"What do you want?"

The anger in his eyes slowly dissipated before her, replaced with sadness, and perhaps a little bit of hunger. "You left." He shoved his hand toward her. A tiny crumpled ball sat in his palm. "You dumped me with a damn letter."

Just like that, the anger rushed back in. She could handle his anger. The sadness, though. She didn't like witnessing that. "Dumped? I'm not sure what we had was enough to say I dumped you. It was just a little fun. It wasn't anything serious."

Wrong thing to say. Way wrong.

Emmett dropped the paper ball, pulled her roughly into his arms, and slammed his mouth upon hers. She immediately opened to him, unable to fight the desire swimming throughout her body. Home. His arms always felt like home, and like a little slice of heaven. Why did he have to ruin everything? Why did he have to doubt her brother? As much as she loved Emmett—yes, loved him—she couldn't be with a man who didn't trust her brother. She just couldn't.

Her body melted into a puddle of desire as his arms wrapped her tightly against him. She moaned into his mouth as one of his hands grabbed her ass and pushed her gently into him. She felt his arousal immediately. The clothes between them needed to go. She wanted to feel him skin to skin. To feel him deep inside her. She missed him so much.

The last two days, while she had fun getting to know her brother again, had been miserable at the same time. Try as she might, she couldn't stop thinking about Emmett.

The hunger in the kiss started to slow down. His lips, instead of demanding, turned soft. He peppered a few kisses across her chin down her neck and to her ear, nibbling on her lobe.

"That was fun."

She blinked, feeling the loss of his heat immediately as he stepped away from her. Fun? That wasn't fun. More like passion, desire, just plain right. Fun didn't even make the list of how to describe it.

"Right. It was." No way was she about to admit that meant more to her than simple fun. She loved the idiot standing in front of her, but she would never tell him. Her livelihood depended on her keeping it a secret.

"Still lying, and to my face." He cupped her chin softly, planting a kiss upon her lips. "You know damn well that wasn't fun. That was love. You don't want anything to do with me, you don't want me in your life, then tell it to my face. Not in a damn letter." He kicked the paper ball. It went shuffling across the pukey-green carpet.

He knew her so well. He could always read her like a book. Yeah, she'd admit it. She took the coward's way out when she wrote that letter. Because she knew he knew that she wouldn't be able to say it to his face. For all the bravado she liked to think she possessed, when it came to Emmett, it slipped away.

"Go on. Tell me you never want to see me again. Tell me what we had was just fun and nothing serious. Tell me I don't mean shit to you."

"You think my brother is a killer. When you think things like that, you think that about me."

His brows dipped as little wrinkle lines formed on his forehead. His anger slowly left once again. "You're right. I was wrong to make assumptions about him. To think the worst about him. I'm sorry about that. I should've thought the same thing about Austin."

"What?" He couldn't have surprised her more. Austin? He wouldn't hurt a soul.

His shoulders fell as he rubbed his jaw. "He said he'd kill Kevin. You were there. You heard him. It was just his anger speaking. I know he'd never actually do it. I should've had the same faith in Dare. Dare said he wouldn't do anything when we told him no, and I should've trusted his word. I'm sorry."

His apology touched her heart. She wanted so much to fling herself back into his arms. She wanted to soak up his love like a sponge and never wring it out. Just keep it filled with love.

Instead, she took a step back. There still wasn't enough distance between them. There might never be enough distance. "Thank you. I appreciate your apology."

"Come back home then. I love you. We can work through this."

"I don't have a home. I never did. It was just a place to rest my head."

A small groan erupted from him. His fists clenched and unclenched. A myriad of emotions crossed over his face within seconds. "It could take years to make you feel like you're loved. To show you that you do have a home, a family that includes more than just Dare. People make mistakes. We made a mistake doubting him for a second, but that doubt is gone. We, not just me, but we want you and Dare to come back home. This motel isn't your home. Being with me, with Sophie, that's where you belong. I'm willing to wait years to show you how much I love you. Doesn't that tell you anything?"

Yeah, it sure did. She felt even more unworthy of his devoted love. Couldn't he see she was all wrong for him? She couldn't trust like he wanted her to. She couldn't love like he wanted her to. She didn't even know what a real home looked like. He said he would wait years, but would he? At the first sign of trouble, would he doubt Dare once again?

She had lied, stolen. She even cheated on a test one time. She was not a good person, no matter how much he wanted to believe she was. That left her with no choice now. She'd lie to save them both from heartache in the future. Sometimes, you just had to rip the band-aid off before the wound was ready. Give it some air to breathe, to heal.

Emmett would heal sooner than he probably thought. She, on the other hand, would probably never love another man as she loved him.

It was better this way. She wasn't sure how to give him the love he so desperately needed. Yes, she loved him. She just didn't know how to say it, to show it, to give it.

She didn't want to hurt him. Now she had no choice. Quick and clean.

"I don't love you, Emmett. It was just a good time for me. Nothing more. I don't want to see you again. I'd appreciate it if you wouldn't contact me again. Is that sufficient to your liking? You said I had to say it to your face. Well, I just did. I'd like you to leave now."

"You're the worst liar in the world. I still don't believe you. You're just saying it to pacify me, to hurt me. Yeah, you're doing a lovely job of that. Congratulations. You're also hurting yourself." He shook his head as if he were battling an internal war. He shoved his hand in his pocket, then pulled a fist out. Grabbing her hand, he shoved something inside it. "You want me to believe your words and I just can't. You're hiding behind those walls of yours built from your childhood. I have no idea how I'm going to break them down, but I will. I'm not giving up on us."

"I don't love you, Emmett."

He let her hand go. "Yeah, you do. You're just afraid."

"I don't scare easily."

"No, you don't, but with this, you're scared."

She shoved him hard, pushing him into the hallway. "Leave. If I see you again, I'm calling the cops."

He had the nerve to laugh. "You don't like the cops. I highly doubt you'll do that."

"Are you trying to piss me off?"

"You are so beautiful when you're angry."

"I hate you, Emmett McCord. With a passion."

"You probably do. You also love me with a passion."

She scrunched her lips as she tried not to scream. Why did he frustrate and aggravate her so? "I do not."

"Are we about to revert to childish games?" He grinned. "Do, too."

How could she make him see she didn't want him? Well, that was the problem, wasn't it? She did want him. She did love him. The stubborn, obstinate man knew it. He read her like a book.

She opened the palm of her hand where the ring he shoved there lay resting like a hot iron and looked at it. "I'm never going to wear this. I don't love you."

"It's yours whether you put it on your finger or not. I don't want it back. I think I am going to leave now because I'm not sure how many times I can hear you lie to my face." He turned to leave, then paused. "But I'll be back. I said it before and I meant it. Get used to this. Get used to me."

Deja watched as he walked away. Not once did he turn around.

See. He was already regretting his decision to love her. He couldn't even give her one last glance.

She closed the motel room door.

That wasn't fair. It wasn't true. He did love her. She probably just upset him so badly he couldn't stand to look at her. Yeah, she had that problem sometimes looking in the mirror.

What was she going to do? Emmett wasn't likely to give up so easily. How long could she continue to lie to him? She believed his apology. Did she believe he'd never do it again? That she wasn't so sure of. Was it fair to hold him to such high standards when it came to her brother? Probably not, but her brother was all she had left. She wouldn't stand for anyone to treat him wrong or with disrespect.

A knock sounded on the door.

He came back. He changed his mind already.

Well, maybe she did, too. She loved him. Maybe they could work through this.

She whipped open the door. The smile on her face fell like an avalanche crushing a mountain.

"Someone called for more pillows?" The short, pudgy-looking teenage girl held out two fluffy white pillows to her.

Deja didn't even bother with a fake smile. "Yeah, thanks."

The girl nodded, snapped a bubble from the wad of gum in her mouth, and walked away. She slowly closed her door.

Would she have the bravery to admit her love the next time she saw Emmett? She honestly didn't know. That might've been a short-lived shot of bravery she just had.

Just another reason why she wasn't worthy of Emmett. It'd be better if he just stayed away.

18

THE KEYS JINGLED in her hand as she fidgeted. "Are you sure you don't mind? Last time..."

Sophie smiled softly as she grasped her shoulder in reassurance. "Of course I don't mind. You and Dare have fun tonight. I just hope the rain stays away and the game's not postponed. Austin and I are going to watch it. Make sure to wave at the camera."

Deja rolled her eyes. "I didn't even think of that. Are we going to be on TV?"

"You are sitting behind home plate. What a great gift. Is Dare excited?"

"He is. It should be a fun night, as long as the rain stays away."

Deja headed for the front door, the keys burning a hole in her hand. She was oddly nervous to drive. Sophie said she didn't mind who drove her car. Maybe she'd have Dare drive once she picked him up from the motel. After almost hitting that deer, the thought of driving just put her in a panic. Was Dare nervous, too? He hadn't driven yet since he was released. Maybe it wasn't such a good idea to ask him.

She'd just suck it up. What were the odds she'd hit another deer so soon? Well, technically she didn't hit the deer the first time. So, she might hit it this—no. She wasn't going to think negatively.

With her hand on the doorknob, she glanced at Sophie. "Have you talked to Emmett recently?"

Sophie hesitated. "I have."

Should she ask? Sophie wouldn't betray her like that. But she had to know.

"He showed up at the motel last night."

"He did?" Her shock wasn't fake.

A sigh let loose. The next day, after feeling guilty for leaving Sophie in such a rush, she called her to let her know where they were staying. She didn't think Sophie would rat her out and tell Emmett where she was.

So, how did Emmett know where to find her?

"What did he say?"

Too much. Everything she wanted to hear. She couldn't say that, of course. "Stuff. It doesn't matter. I can't figure out how he found me, though."

"I didn't tell him."

"I never thought so." Sophie raised a brow in disbelief, a mingling of hurt mixed in. "Okay. Maybe I wondered a little if you said something."

"He loves you, Deja. I have no idea how he found out, but he's a man in love. That makes him very resourceful. Do you love him? Because I think you do." Her cheeks turned red, a bright contrast with her light-blonde hair. "I don't mean to be so bold, or put you on the spot."

"We're friends, Soph. It's okay. You can say what you want." Deja grinned, trying to make Sophie feel better. Like she shouldn't be ashamed for saying something.

"So, do you love him?"

Biting her bottom lip, she smoothed it out with her tongue after she realized what she was doing. "I'm just confused right now. I'm not sure I know how to love."

Sophie scoffed. Something she did very well, but rarely. "That's a load of crock and you know it."

"Wow. That's the closest I've heard you swear before. Naughty."

She propped a hand to her hip, mimicking the gesture Deja displayed on occasion. "Yeah, well, you just might make me let loose a real curse word if you don't start being honest with yourself." She dropped her hand as her face softened. "Emmett did ask if I knew where you were, and I would never do that to you. But I wanted to tell him because he asked a few times. Every time he asked, I really, really wanted to tell him."

"Why?" The word fell out in a whisper.

"Because I know you love him just as much as he loves you. You're good for each other and you deserve happiness, Deja. You deserve everything. I hate seeing you so unhappy."

"I'm not—"

"Don't." Sophie pursed her lips. "Don't lie to me. I dislike it when Austin does it, and I don't want to hear you do it either."

"Austin hasn't lied to you in a very long time. Almost a year ago when he nearly screwed it up between you two."

"Don't try to steer the conversation in a different direction. You're unhappy. When Emmett's around, your face lights up so brightly."

Deja pulled open the door. "I should go."

Sophie wrapped her arms around herself. "Have fun."

Just like that, the conversation was over. Sophie knew she didn't want to talk about it, and she respected that. As long as Deja quit spewing lies, Sophie was okay letting it go. She abhorred lying. Truth be told, Deja felt sick to her stomach even voicing a tiny lie. It was better if they just dropped the conversation altogether. She wasn't sure how to process her emotions, let alone voice them to another person.

"I'll make sure to bring your car back without a dent."

"I trust you. Wave to the camera." Sophie offered a smile, but sadly, it didn't reach her eyes.

Deja did that. She made Sophie unhappy. Well, didn't that just make her a horrible friend. Shit, she never kept any friendships growing up. Why would the one with Sophie last forever? She never did anything right. She was hurting her friend and she could do nothing to stop it.

"Right, I will. Bye, Soph."

"Bye, Deja."

The door closed with an audible click. Walking briskly to the car, she jumped inside way too fast and pulled away from the house without glancing behind her. Not that she had anything to glance at. Well, maybe her house. No. It was Sophie's house. So what if she started to think of it as her house. It's not as if she ever made it a true home. Everything in the house spoke loudly of Sophie's tastes rather than her own.

Asking Sophie, even knowing she wouldn't need permission to decorate it, would have admitted she was finally settling down. Making a home.

Doing that scared her. She didn't know how to make a home. She didn't know the first thing what to do. Pretending was her forte. Making herself believe everything was okay in her world was what she did well. Creating a home? Totally clueless.

"Shit."

She hurt her friend. Her only real friend she ever had. She should've just admitted she was scared.

Scared to love. To open herself up. To let love in. That was her problem. She did love Emmett. When would it fall apart? Everything in her life always did.

Look at her friendship with Sophie. That suddenly fell apart within a space of less than five minutes. All because she couldn't admit the truth.

Enough.

She had a baseball game to look forward to. Thinking about what happened with Sophie, what could possibly happen with Emmett, wasn't going to help lift her mood. She needed to think about Dare and the fun they would have at the baseball game.

She started to slow down as she neared a red light. It suddenly changed to green. Lifting her foot off the brake, she continued with her usual pace. She crossed over the white line, her eyes straight ahead, her mind dancing around her issues like a crazy hip-hop song.

She needed to call Sophie before they left for the game. She didn't feel right with how she left. For once in her life, she needed to start talking things out. She needed to let people in that cared about her. Sophie cared a great deal.

Boom!

Her body jerked. The sound of crunching metal and glass breaking barely registered as her head swung violently and connected with the door window. Her mind spun in a circle.

No, wait.

She was spinning. The car was out of her control.

The large metal post looming ahead should've scared her. Not that she wasn't already scared as she continued to spin, the car jerking her around. Her mind was so disoriented, she had no time to feel fearful.

Emmett. She should've said so much to him. More than what she had.

Liar. That's all she was.

The front end crashed head-on into the metal post, forcing the momentum of the car to a screeching halt. Her head jerked forward, the force of the impact imploded the airbag in her face.

Barely able to move, unsure of why her legs felt trapped, she tried to look around to see how bad it was. Except, she couldn't see anything. Her eyes were coated with wetness. With her blood.

She wanted to lift her hand and feel for a wound to figure out where the blood was coming from. She managed a soft groan before the blackness took over.

THIS FELT like a reoccurring thing he had been doing way too much. Yet, he didn't know how to stop himself. Of course, he knew stopping over to Sophie and Austin's house he'd have zero chance of running into Deja because she moved. Left. Gone away.

God, it hurt to think about.

He missed her so much. Seeing her last night had been breathtaking and painful all at once. He had a hard time walking away. It had been even more difficult not to look back. It was for the best. She needed time to think about everything he said and hopefully realize on her own that they were meant to be together. That he loved her no matter what.

Patience. That's what he needed. Something he sorely

lacked. Which would explain why he was knocking on Austin's door. To occupy his time. He didn't want to go rushing to Deja just yet. She needed a little more time to think about what he said. He didn't want to come on too strong. Or should he?

Indecisive. He seriously needed to get over that shit.

"Emmett. Hi."

Sophie didn't look happy to see him.

"Is it a bad time?"

"No, no, come on in." She backed away from the door and let him step inside. Closing the door, she then headed for the kitchen. "Do you want a drink?"

"Sure." He glanced around the living room and listened for any other sounds in the house as he followed her to the kitchen. "Austin's not home?"

"He's still at the farm." Sophie pulled a pitcher of iced tea out, then grabbed two glasses from the cupboard. Her hand slightly shook as she set them on the counter.

"Everything okay, Soph?"

Her back faced him. "Why are you here, Emmett?"

"You're upset at me. I wasn't going to ask where Deja is anymore. I swear."

Sophie whipped around, the anger clear. "Of course not. You already know where she is. How?"

So, Deja must've talked to Sophie today. Did she accuse Sophie of spilling her secrets? That was the last thing he wanted to happen. He was clearly screwing up every step of the way.

"I hired a PI. I'm sorry, Sophie. I'll just leave." He started to walk away. He wasn't even sure why he came in the first place. He really had no good excuse for showing up.

"Don't go, Emmett. I should apologize. I feel like Deja

and I sort of argued and it's bothering me. I didn't mean to take it out on you."

He turned around, already halfway to the front door. She stood a few steps away. He closed the distance and pulled her into a hug. "You never have to apologize to me. I'm the idiot here."

The front door opened. "Why do you have your hands on my pixie angel?"

Emmett let Sophie go and stepped away. Austin shut the front door, not looking amused whatsoever. Emmett couldn't help but chuckle. "It was a friendly hug. Do you get jealous with everyone, or is it just me? You know I love Deja."

Sophie's laughter filled the room, and his heart soared a little, lifting his mood. "He's like that with everyone."

Austin pulled her into his arms, snuggling his head into her neck. "That's because I love you so much." He looked at Emmett. "So, what lame excuse do you have for visiting us today?"

He shrugged. "I don't have one. I'm...I'm..." He shrugged again.

"I want to say she'll come around, but I'm honestly not sure, Emmett. I truly do believe she loves you." Sophie rested her head onto Austin's shoulder.

"She's scared. I might've handled it all wrong last night with her—again. I'm always screwing it up."

"Keep at it, man. If you give up, that's when you lose her for sure." Austin kissed the top of Sophie's head. "I never gave up."

She snuggled closer to him. "I'm so glad you didn't."

"Yeah, maybe this wasn't the brightest idea showing up here. I can't handle seeing you two like this." Emmett chuckled to show he was teasing, when in reality, he wasn't. It was hard to see them so in love, acting lovey-dovey. He wanted that. With Deja.

Sophie softly laughed, but her eyes betrayed that she understood his pain. "I was about to start supper. You should stay."

"Na. I think I'll just go brood in my own house."

"Dude, that's not healthy." Austin grinned. The doorbell rang. "If that's Ethan or Gabe, you're staying. You won't be able to sulk like you want to."

Austin swung the door open and his stance faltered a bit. Officer Dorscher stood on the porch, his expression a morose one.

Emmett's stomach gurgled. A deep dread filled every pore. Why did he look that way? Why was he here?

"Can I come in, Austin?"

Austin gestured him inside. "What's up, Brian? Last time you were here, you dropped the bomb about Kevin. Did you find the people who killed him?"

Officer Dorscher shook his head as he glanced at Emmett and then away too quickly. "I'm afraid we're still looking. I'm here for a different reason." His eyes sought him out again. The look unnerved him. "I'm glad you're here, Emmett."

He didn't want to know why. That look said way more than he wanted to know. Somehow his voice found a way out. "What happened?"

"I don't know how to say it, so I'll just say it. Deja's been in a car accident."

Emmett's knees buckled. If not for Austin standing so close, he would've fallen to the floor. His arm swooped around him, holding him upright. "Is she...is she..." He couldn't even get the words out. His eyes swiveled to Sophie, who had gone deathly pale. His body jerked upright and stiff, telling Austin he wouldn't collapse to the floor.

Austin immediately rushed to Sophie's side, holding her as they waited for Officer Dorscher to tell them more. He knew what Emmett had been trying to ask.

"I'm not sure. I wasn't the first to arrive to the scene. They had to extract her from the car carefully. Her legs were pinned between the steering wheel and the seat. She hit a post pretty hard. It crushed the front end. She was unconscious but alive when they rushed her to the hospital. As soon as I knew who it was, I told the lead officer I would notify you guys."

"She..." Sophie paused as her breath hitched. A tear fell down. "She was very concerned about driving my car. She wouldn't be driving recklessly. I don't understand."

Officer Dorscher's throat bobbed as he swallowed hard. "She wasn't driving reckless. She didn't do anything wrong by all the accounts of the witnesses. Someone ran a red light and T-boned her. It sent her car into a tailspin where she crashed head-on into the pole. They hit her pretty hard. Crushed the side of the vehicle. I'm sorry, Sophie. Your car is totaled."

She hiccupped in between the soft tears rolling down. "I don't give a shit about my car. She can't die." She buried her face into Austin's chest. He started to rub his hand up and down her back.

Sophie was right. Deja couldn't die. In all his time knowing her, he had never heard her swear once. That alone made him extremely nervous. She seriously thought Deja could die. That was unacceptable.

"The driver of the other car...what..." He couldn't even form coherent sentences. She couldn't die. She just couldn't.

"He's in custody. It's not looking good for him." Officer

Dorscher propped a hand onto his service weapon in a gesture that looked very comfortable and like he'd done it a million times. "He's intoxicated. Way over the limit. I'm sorry. I know Deja means the world to all of you. They were bringing her to the St. Cloud Hospital. Do you need me to take you there?"

"Yeah, that'd be great. Thanks, Brian," Austin said, as he continued to soothe Sophie as best as he could.

"I'll meet you guys there."

Austin looked surprised. "I think it's best we ride together. You're probably not in the right frame of mind to drive, Emmett."

Emmett tried to focus on Sophie. Anything other than his cousin's knowing eyes. Austin had a point. A very good one. His knees wanted to buckle again. He wanted to fall to the floor and scream in pain from the unfairness. If he lost the woman he loved before he truly had a chance to have her, he'd never survive.

He made eye contact with Austin. "Someone needs to tell Dare."

———

DARE RUBBED his hand back and forth over his hair. A buzz cut. He hadn't had his hair this short since he was nineteen. But it was time for a change. Time to start life anew. To make things right.

His sister was miserable. She played it off well enough, but he knew. He sensed it right away the same night they left. He also knew the reason why she was so miserable.

Emmett.

She didn't know it, but he heard the entire conversation

between them. Emmett didn't issue the apology to him, but he had accepted it, nonetheless. After he thought about it, he couldn't blame them all for thinking the worst. He had been forceful with his words that night when he offered to teach Kevin a lesson. When Austin declined, he was hard-pressed to ignore his words. He wanted to pretend he never said such a thing. He wanted to have his friends give Kevin a beating of a lifetime so he would know that it could happen again at any moment if he didn't stop whatever he was doing to make the case go haywire for Sophie.

Except, he didn't. He never called his friends. He respected Austin's wishes. But with his background and how he sounded that night, he honestly couldn't blame them for thinking he went against his word.

He let his pride and emotions get in the way. Like usual. Like he always did with his sister. He pushed her away for ten years. And why? Because he was afraid to see the accusations, the guilt in her eyes. It was his fault, no matter what anyone said, that his parents died. He didn't want to see the confirmation in her eyes.

He was still waiting to see it. That's what was so damn funny. He pushed her away for ten years and he was still waiting to see that look in her eyes. Damn it, he probably never would. Because she didn't blame him.

For that, he needed to make things right. She was miserable, and it was his fault. She only pushed Emmett away because of him. She might not like it, but he would try his damndest to convince her to go back home. Home, as in Sophie's house. Home, as in Emmett's arms.

The guy could still rankle him sometimes, but overall, he was perfect for his sister. They made a good couple. Not that he could call himself an expert on what made a good couple. He just knew. The spark he saw in her eyes, or the way Emmett glanced at her, he just knew.

He wouldn't convince her tonight. No. Tonight was all about them. They'd enjoy the baseball game, and then tomorrow, they would talk about it. He was even going to man up and do the right thing.

He'd make Deja go back home, then he planned to talk to Ethan. Apologize for acting like an ass and almost hitting him when all Ethan did was be a good friend. He let him in his home without batting an eye.

It sucked to admit he was wrong. But he was man enough to own it.

A loud knock interrupted his thoughts. Shit. Did Deja lose her key card?

He glanced through the peephole, raising a brow when he saw Emmett standing on the other side.

Tonight was supposed to go without a hitch. Emmett was suddenly putting a damper in the plans. As much as he wanted them to work it out, Emmett would have to wait until tomorrow. Tonight was brother and sister time.

He swung open the door. "Not a good time."

Emmett cleared his throat. "I'm sorry."

"I heard you last night. It's not necessary to dish out more apologies. I was wrong. So, I'm sorry. I'm on your side and I'll try to help you with Deja, but tonight we're going to a baseball game and I really don't want you to ruin her mood. We good?"

Dare even cracked a smile, hoping to show he didn't hold any hard feelings and that he was sorry for acting like a sour child. Emmett didn't beam with delight like he figured he would've. Instead, his expression turned worse.

"Shit." Emmett rubbed a hand over his face, then

cleared his throat again. His hand fell away, his eyes glistening with unshed tears.

"I don't...Emmett?" Was he about to cry? This visit made no sense.

"Deja's been in a car accident and it's not looking good." His voice cracked. "I'm sorry."

Yeah, his apology made a lot more sense now. Yet, he didn't want his damn apologies. He didn't want to hear what he just said. Losing his sister—no, he couldn't think like that. He wouldn't think like that.

"Dare? Did you hear me?"

His head bobbed up and down in a nod, yet he felt so disjointed from his body. Nothing made sense. They were going to a baseball game. They were going to have fun tonight.

His hands started to shake, that empty feeling filling him up. That same feeling he got when his parents started to get on his nerves. That same feeling that made him turn to pills to dull the pain.

He had been so strong the last ten years. Sure, partly because he had been locked away in prison. It didn't mean he couldn't have gotten high as much as he wanted. He could've gotten anything inside those walls. You just needed to know the right people. He never touched one thing, though. He stopped having the urge the first time the bars slammed shut in his face. The moment they slammed closed, his mind conjured only one thing.

His sister.

He knew he had to stay clean for her.

Rapid images flashed before his eyes. Blood. Glass on the dirt ground, weeds mingling around. His mother's body.

Oh, to lose himself in the deep abyss. Numb his entire body. He couldn't handle this. He wouldn't survive losing his sister. Especially that way. Any way but that. Not a car accident.

If she never bought him these dumbass tickets, she never would've been—

Whack!

His cheek stung from the hard slap delivered by Emmett. Rubbing the tender part of his face, his eyes searched for Emmett's.

"What the hell?" There was no anger behind those words, just complete wonder.

"Snap out of it, man. I don't know where you went, but you weren't here with me. Did you hear a damn word I said? I need you to keep it together. Your sister is one of the toughest women I know. She'll survive this. She's not a quitter. Do you hear me?"

"I haven't touched any drugs. I haven't wanted to. I need—"

Emmett grabbed him roughly by the shoulders and dragged him out of the motel room, letting the door shut behind them. "You need to come to the hospital with me. That's all you need to do. Just...shit...lean on me because I'm barely holding on myself. The only thing you don't need to do is think about drugs. Get it out of your head. You're stronger than that."

Dare puffed his chest out and shrugged off Emmett's arm that had been wrapped around his shoulder. "You're right. I'm a badass mo-fo. I need to start acting like one."

A deep laugh flew out of Emmett's lips. "Not really what I said, but sure, we'll go with it."

"Thanks, Emmett."

His steps stalled as they neared the stairs leading to the parking lot. "For what?"

"For coming...instead of a bunch of cops. I...my sister..."

A strong hand clamped onto his shoulder. "I know. You don't have to say it. Let's get to the hospital. I don't know much other than the wreck was pretty bad."

So was the accident ten years ago. Only one survived. Him.

Would his sister?

19

THE HAND he held was warm and soft, yet nothing else indicated she would wake up any time soon. In all his years, he never imagined he would lose his sister like this. The same way he had taken the lives of their parents. It was almost as if a cruel fate was weaving its way to right what should've happened years ago.

Deja never went out often when they were kids. She had started to date some asshat a few weeks before that fateful night everything changed. He could come on strong when it came to certain things, namely boys. He didn't like the jerk she was dating, but he stepped back for once to let her live her life as a teenager. It probably saved her life.

If she would've been home that night. She would've insisted on coming to the hospital with him and their parents, and in all likelihood, he probably would've killed his sister, too. Now fate was finishing the job.

Life was so unfair. Complete shit.

"Dare?"

The small hand resting on his shoulder made him shiver. Not from the coldness of her touch because he could feel the chill straight through his shirt, but from the kindness and sympathy in that little touch. He didn't want either. He just wanted to be left alone with his sister.

"I'm sorry. It's all my fault."

He jerked his head to Sophie, prepared to ignore her until she left. At those words, he couldn't do anything but stare at her.

"What kind of bullshit is that?"

She flinched. "The truth."

Shrugging, mostly to dislodge her hand without acting like a complete jackass, he turned his head away. She had no clue what she was talking about. A drunken idiot hurt his sister. He hurt his sister. She was on the road that night because she wanted to take *him* to a baseball game. Nobody was to blame but him.

"I hope...hope you can forgive me."

The tears mixing with her words had his heart cracking into pieces. He had slowly started to get to know everyone in Deja's life. Not by much, but enough to know what a kindhearted sweetheart Sophie was. She was killing him with her dejected words. He had no idea what to say because all he wanted to do was spew nasty words. Not at her, of course. Just let loose with words that would have her washing his mouth out with soap for a week. He already made her flinch once with his swearing, yet she said nothing to berate him for it.

"She'll wake up. She's so tough."

Dare rubbed the top of his sister's hand, willing her to wake up at that very moment. He couldn't have this conversation with Sophie on his own. He had no idea how to make her feel better. That's all he wanted to do. Just make her feel better somehow, make her realize that none of this was her fault. He couldn't even ask why she thought it was her fault.

"I know...I know I'm the last person you probably want to speak to right now, but you need to rest. You've been here the last three days and haven't left once. You and Emmett both need to rest."

A deep breath released. No words, though. He still had none. Not even to Emmett, who usually sat on the other side of the bed since they wheeled her out of surgery and put her in the ICU. She had yet to wake up. Three long, torturous days of nothing. Just her in a deep sleep. The doctors couldn't give a definite answer if she would ever wake up. She had swelling in the brain and quite a few internal injuries that almost took her life on the table itself. Whatever other mumbo jumbo they told him, he couldn't recall. All he heard was, "It's not looking promising."

Who said shit like that? Were doctors supposed to say it so depressing and unsupportive?

They had some strict rules in the ICU. Yet they overlooked the rules when it came to him and Emmett. Maybe it was the dangerous glint in his eyes when he told each and every nurse, the doctor himself, that nobody would tear him away from his sister's side until she woke up. Emmett had stood next to him, quiet as a clam, but with that same fierce look in his eyes.

Maybe it was how every time they stepped out of the room for a small breath or a bathroom break or just a quick bite to eat, her vitals seemed to plummet. The minute he picked up her hand, they surged back to life just as quickly.

That said everything he needed to know. His sister needed him right by her side. She'd wake up. She had to.

"Stop acting like a jackass."

His head whipped to Sophie again.

Her eyes were filled with water, but the hands on her hips and the defiance in her stance said a lot. "That's right.

You made me swear. That's twice now in the past three days. And I don't like doing it."

"What do you want me to say? This isn't your fault, Sophie. I'm sorta baffled why you think so."

"She was upset when she left me. It probably made her distracted." Her hands fell to her sides as her bottom lip trembled like a mini earthquake. "I...I..." Her entire body crumbled when a strong pair of arms wrapped around her. She turned immediately into Austin's chest.

"Shh, my pixie angel, stop blaming yourself." Austin rubbed his hand up and down her back as his eyes connected with his. "Any change?"

His head barely moved back and forth to say no. "You should take her home."

Austin nodded. "Emmett's almost done on the phone. He'll be back in a few minutes." He pulled Sophie tighter in his embrace. "We'll be back after supper."

Dare's eyes trained on Sophie, then they shared a look. "Maybe..."

"Don't let her fool you. She's a little piston. I'm wrapped around her little finger. If she says we're coming back, we're coming back." The sweet grin on Austin's face as he angled his stare at Sophie made Dare smile.

"Well, at least convince her none of this is her fault."

Sophie shoved out of Austin's arms, almost making him fall in the process as she turned toward him and wagged her finger in his face. "Then you better understand it's not your fault either. I know you're doing the same as me. Don't try to deny it."

Dare held his one hand up in surrender, refusing to let go of Deja's hand. "You got me."

Her hand brushed his cheek softly. "We do. And we're never letting go."

"I didn't mean—"

"You're part of this family. Just accept it. Quit blaming yourself."

"Listen to your own words then. Deja would be pissed thinking you're blaming yourself."

"Ditto."

The cocky smile, which looked so foreign on her sweet face, made him chuckle and relinquish control. "I know better than to keep arguing with a beautiful woman."

She nodded as if they'd settled the conversation, although the sadness cloaked her eyes once again. "We'll be back soon. Then I want you to leave for a break. No arguments. You won't win."

Austin gave him a funny look, as if saying he'd make sure Sophie stayed happy and not to mess with her, which would inadvertently be messing with him, then followed Sophie out of the room.

He turned toward Deja and rubbed her hand one more time.

"How is she?"

Dare glanced at Emmett as he took a seat in the chair on the opposite side of Deja. "Same. Sophie swore."

Despite the seriousness behind that simple statement, Emmett chuckled. "Kinda makes her more adorable when she does."

Dare's laughter joined Emmett's. The room became silent as they both looked at Deja.

"She'll pull through."

Dare hesitated. "You really believe it?"

"I have to." Emmett sucked in a harsh breath. "Because the thought of losing her is unfathomable."

EMMETT SCOOTED his chair closer to the bed. His arm was starting to ache from reaching out to hold Deja's hand. He refused to let go, though. If he wasn't holding her hand, Dare was. Someone had to hold her, no matter what. He couldn't explain it. Dare probably couldn't either. They both just felt compelled to make sure she knew they were here. They weren't going anywhere.

Five days.

She'd been in a coma for five days. The swelling in her brain had gone down and her vitals had improved significantly. Everything in surgery had gone well, repairing all the internal damage from the crash. Yet she refused to wake up.

Emmett liked to consider this being her usual stubborn self. She'd wake up when she was ready. Thinking any other option was unacceptable. He couldn't think any other alternative.

He kept reliving the last time he saw her. The things he said. The things he didn't. Why did he walk away? He should've fought harder to make her understand—realize— how much he loved her. How much he wanted her in his life.

Of course, none of that would've prevented the accident. She still would've gone to Sophie's to borrow her car. She still would've been driving through that intersection.

Or not.

He could've let her borrow his truck. He could've even driven them to the Cities himself.

Could've. Would've. Should've. It didn't change anything. He couldn't change anything, and that's what upset him the most. He'd change places with her if he could.

Leaning back, his hand still clasped securely with hers, he closed his eyes. Just a little shut-eye. Taking turns staying awake with her took a lot of energy. But between him and

Dare, one of them always wanted to be awake, waiting for the moment she would open her beautiful blue eyes.

She had to.

THE PRESSURE on her hand wasn't as bad as the pressure on her chest. Why did she feel like she was being weighed down? And her legs. She couldn't move her legs.

Suddenly, pain ricocheted up her legs and straight to her head. Her hand wanted to lift to cradle her head, yet the strain wouldn't ease. Her muscles felt almost locked in a death grip as she exerted as much energy as she could to move even a tiny inch.

Why couldn't she move?

Why couldn't she see anything?

Like her hands, chest, and legs, her eyes were burdened with heaviness. A simple blink wouldn't erupt.

Why couldn't she even open her eyes? What was happening to her?

A light whisper floated to her.

Who was that?

Emmett?

Yes, it sounded like Emmett. Why did he sound so far away? Why couldn't she hear what he was saying?

It didn't matter. Not really. His voice, regardless of the words, was soothing. Slowly, the pressure in her chest felt lighter.

A deep breath escaped.

"Deja?"

Exerting all the power she had, she opened her eyes. Everything was a blur, even Emmett's face as he leaned closer. He was leaning, wasn't he?

"Oh, sweetheart, talk to me. Open those beautiful eyes again."

His warm breath tickled her cheeks. He was definitely leaning over her. Listening to his sweet words, she tried to open her eyes again. This time she managed to keep them open longer than a second.

Her mouth opened, but nothing came out but a croak.

"Take your time. Let me get you some water." Emmett reached to his left to a small table near him and swung back with a large cup with a straw.

She took a small sip, not managing more than that.

Warm lips touched her cheek as her eyes fluttered closed once again. "You had us all so worried. You have no idea what it means to see your beautiful eyes shining back at me. I love you so much. God, I love you."

Eyes still closed, she whispered, "Shut up, Emmett."

A soft chuckle floated around her, making her want to smile, yet her lips wouldn't cooperate.

"I love hearing you say that. I love hearing you say anything. Five days..."

Opening her eyes again, she knew she must've given him a puzzled look because he continued, "You've been in a coma for five days. Do you remember what happened?"

Intense pressure zapped her body once again. The horrible memory assaulted her. Someone hit her while she was driving. A crash. A pole. Unable to move her legs. The steering wheel almost crushing her upper body. How in the world did she survive that?

She realized she didn't answer Emmett, who stared at her intensely, patiently waiting for an answer. She nodded, unable to vocalize anything.

"Dare's here. He left a little bit ago to get some food. He'll be right back. He'll be just as happy as I am that you're finally awake. You gave us quite a scare." He squeezed her hand, not too tightly, but she wouldn't have cared. She liked the feeling. "I should get the doctor or the nurse."

She tightened the grip with his hand when he started to stand up. "No."

He sunk back into the chair as he cracked a grin. "I didn't want to leave you anyway."

"Shut up." Her voice felt so weak. She wanted to say more, but she didn't know how.

A hand brushed her cheek and across her hair. "I love you, too."

"Emmett..."

"Shh." His finger touched her lips. "It's okay. Let's not talk about that right now. I just need you to know that I love you and I'm not going anywhere. I haven't gone anywhere for the past five days. There's no way I wanted to be away from you for one second. Neither has Dare."

She kissed his finger. "I want to say shut up again."

"I know. I'm talking too much right now. You need to take everything slowly, and here I am bombarding you with word after word. I'm sorry."

"No, that's not it. It's because that's the only way I know how to say it."

His brows puckered. "Say what?"

"I love you."

20

A WARM HAND CLUTCHED HERS. "You okay?"

"I'm fine."

"Comfortable enough?"

She squeezed his hand in reassurance. "Emmett, I'm good. I just want to go home." Glancing at him, she brought his hand back to his side. "Please use two hands."

He looked aghast, jamming both hands to the steering wheel. "I'm sorry. Are you nervous?"

"I don't know. I just know that I'm feeling a little jumpy being a passenger. I just want to get home."

"We'll be there soon, sweetheart."

Ah, an endearment—again. He had been calling her sweetheart or honey a lot the past two weeks. It sounded lovely every time she heard it. She never was one who needed that kind of affection from a guy, but she was glad Emmett felt compelled to call her sweet names.

Leaning her head against the headrest, she closed her eyes. The ride was fairly smooth. Closing her eyes helped the anxiety rushing through her veins of sitting in a vehicle since the accident. If she couldn't see what was in front of her, then she wouldn't worry as much. Not that she saw the car coming that day. It came out of nowhere, smacking the side of her vehicle with such force, she could still feel how her head slammed into the driver's side window.

Thinking about that wouldn't help her now, especially while sitting in another vehicle. She trusted Emmett, though. She knew he'd get her home safely.

A hand touched her shoulder. A loud crunching sound reverberated around them.

"Emmett!" Her eyes shot open, bracing herself for the impact.

"Whoa, sweetheart. It's okay. We're okay. We're home. I didn't mean to frighten you. I'm so sorry. I should've waited to close the garage door until you opened your eyes."

It took her a full minute before the shaking that consumed her stopped. Emmett didn't say another word. He just knew she needed to sit there and calm herself down.

"I'm okay."

"I know you are."

Her eyes turned to his, the understanding reflecting brightly. He knew she needed time to deal with everything, but he also knew she'd be okay. She was very thankful for that.

"I'll help you out."

He jumped out of the truck before she could protest. He'd been coddling her since the moment she woke up. She enjoyed him being near, spoiling her, making sure she was comfortable in every possible way, but she wasn't sure how much more she could take.

The minute he opened her door and scooped her into his arms, she disregarded that ridiculous thought. She loved his arms around her. His sweetness. His desire to make her as happy as possible. Who wouldn't?

But did she deserve it? It always came down to that.

After everything that happened between them, she still wasn't sure she did.

"I can walk, you know. I didn't break my legs."

"Yeah, but they're plenty bruised." He opened the door to the house, very awkwardly but successfully, and slammed it shut with his boot. "Besides, I like holding you."

She started to say she liked it, too, when the surroundings finally registered with her. "Emmett, this isn't my house." Then she realized what she said. She didn't have a home anymore. She had given Sophie the keys to the house and left. She and Dare had been living out of a motel.

Why did Emmett bring her to his house? Why would he call it home?

He gently set her on the couch, then sat next to her, grabbing her hand. His fingers brushed hers, up then down, soft as a feather. His touch sent a rush of desire straight through her.

"You asked me to take you home..."

She couldn't even look him in the eye. "I don't have—"

He turned her head and brushed his lips to hers. Being greedy, she stayed locked to him, making the kiss hotter than any of the other ones he'd delivered in the hospital. Turning his body, he pulled her closer. She didn't need any further signal he wanted her just as much as she wanted him. She rolled onto his lap, her hands to his chest.

He pulled away, drawing in heavy breaths. "I want to... but later. We need to talk."

"We can talk later." She went to kiss him again, but his hands squeezing her hips had her halting any movement.

"We'll talk now." He sighed heavily, then started to

rummage in his pocket as best as he could with her sitting on his lap. "You asked me to take you home. So I did."

Her mouth dropped open as she stared at the ring he'd given her.

"One of the nurses gave it to me. She said you were wearing it around your neck. Your heart knows what it wants. Your mind is fighting it." He rested his forehead against hers. "Quit fighting me. Just let me in. I know you said you love me, but you're still fighting it."

"Emmett..." She didn't know what to say. What could she say? He was right. Every single word. She didn't know how to stop fighting it. She felt like she'd been fighting her entire life. Stopping just like that would take a miracle.

"Deja, I love you. I always will." His voice dropped to a whisper. "I'm not perfect. I'll more than likely piss you off at times. But I will always love you. Make a home with me. Marry me."

She wasn't perfect either. And she knew without a doubt she'd probably piss him off as well.

"Talk to me. Say anything." He chuckled. "Well, not anything. You can't say no."

How could she not love this man? He made her laugh when she didn't want to laugh.

"I don't know how to stop fighting. I don't think I deserve you."

The sweetest smile filled his face as he took the ring off the chain and grabbed her hand. "And I don't deserve you." He slid the ring onto her finger.

"I never said yes."

"You never said no."

"You said I couldn't."

He winked.

She couldn't help but laugh as she squeezed his hand

and kissed him. This time he let her. A brief one. But it was enough. It said enough.

"I'm scared, Emmett." She never admitted things like that. Even saying the words out loud scared the shit out of her.

"Me, too. Love is scary." He cradled her face, his thumbs rubbing her cheeks softly. "But it's also exhilarating and fun and something I want to feel every day of my life. With you. Nobody but you." He kissed her again, hard and unyielding. "I almost lost you, Deja. That feeling...it was horrible. I never want to feel like that again."

She never wanted to make him feel like that again either. She could relate. When the bailiffs walked Dare out of the courtroom ten years ago, her life felt like it was ending. She lost her brother. Even though he was alive and breathing, she had lost him. Now he was back. She never wanted to lose him again.

If she could love Dare, frightened for the day she might lose him once again, why couldn't she do the same with Emmett?

She didn't think she deserved him. He thought the same thing. But they both deserved love. Didn't they?

Grabbing him by the shirt, she yanked his mouth to hers, delving deep, throwing all her erratic emotions into the kiss, letting him know how crazy he made her.

"I love you, Emmett McCord. I wouldn't want to love anyone else."

"That's all I needed to hear." He smiled. "Welcome home, sweetheart."

He pushed the doorbell, then took two steps back. One step for some air he needed desperately. Another step just in case a fist came at his face.

Less than thirty seconds later, the door swung open. Ethan stared at him, not giving much away what he was thinking.

"Want a beer?"

Dare didn't know what to think, but nodded and followed Ethan inside. He took a seat on the couch, his normal spot when he lived with him, and waited for Ethan to come back with their beers.

He had seen Ethan quite a bit at the hospital while Deja was there. Especially in the beginning when she was in the ICU. The entire McCord family took turns visiting, making sure he and Emmett were never alone. They weren't allowed to stay in the room as he and Emmett were, but they hung around until the next person arrived to relieve them. He honestly didn't think they stayed there just for moral support for Emmett. They stayed because they considered Deja a part of their family.

Ethan plopped down next to him and handed him a beer. He took a sip, his eyes glued to the television where Minnesota was playing. He hated to admit he was afraid to look Ethan in the eye.

"I'm sorry—"

"I acted—"

They both laughed, then Ethan cleared his throat. "Let me go first." He opened his mouth to dispute that, really wanting to be the one to go first, when Ethan shook his head. "I need to go first. You had every right to get upset. We should've never questioned you, accused you like that. I'm sorry, man."

Dare fiddled with the beer bottle before looking him in

the eye. "I wanted to make him feel the pain. I wanted to sic my friends on him. I wanted to so badly."

Ethan nodded. "But you didn't."

"No, I didn't. I reacted badly—"

"No, dude, we did."

He chuckled and held out his bottle. "I'm ready to move on and forget about it. You?"

Ethan tapped his bottle with his, then they both took a sip. "Wanna watch the game?"

"Yeah, sure."

They sat in silence for a while—a comfortable silence—watching the game, cheering when it called for it, booing when it warranted it.

"Shit, that ump is making the worst calls." Ethan stood up. "Another beer?"

"Yeah, just one more. I should go soon."

Ethan nodded and walked out of the room. When he strolled back in, he handed him a beer, his face drawn in a hard frown.

"You okay?"

"You aren't still staying in that motel, are you?"

"I'm still in a motel near the hospital. Sophie..." He took a sip of beer. "She's a sweetheart, but I don't want to live in her house. It's too big."

"I didn't know Sophie offered her house to you." Ethan rubbed a hand over his chin. "Well, you know you can have your old room back."

He chuckled. "Old room? I didn't know I stayed here that long for it to be considered my old room."

"Well, the offer stands." He sighed. "I should've offered days ago. I just didn't know how pissed you were still, and the thing with Deja...your old room is available is all I'm saying."

Dare clinked beer bottles with him again and smiled. "Then I guess I can have another beer after this one. Thanks, Ethan."

"Hey, man, anything for family. You know it'll be official as soon as Emmett convinces Deja to wear the ring again."

"Don't think it'll take much convincing this time."

"Yeah, you're probably right."

21

EMMETT RAISED his glass with a huge smile. He didn't think his smile could get any larger, but when he looked into Deja's eyes, he knew it could. Just looking into her beautiful ocean-blue eyes made him smile like a man in love with the best woman on the planet. And he was. To think he dragged his ass for so long, hiding his feelings for her, afraid she'd reject him and lose her from his life altogether.

Now look at his life. It was perfect.

He cleared his throat. "I want to make a toast. Just a few words." He glanced across the living room to where Deja sat next to Sophie and Ava, holding little Jimmy in her arms. The picture sent an immediate sense of rightness and impatience. He wanted to kick everyone out and make sweet love to his fiancée. Without any protection. She looked so beautiful holding a baby, it almost made his heart hurt.

"Any day now, Emmett," Ethan joked.

"Right." He held out his glass a little more. "I just want to say that I'm happy you could all be here. This party was a last-minute idea, but both of us were excited to share the news of our engagement."

"Again." Austin winked.

"Right." He gave both Ethan and Austin a glare to shut the hell up. "Deja is the most courageous, strongest woman I have ever met, and I couldn't imagine my life without her. The last few weeks, especially those first few hours after the accident, were probably one of the most horrifying moments of my life. I think we can all agree it would've been another huge loss to this family if she would've never pulled through."

His voice started to crack as water filled his eyes. Damn it, he wouldn't cry in front of his family. Steeling his features, he cleared his throat and willed the water to dissipate. "I'm blessed to have such a wonderful family, and I'm excited to start a new one with you. I love you, Deja."

Deja handed little Jimmy to Ava and stood up somewhat wobbly. Dare was by her side in an instant.

"I'm fine."

"You're still healing. Take it easy. He ain't going anywhere."

Deja laughed and playfully shoved Dare out of the way. She was in his arms within five steps. "Why did you have to get all sappy?"

"I have no idea." He pulled her closer, sinking his head into the crook of her neck. "All I know is I saw you sitting there and I just felt compelled to say something. I know the last few weeks have been crazy, but I just need you to know how much I love you. How much I want to take care of you." His voice dropped lower as he pressed a few kisses in between each word. "How much I want to make love to you. With no condom. No pill."

Her breathing became heavy as she snuggled closer. "Emmett, your family is in the room."

"I know. I wish they'd leave."

She giggled, then stepped back. Which was probably for the best. He didn't trust himself not to continue taking advantage of her.

"Thank you everyone for coming tonight." She let out a huge breath. "Thank you for being there for me. If I was cranky at any point, well, you know I didn't mean it."

Austin stood the closest and pulled her into a hug. "We love you, Deja."

Without warning, everyone decided to grab a hug from him and Deja, congratulating them once again. Soon after, they all said their good-byes and left. Ethan couldn't hold back when he walked him to the door.

"Have fun having some hanky-panky."

As much as it annoyed him, it also made him laugh. He *was* about to have some fun making sweet love to his fiancée. Or, in the words of Ethan, hanky-panky.

Emmett locked the door, then scooped Deja into his arms and all but ran to the bedroom. Playfully, he threw her onto the bed and covered her body with his.

"I shouldn't have done that. You just got home from the hospital, and here I am, throwing you around."

"And ravishing me silly at all hours of the night. What is wrong with you?"

The twinkle in her eyes had him laughing as he took her shirt off. "Would it be corny to say I'm crazy in love?"

"Yeah." She chuckled as she helped him take his shirt off. "But I like hearing it." Her hands ran up his chest and up and over his shoulders, then down his back. "So, no pill or condoms, uh? Are you sure?"

"Only if you're okay with it. If you're okay with possibly getting pregnant before we're married."

"When are we getting married? Here we had this

impromptu engagement party and we didn't announce a date."

"Whenever. You can plan it all. I just want to say I do."

"I guess I could ask Sophie for help. I don't know the first thing about planning a wedding."

He started to layer kisses up and down her neck. "We could always see if Austin and Sophie want to have a double wedding."

She shivered, whether from his kisses or his words, he didn't care. He loved when she trembled like that. "That would be great. I would love that."

He lifted his head, kissing her on the lips. "You know what? I think Sophie would, too. I'm sure Austin isn't going to argue about it. I know I won't."

"It was your idea."

"Yeah, but it also makes you happy."

She grabbed his face, landing a kiss of all kisses on his lips. They tangled tongues, their bodies molding together as if they were one. They didn't even get to the best part yet, but in that moment, he didn't need to be joined in that way. Kissing her, holding her, was enough.

"No pill or condom."

Her whispered words echoed around the room. He had hoped she'd say that, but honestly didn't know if she would.

"Have I told you how lucky I am? Because I am the luckiest guy in the world to have such a beautiful, amazing woman like you."

She chuckled as her fingers grazed down his back. "Remember that tomorrow when I walk back in the office and see what kind of mess you made."

He tried to stop the wince, to hide the truth in those words.

"It hasn't been that long. Please tell me you didn't make the office a complete disaster."

Shrugging, his face lit up with laughter. "I didn't take it well when you left."

Her face scrunched up as if she were irritated, then suddenly her fingers attacked him under the armpits. He started to squirm as their laughter rolled around the room.

"I'll help you put it back together. Just stop tickling me."

She let go as his body sunk down, resting in the perfect spot. He lowered his mouth close to hers, then his hands cradled her face. "I love you."

She sighed happily. "Shut up, Emmett, and make sweet love to me."

He did just that.

Don't miss the next book in this angsty, yet
heartwarming series!
Always Kind of Love

He wanted to hate her.
She needed his forgiveness.
Love has a way of healing even the deepest wounds.

Zane McCord has always been there for his brothers, no matter what. But when his brother Jimmy dies, leaving unresolved tension hanging between them, he turns all his hatred and blame onto Ava Rainer— the woman he holds responsible for Jimmy's death. He doesn't want anything to do with her, but when she unexpectedly shows up on his farm, needing his help, Zane finds himself drawn to her, despite every effort to push her away.

Ava can't escape the guilt weighing heavy on her shoulders, and she's desperate to make amends. Working together gives her the perfect opportunity to break down the walls he's built around his heart and set them both on a journey of forgiveness, healing, and unexpected love. But with the painful memories of the past looming, can they ever truly move forward and find happiness in each other's arms, or will the guilt prove too much and destroy everything?

*Grab your copy of **Protecting You** today and witness the power of forgiveness and love.*

FOR AUSTIN & SOPHIE'S STORY
TRUST IN LOVE
A MCCORD FAMILY NOVEL, #2

He wasn't looking for love.
She was afraid to trust again.
When fate brings them together, will they take a chance on
forever?

Austin McCord has always enjoyed the company of women, but he's never been one for commitment. Until he meets his neighbor, Sophie. With her angelic face and kind heart, she's everything he never knew he wanted. But there's a catch—Sophie is the type that has marriage written all over her, making her untouchable.

Despite his best efforts, the temptation proves too much. Austin is drawn to Sophie like a moth to a flame, but every time he tries to get close, she pulls away. It's obvious that she's been hurt before, and for the first time in his life, Austin finds himself in hot pursuit.

As he tries to break down her walls, the past looms ahead, threatening to tear them apart. With danger closing in, Austin finds himself fighting for not only Sophie's heart but also her safety.

Will they find the courage to take a leap of faith on love before it's ripped away from them forever?

Fall in love with Austin and Sophie's story today and discover if they can overcome their fears and forge a future together.

For Ethan & Penelope's Story
Always Kind of Love
A McCord Family Novel, #4

He wanted to forget her.
She longed for a second chance.
The flames of their love never died.

Ethan McCord has spent the last ten years trying to forget his high school sweetheart, Penelope. When she left town for college, she took his heart with her, leaving him to pick up the pieces. Now, while battling burning blazes and an arsonist bent on destruction, Ethan finds himself face-to-face with the woman he's never forgotten.

With danger lurking around every corner and the temptation of rekindling past desires growing stronger every day, can Ethan and Penelope overcome heartbreak and reignite the spark they once shared, or will the pain and danger of the present consume them both?

*Get your copy of **Always Kind of Love** and experience the heat of second-chance romance mixed with heart-pounding suspense as Ethan and Penelope struggle with the flames of the past and present to find their way back to one another.*

Note: This story was previously a part of the Risking Everything Charity Anthology.

FOR GABE & OLIVIA'S STORY
FINDING YOU
A MCCORD FAMILY NOVEL, #5

What happens in Vegas doesn't always stay in Vegas. One wild mishap could be the best thing that ever happened to him.

Being shy makes it hard for Gabe McCord to talk to women, but throw in a fun, wild night of drinking and it's not so hard. Until he learns he didn't just wake up next to a gorgeous woman—he married her. Nine months later and he's still trying to find her...when she accidentally finds him.

Olivia Brenson is the new arson investigator in town trying to find the person responsible for multiple fires, the latest one which almost took a life. When she learns they're married—because neither remembered their nuptials—Gabe finds himself on another fun adventure. She wants to stay married for a short time to keep her overprotective, demanding father off her back. He doesn't protest as it gives him a chance to prove he isn't always the shy guy. But if he's not careful, he might lose more than just his reserved tendencies. He'll lose his heart along the way. Because he's finding Olivia is the woman he never knew he needed in his life.

With nail-biting suspense and smoldering romance, dive into the danger and desire with Gabe & Olivia's story!

For Dare & Julie's story
DARE YOU TO LOVE
A McCORD FAMILY NOVEL, #6

He's looking for a fresh start.
She only wants to unwind and relax.
But when opposites attract, anything can happen.

He's done his time, but once a felon, always a felon. Nobody lets him forget that. Dare needs to leave town, get a new start somewhere else where no one knows him and what he's done. If only it were that simple. Not only is it impossible to find the right time to tell his sister he's hitting the road, he meets a woman who gets under his skin without even trying. There's something about her that he can't resist. And she knows it. So when he's asked to do something that could send him spiraling back into his old life, he wants to say no. He wants to run in the opposite direction and never stop. If only she'd let him.

Vacation time is meant to relax, not bring the stress and tension bearing down on her. Of course, meeting a man who challenges her in so many ways, well, Julie can't ignore that. Nor can she combat the desire that attacks her body every time he looks her way. Fighting comes easy to them, and so does the pleasure. It should be just sex, yet it's turning into more than she bargained for. It would never work between them. She works for the law, and he...is only trying to find a new path, and she respects that. If only it were that easy.

ABOUT THE AUTHOR

I'm a *USA Today* Bestselling Author that loves to write contemporary romance and romantic suspense novels, although I am partial to romantic suspense. I even dabble in paranormal. Honestly, I love anything that has to do with romance. As long as there's a happy ending, I'm a happy camper. And insta-love...yes, please! I love baseball (Go Twins!) and creating awesome crafts. I graduated with a Bachelor's Degree in Criminal Justice, working in that field for several years before I became a stay-at-home mom. I have a few more amazing stories in the works. If you would like to learn more about me and my books, head to my website by scanning the QR code. Thanks for reading!

Scan me